Lament the Common Bones

Also by Jen J. Danna and Ann Vanderlaan

<u>Abbott and Lowell Forensic Mysteries</u>

Dead, Without a Stone to Tell It
No One Sees Me 'Til I Fall
A Flame in the Wind of Death
Two Parts Bloody Murder
Lament the Commons Bones

<u>FBI K-9s</u>
(Writing as Sara Driscoll)

Lone Wolf
Before It's Too Late
Storm Rising
No Man's Land (coming December 2019)

Kindle™ editions available through Amazon.
Also available in Kobo™/Nook™ e-book formats.

Lament the Common Bones

Abbott and Lowell Forensic Mysteries

Jen J. Danna

with Ann Vanderlaan

ISBN: 978-1-7751578-0-9

First Edition: November 2017

Printed by Kindle Direct Publishing™, An Amazon.com Company.

AUTHOR'S NOTE

The title of this novel comes from the eighteenth poem in a collection translated by Red Pine. The poems are attributed to Hanshan, who referred to himself as Cold Mountain, and are believed to have been written during the Tang Dynasty (618 – 907 A.D.). Hanshan fled with his family during the An Lu-shan rebellion to the Tientei mountains and created a new identity for himself. The translator Red Pine states, "In the entire history of Chinese culture, no other poet has managed to preserve the veil of mystery concerning his true identity as well as Cold Mountain, and I propose that this was not literary conceit but a matter of life or death."

> *I spur my horse past ruins;*
> *ruins move a traveler's heart.*
> *The old parapets high and low*
> *the ancient graves great and small,*
> *the shuddering shadow of a tumbleweed,*
> *the steady sound of giant trees.*
> *But what I lament are the common bones*
> *unnamed in the records of immortals.*

ACKNOWLEDGMENTS

While writing this fact-based novel, we've been extremely lucky to have the assistance of many experts in their fields to ensure our accuracy. We could not have managed without them and are very grateful for their assistance: Detective Lieutenant Norman Zuk, for once again graciously sharing his time and knowledge regarding police protocols, especially the challenge of finding a legal way to set the beginning of the case in Middlesex County while still keeping it an Essex County case. Jeff Romano, author of *Best Loop Hikes: From New Hampshire's White Mountains to the Maine Coast, 100 Classic Hikes in New England,* and *Day Hiking New England,* for his assistance in planning the location of the final scenes, helping to plan a research trip to Mount Holyoke Range State Park, and for sharing his personal experience and photos of the area. Detective Lieutenant Michael Holleran for arranging a tour of the Massachusetts State Police Springfield Crime Lab where he shared many of his unique personal experiences in both the field and the lab. Sergeant Ken Heffernan for taking the time to run us through the details surrounding evidence collection and processing, fingerprinting, and tire and shoe casting. Lieutenant John Crane for taking us on a tour of the ballistic division of the Springfield Crime Lab—it was a fascinating look at firearms, the evidence they leave behind, and the science concerning that evidence. It was also more guns than this group of Canadians had ever seen in our lives! Erica Nadeau, a forensic scientist in the Springfield criminalistics unit, for walking us through her lab, covering blood and body fluid processing, evidence collection kits, and techniques at crime scenes. Dr. Bruce Wainman, Director of McMaster University's Education in Anatomy Program, for sharing his experiences in skeleton processing and acquisition.

Once again, our critique team eagerly joined us in preparing this manuscript. To Margaret Isaacs, Jenny Lidstrom, Rick Newton, and Sharon Taylor, thank you for your time, your questions, your corrections, and for cheering your way through the manuscript. As always, you helped us produce a stronger, tighter story. To Lisa Giblin, Matt Tribur (Tribe), Ray Spear (Spear), and Matt VanVoltinburg (Van), thank you for ensuring our medical details were correct, especially with the challenging scenario we sent you! Thanks to Marianne Harden who leant her considerable skills on a deep copy edit of the manuscript. Many thanks, also, to Rick Newton who spent untold hours working on formatting both the print and electronic versions of this novel.

To our agent, Nicole Resciniti, thank you for always being in our corner with words of encouragement whenever we need it. And to our editor, Gordon Aalborg, thanks for your eagle eye and amazing ability to pinpoint issues and know exactly how to fix them.

J.J.D. and A.V.

To my son Paul and my daughter-in-law Shelly for their encouragement, enthusiasm, and willingness to share this adventure. To my friends who rescued the members of The Thundertail Tribe and also read our books.

A.V.

To my daughters Jess and Jordan for once again being the best of sports as I dragged you around Massachusetts while planning and plotting another novel. From touring the crime lab to climbing all 1,100 feet of Mount Norwottuck so I could get the end of this book right, a writer couldn't ask for better partners in crime!

J.J.D.

PROLOGUE: FIRESTEEL

Firesteel: a piece of high-carbon or alloyed steel used to start fires. When struck with a chert or other sharp-edged rocks, the resulting sparks ignite the tinder.

Sunday, 3:10 p.m.
Amherst, Massachusetts

The victim's breath gurgled a strangled cry as blood flowed hot and fast over dirty skin. Over the blade. Over fingers clenched surely around the handle.

Crimson spurted in a wide arc over new leaves, clinging briefly before the falling rain swept it away. Washed clean by Nature herself.

The body went limp and fell spread-eagled in the bright new grass, already lifeless. The man stood over him, the blade hanging at his side while blood dripped from the razor-sharp edge to spatter in a dark stain at his feet.

In spring, life began anew. And so it would for him.

He looked around, surveying his land. Those who had no right tried to take everything from him. But it was his land and his laws. His right to live as he chose. His right to protect his own. And to wreak his vengeance on those who would ruin him for their own gain.

With a practiced hand, he wiped the blade on the dead man's worn flannel shirt and then slipped it into its sheath for later scouring. A neglected tool, dull or nicked, could be a death sentence. And he meant to live.

He dug the toe of one boot under the torso and rolled the dead weight of the corpse. Then he seized a ragged shoe in both hands and dragged the body deeper into the cover of the nearby woods. There he would set the scene and let Nature take its course.

Nature knew how to make man one with her, so all would be clean and new.

He looked down at the face frozen in death. So old for his age, so jaded. A life squandered before it had barely started.

Now he had paid.

And would pay again.

CHAPTER ONE: BATTLESPACE

Battlespace: the entire field of combat—air, ground, sea, satellite reconnaissance, human intelligence, and environment.

Thursday, December 5, 3:24 p.m.
Washington Street
Haverhill, Massachusetts

A furious whine streaked past Leigh's ear, close enough to stir the air. She threw herself against the grimy wall, her heart pounding. She flattened against the crumbling surface as the sound of gunfire exploded around her again. *Damn, that was close.* Another inch closer and she'd have a scar all too similar to Matt's.

The air reeked of sulfur and profanities rang from the far end of the building. Across the dim hallway, Brad Riley peered at her through an open doorway. She answered his unspoken question with a hurried nod and jerked her head toward the corridor branching to their left. *Cover me.* He nodded and swung into the hallway, gun clenched in both hands. The newest member of the Massachusetts State Police Essex Detective Unit, this was Riley's first gang op. The pressure showed in his sheet-white face, but his Smith and Wesson M didn't waver in his grip. He slid across the hallway, his shoulder to the corner, and only paused long enough to take a deep breath before darting into the open, firing toward the end of the hall.

Leigh sprinted around the corner behind him, aiming for the open door on the far side of the corridor. She nearly plowed into another Essex officer, Chris Tapley, as she bolted for cover.

Leigh took advantage of the few seconds of safety to catch her breath. "How did they know we were coming?" she gasped.

"No idea." Tapley pushed sweaty hair out of his eyes. "But from the way this went south from the get-go, someone tipped them off."

Now they were pinned down in the middle of a firefight.

"They're holed up at the end of the hall." Tapley jerked a thumb toward the rear of the building. A former shoe factory, the once open space of the second floor had been divided by cheap drywall into smaller sections. The walls now showed their age in crumbling patches, stains, and creeping splotches of mold. Abandoned for over twenty years in a run down, graffiti-laden neighborhood, and surrounded by more empty buildings, it was a perfect gang hideaway.

"Trapped is more like it," Leigh said. "And trapped is desperate and dangerous."

As if in reply, more gunfire erupted, accompanied by a cry of pain and the sound of someone falling heavily to the ground.

"Time to end this." Tapley readjusted his bulletproof vest. "You with me?"

She nodded. "Riley's just across the hall, so he's with us, too. Do you know where everyone else is?"

"STOP went first," he said, referring to the state police Special Tactical Operations, their version of a SWAT team. "The Haverhill cops were in front of me. They took cover further up the hall. I came in with several FBI agents but lost them when we took cover." He cocked his head at the sudden silence, unease etched into his expression. "Let's go."

He moved to the doorway, angling his body to peer down the hallway, and then he stepped through the door. Leigh followed close behind, and Riley shifted from the opposite wall to join them.

All hell broke loose.

Volleys of gunfire came so fast they sounded like cannon fire rather than multiple rounds. Tapley jerked, his hand flying upward, his finger reflexively clutching the trigger to loose a round at the ceiling. Blood flew, splattering in a warm spray across Leigh's cheek. She jerked in shock, watching in horror as first Riley flew backwards, and then Tapley did a jittery dance before crumpling into the hall.

It only took seconds, but it felt like minutes to drag air into her shocked lungs. She ripped the radio off her duty belt. "Officers down! Second floor, west side." She jammed the radio back into place.

More gunshots, followed by a wave of running feet and bellows of rage. Riley sprawled just ten feet away, but that distance might have been ten miles with the bullets screaming down the corridor. But Tapley was within reach—he'd fallen with his left foot across the threshold. Leigh re-holstered her gun and grabbed his boot. She grunted with effort as she dragged two hundred plus pounds of dead weight into the room.

"Come on, Tapley, help me out here." She focused on his pale face—his eyes were open and his mouth moved soundlessly. Red drenched his shirt collar and spread in a dark patch above the vest. She fell to her knees beside him and yanked his vest open to see where he was hit.

As she uncovered the wound, blood spurted and then pooled at the edge of the vest, just under his collarbone. Frantic, she searched for something to staunch the blood, but the room was empty except for rusted beer cans, a broken bottle, and splintered two-by-fours lining the wall. Leigh planted both hands over the shredded flesh and applied pressure.

"Come on, Chris. Stay with me." Her voice shook and she swallowed hard, steadying herself in an attempt to camouflage her fear. "Your wife will kill you if you don't hang on."

She pushed harder, ignoring both his groans and the slip of slick blood under her palms. Shadowy forms sprinting by the open doorway drew her attention. As they ran past, she saw Riley commando-crawling into the opposite room under his own power. Relief was like a bucket of warm water poured over frozen flesh. *Hit, but still in the game.*

Her relief lasted for only a few seconds as Leigh returned her attention to Tapley to find his head lolling and his eyes open and staring. She focused on his chest, but couldn't tell if it was rising and falling in the watery light filtering through the grimy window.

"Chris!" She crouched over him, an ear over his mouth, but

she couldn't hear over the shouts, gunfire, and the frantic heartbeat in her ears. She searched for a pulse, pressing two fingers deep into the clammy flesh of his throat. Nothing. "Damn it, Tapley, don't you dare die on me."

Making the nearly impossible choice between blood loss and the lack of a pulse, Leigh layered her hands over his breastbone and started CPR. Fingers laced together, she counted, trying to ignore the weakening blood spurts from the open wound.

"On your knees!" The bellowed order came from down the hall, followed by the sound of more running feet as Riley came through the door.

"It's over." Riley's gaze fell on Tapley. "Shit, Abbott."

"I'm holding him. I've radioed for help, but I need you to meet the paramedics if the coast is clear." Leigh's words jerked out in a steady rhythm, punctuating the chest compressions. "You okay?"

Riley crouched down on the other side of Tapley. "Bullet hit the vest. Knocked the wind out of me and will leave a bruise, but that's the worst of it. Abbott . . . look at him. It's too—"

"Get help." She ruthlessly cut him off, pinning him with a razor-sharp glare.

He must have read the edge of panic in her face because he pushed to his feet and backed away, his eyes fixed on the fallen officer. "I'll get the paramedics."

Leigh turned back to Tapley to take in his pale waxy skin and lifeless blue eyes. She squeezed her eyes closed, shutting out the specter of death, and continued compressions.

One, two, three, four, five . . .

Thursday, December 5, 4:13 p.m.
Interstate-93
Reading, Massachusetts

She's all right.
She's busy, that's why you can't get a hold of her. She needs

to do her job, not answer the phone. *She's all right. You'll see.*

Matt Lowell signaled the lane change a millisecond before cutting left, slipping through the increasingly sluggish rush hour traffic. As he slid in behind a minivan loaded with roughhousing kids, their heads bobbing in the rear window, he forced himself to ease off the gas and leave a safe distance. But the internal battle between his need to be there *now* and his need not to kill himself or anyone else on the freeway manifested in the machine-gun tapping of his fingers against the steering wheel.

He drew in a deep breath and then forced a slow exhale, trying unsuccessfully to blow out some of his tension. It only left him wound tighter than before.

It had been a normal day until an hour ago—sitting at his desk, tuning out the usual noise and conversation of his grad students as they worked in the lab while he contemplated the direction of his newest manuscript for the *American Journal of Physical Anthropology*.

Before the bottom fell out of his world.

Paul ran full-tilt through the door of the lab, clamping one hand on the frame in a futile attempt to control his wild careen through the gap. His gangly frame was an off-balanced windmill of flailing limbs until he abruptly stopped himself by jamming both hands against a lab bench. All conversation halted in shock.

"Where's Leigh?" Paul spoke so quickly his question came out as a single word.

Ice slid through Matt's veins at the panic in Paul's eyes, at the pallor of his skin. His chair slid back from his desk with a screech as he shot to his feet. "On assignment in Haverhill. Why?"

"Can you get in touch with her?"

Kiko and Juka crowded closer, their eyes locked on Paul's pale face.

"She's on assignment. That's cop-speak for 'I'm busy, don't bother me'."

"Was she working the gang take-down?"

"She didn't say. When I'm not involved, she can't tell me

classified details. Why?" Matt struggled against the need to grab Paul by the shoulders and shake him for information.

"Went to the lounge to make coffee. TV was on. A special news bulletin. There was a firefight in Haverhill, multiple injuries. Several gang members dead, and at least one police officer. Didn't say who or what force. But several agencies were involved—FBI, Massachusetts State Police, ATF." Paul stopped and took a deep breath. *"Haverhill is in Essex County, so it would be the Essex cops investigating."*

Matt already had his phone out, speed dialing Leigh's number. His heart beat triple time to the rhythm of the rings at the other end.

"You've reached Trooper Leigh Abbott of the Massachusetts State Police—"

He cut the connection. *"She's not picking up."*

Kiko stepped forward and laid a hand on his arm. Her voice was calm and reasonable, but he could hear the effort it took to keep it that way. *"You know something's happened, but that doesn't mean she's dead or even injured. She might just be busy."*

"I have to find out what's going on."

"Go. We'll see what we can find out from here. Keep your cell on and we'll let you know the moment we learn anything."

He already had his ski jacket in his hand and was sprinting for the hallway.

Up ahead, road signs warned of the upcoming interchange with the I-495. Nearly there. He glanced over his shoulder, but the traffic jammed around him, trapping him helplessly behind the soccer mom.

This is what she does. You knew it when you signed on with her. She has a dangerous job but she's smart and can take care of herself.

He jerked when his cell rang. He pushed a button on the steering wheel to bring the call in through his sound system. "Lowell."

"It's Tucker." Rob Tucker was the Essex Detective Unit's computer genius. Matt and Leigh had worked cases with him, and

Tucker was currently involved in an off-the-books investigation with them. As far as Matt was concerned, he was the 'go-to' inside the department for information. If there was something to uncover, Rob Tucker was the man for the job. He'd been Matt's first call as he jogged to his SUV.

Soccer mom and her van of kids suddenly jockeyed for a position in the middle lane, earning a blast of horn from a hatchback she cut off. Matt took advantage of the gap in the snarl of cars and shot past them. "What have you got?"

"Nothing much so far. It's pure chaos up there, and the radio calls reflect the confusion. I can't reach anyone on their cell and the reports coming in are jumbled. What I can say is the op went wrong and every on-duty cop in Haverhill is there now along with half of Field Troop A. Every ambulance in the area is also on site, but I can't get confirmation of who's injured, who's down, and who's in one piece. Are you almost there?"

"Nearly half way. I'll be there in about twenty minutes if I don't get pulled over for going eighty in a sixty-five."

"If someone pulls you over, call me, and I'll get them to escort you. Now get the hell up there and find her. Call me if you hear anything; I'll do the same."

"Done." Matt ended the call.

Leigh always considered herself the square peg in the round hole of her department. But Tucker's blatant concern for her settled some of the jagged edges in Matt's gut.

The sign for his exit flashed overhead and Matt jammed his foot down on the accelerator, shooting ahead to weave deftly through traffic and finally swing onto the off-ramp to head east.

She has to be all right.

Thursday, December 5, 5:02 p.m.
Washington Street
Haverhill, Massachusetts

Even from inside the old factory as she escorted a handcuffed gang member outside, Leigh could hear Matt's insistent voice through the open door before she saw him.

"Get out of my way before I move you myself."

"This is a crime scene. Civilians aren't allowed."

Pausing near the door, Leigh's heart sank at the snarl that could only be Trooper Len Morrison, another Essex Detective Unit officer and the bane of her existence. Morrison would delight in making Matt's life difficult simply because of his connection to Leigh.

"Goddamn it, you know I'm not a civilian." Frustration darkened Matt's tone. "I'm her partner and I need to see her. Where is she?"

"You're a *consultant* and this isn't a case for you."

"That may be, but I was also a medic. I can help those needing medical assistance if you're shorthanded."

Leigh stepped out of the building, swallowing an involuntary gasp of shock as the biting winter wind sliced across her skin. Dark had already fallen, but headlights and flashing emergency lights lit the area as if it were daytime. Twenty feet away, Morrison faced down Matt outside the police tape, his stocky frame blocking the way. Behind them, reporters shouted out questions and cameras flashed as they tried to get story tidbits from anyone inside the scene.

"You help the dead." Morrison's tone was scathing, his weight tipped onto his toes as if inviting attack. "We don't have your kind of dead here."

Even though she was exhausted, emotionally wrung out, and desperate for the world to go away, anger flared through Leigh. She knew what Morrison was doing: barring Matt from the scene while implying there were dead on site—fresh dead, not the decomposed or skeletonized remains that were Matt's specialty.

Matt would be frantic. Knowing Morrison, he loved every minute of it.

How can he play games like this considering what's happened? She turned to a tall officer wearing a heavy navy winter coat, a knit cap pulled low on his forehead, as he settled another handcuffed man into the back of a cruiser.

"Carmichael, have you got this for a second? My partner's on scene and I want to bring him in."

Carmichael slammed the door and reached for Leigh's prisoner. "I've got him. Go."

Leigh turned into the wind, wincing as the cold snaked inside her open jacket. She glanced down, numbly cataloging the dark smears of blood barely visible against the navy and the brighter splashes contrasting against her pale blouse. Dried blood caked her hands, disappearing beneath her cuffs.

Tapley.

She looked away, shuttering the pain and sorrow. Experience had taught her that those who didn't allow themselves to work through their feelings burned out early. But this kind of grief was intensely private. Today, she needed to reflect the public face of the department; later, she'd allow the emotion free rein. Her throat tightened as she swallowed and blinked a few times to beat back the moisture burning at the edges of her eyelids.

She circled a squad car, its lights flashing in blinding bursts of red and blue, and took in the scene. The two men were still standing chest to chest as she'd seen once before: Matt with the advantage of several inches of height, Morrison with considerably more bulk. Matt stood with both boots planted, one hand clenched at his side, and, for a moment, Leigh thought he was going to lay into Morrison. Past dealings with Morrison might automatically put Matt on the defensive, but he wasn't the type to haul off and hit someone without cause. The fact he was walking that line spoke volumes about his level of desperation.

She stepped into his line of sight. "Matt."

Matt started and then jerked his head toward her. Beneath the tousled dark hair worn long over his forehead to hide a battle scar, emotions spilled across his face at lightning speed—relief, joy, concern, and finally alarm. His gaze shifted from her bloody hands to her ruined clothes and up to her blood-splattered face, rapidly cataloging the disconnect between her appearance and physical state.

She waited until his gaze finally settled on her face, seeing the fear in his eyes morph into deduction. "It's not my blood. Morrison, let him through."

"He's not supposed to be on site."

Enough of this bullshit. She shouldered past Morrison, forcing him back with a low curse. She lifted the yellow tape and stepped aside to allow Matt to duck under into the crime scene.

"Next time you want to be a bastard," she said with a hiss to Morrison, "pick a less disrespectful moment. Tapley's dead." She indicated her bloody shirt with a crimson-stained hand and felt a rush of satisfaction as Morrison jerked, the color leeching from his cheeks. "Back off." She spun away, not able to look at him anymore.

Clamping her lips together to keep from tearing a strip off Morrison in front of the media, she marched to Matt. "This way," she snapped.

He followed in silence, but she could feel the weight of his gaze on her back. They rounded the corner of the factory and stopped a few feet down a shadowed alley. Only then did she turn to him, desperately searching for the calm that continued to elude her. "I'm sorry about Morrison."

"Screw Morrison." He stepped closer and took her icy hands in his.

"Matt, don't. My hands . . ."

Ignoring her protest, he squeezed tighter, the heat and strength in his grip nearly making her whimper. "Who's Tapley?"

"Trooper Chris Tapley. He's . . ." She caught herself. "He'd been with the department for seven years. He sat in front of me in the bullpen." Anguish crowded in on her. She wanted nothing more than to lean against Matt, letting him absorb some of the emotions raging through her, but she was a cop and this was no time to fall apart. Later, she would tell him everything in detail, but for now, just the highlights. She owed him that much. "It was an op to take out Haverhill's most violent gang—*Chacal*—to not only stop the drive-bys, but also to dam the flood of crack, heroin, firearms, and live rounds out onto the streets. DA Saxon put together a task force out of the Essex Detective Unit, the FBI, the ATF, and Haverhill PD. A tip came through about a meeting of the top members of *Chacal* here, and the decision was made to go in and take them out. It was a way to cut the head off the snake in one strike, so to speak."

"But you're homicide. Why are you involved in a drug bust?"

"Homicide is almost exclusively what I do, but the unit also handles sexual and physical abuse cases, kidnapping, gangs, and white-collar crime. Tapley was the Essex cop working this case, but when the op was called, more hands were needed, and Riley and I were sent in as support."

She took a moment to breathe in an attempt to find calm before she told him more. "Someone tipped them off, because they knew we were coming. It was a clusterfuck from the start. We were pinned down and then Tapley got hit."

Closing her eyes, she rested her forehead against his chin. A small hank of hair escaped the knot at her neck to slide forward, clinging to the drying blood on her jaw. "The bullet slipped through just above the chest plate. I managed to drag him into a side room while everything went to hell around us. I did CPR for ten minutes until the paramedics came." Matt's jaw tightened as he winced. As a frontline Marine medic in Afghanistan after 9/11, he likely recognized it was a lost cause right from the start. "I just couldn't let him go. Not on my watch." Her voice cracked and she gripped his hands a little tighter, her nails biting into his skin as she struggled to maintain.

"You did everything you could. That's all we can ask from any first responder." He rubbed his thumb over the back of her hand. "God, Leigh, I was absolutely frantic. Paul burst into the lab with news of the op. All we knew was an officer had been killed, but we didn't know who. I couldn't get you on the phone. Tucker was sifting through radio calls but couldn't get anywhere."

Matt drew her closer, holding her hands against his chest. She felt his need for contact as if he'd voiced it, but knew he struggled to keep a professional distance; he was well aware she was on duty and this was a crime scene.

"I'm sorry you lost someone today, but I'm not sorry it wasn't you." He pressed a kiss to her forehead. "Can you tell me about it once the scene is secure, or do you need to go back to the Unit?"

"I do, and the paperwork will likely take hours. You have a key to my place. Meet me there. I need a shower, but I'd like to tell you the whole story. Then I need to let it go."

"I'll be there. But first I need to call Tucker. Then I need to call the students and my dad. They're all waiting for word."

Leigh's heart lightened a little bit. It was amazing how family came in many forms. This was hers. "How does your dad know?"

"I called him on my way here. I didn't want him to worry when I didn't show for dinner. He told me to call him the moment I knew anything." He gave her a sympathetic smile—he was all too familiar with the hell of losing a brother-in-arms—and then released her hands. "Come home when you can. I'll be waiting."

Leigh looked down the alley, back toward flashing lights and the reality of a fallen officer and dead perps. But she took a little of Matt's warmth, held it tight, and let it bolster her.

Squaring her shoulders, she walked back into chaos.

CHAPTER TWO: FOG OF WAR

Fog of War: a lack of situational awareness because of numerous confusing or contradictory sources of information.

Friday, December 6, 3:46 a.m.
Abbott Residence
Salem, Massachusetts

The car was a mangled wreck, steam pouring from under the crumpled hood where it had speared into the trunk of a massive oak. Inside the car, two men lay beneath the ruins of the air bags, splattered with a mixture of blood and explosive white powder from the bags.

Leigh sprinted toward the car, but each step seemed to only cover inches instead of feet. "Hang on, help is coming!" Her voice was hoarse, as if she'd been screaming for hours.

Finally reaching the car, Leigh wrestled with the jammed handle before she wrenched the passenger door open. Inside, the driver turned and stared at her with dead eyes. And smiled.

Terror shivered down her spine at the expression of unearthly joy.

"He's already dead, you know."

The voice drew her attention down to the passenger pushing free of the wreckage. She staggered backward as he straightened, his clothes splashed with blood. "The driver?"

"Morgan. You've already killed him."

Leigh's gaze flew over the roof of the car to the young man in a state police uniform sprinting toward them. She wanted to scream for him to stop, but the cry remained trapped in her breathless lungs.

"He just doesn't know it yet." When the man turned, Leigh's gun was in his hand. She clapped one hand to her now empty

holster in disbelief. An ear-ringing explosion and Morgan's body jerked as the force of the bullet knocked him off his feet.

The car separating them suddenly gone, Leigh covered the ground to him in just a few steps and fell to her knees beside him. His neck was a ragged wound and blood spread in creeping fingers around his body. She tried to cover the wound with her hands, but blood continued to ooze through her grip.

Beneath her horrified gaze, Morgan's face changed, the close-shaved blond hair growing longer, darkening. His nose lengthened, his eyes muddying from blue to brown as Tapley's face took shape. Blood gushed through the gap of his open bullet proof vest and Leigh found herself once again kneeling in the filthy, abandoned room, counting off beats as the man's life blood rushed over her hands and down onto the floor to puddle around her knees, flowing over the blade of a serrated knife.

A knife?

A movement in her peripheral vision caught her eye and she swung around to see Sergeant Daniel Kepler, all rich fabric and shiny buttons in his ceremonial dress blues, standing in the corner of the room, his eyes fixed on her. "Sir? Help me!" But he simply continued to stare at her, unblinkingly, never sparing a glance for the man dying on the floor. His man.

She turned back to Tapley to find the vest gone. Instead, a long diagonal slash ripped across his belly, spilling intestines out onto the floor.

Still she kept doing compressions as the blood seemed to pump even faster from his body. So much blood. Where was it all coming from?

The blood welled faster, unending thick streams of it, soaking into her clothes and climbing up her body. Tendrils wound over her cheek.

She screamed as the acrid blood rushed into her open mouth and down her throat . . .

"Leigh!" A man's voice penetrated the screaming in her head. With a gasp, she broke free of the dream, jerking upright, struggling hard against the hands that held her. She tried to draw in a breath, but her lungs were constricted, as if wrapped tight. Kicking out, she tried to free her lower body, but concrete seemed to encase her limbs. In desperation, she threw out an elbow, trying to break free from whatever held her. Pain lanced through her elbow as she connected with something solid.

Matt's grunt of pain cut through the fog, through the confusion and agony, drawing her into the present. Her chest heaving and her throat tight with suppressed sobs, she peered through the blond hair tumbled over her eyes. The lit room seemed blindingly bright as she squinted up at him.

Matt was braced on one arm above her, his eyes clenched tight as he pressed a hand against his jaw. The weight of his lower body held down her legs, while his chest pressed against hers.

"Matt?" Her voice rasped harshly, even to her own ears.

Hazel eyes flew open and his hand dropped away to frame one side of her face. "You're awake. That was a bad one."

She ran her fingertips along his jawline, his five o'clock shadow a rough rasp against her skin. "I hurt you."

"I'll live. You okay?" He eased back slightly, lifting some of his weight from her.

With relief, she pulled a deep, shaky breath into her lungs as she fell back limply on the pillow. "I don't know." She rubbed her hands over her face, trying to clear away the last of the heavy fog.

Matt rolled away, and the room darkened as the bedside light clicked off. His weight settled back on the bed. "Come here."

She pressed against his side, his arms coming around her to pull her in against him as her head naturally found the spot just below his shoulder where the beat of his heart soothed her. Burrowing further, she pressed her face into the curve of his throat, his skin still warm from sleep. She allowed herself a slow breath, pulling in his familiar scent, letting it push away the images of blood and death. With a long sigh, some of the tension flowed from her body.

His fingers threaded through her hair, stroking gently. "Who's Morgan?"

Just like that, the tension returned, stiffening her limbs as she braced both hands against him to push away.

"Whoa, hold on." His arms banded tighter around her, holding her still. "What's wrong?"

She tried to wet her suddenly dry mouth. "How do you know about Morgan? I never told you about him."

"You called his name. Who is he?"

Indecision froze her tongue. If she told him, would he leave her bed and walk out in disgust? Would he join the ranks of so many others who held her responsible?

Men like Morrison.

She could hear his venomous words in her head as if it had only been yesterday: *I don't know how you live with yourself. You killed a cop, a fellow officer. You might as well have pulled the fucking trigger yourself. If you'd been anybody else's kid, you would have been gone after that. But daddy's girl got off with a pat on the head and an early transfer into the Detective Unit like it was some kind of reward for your failure.*

"You know there isn't anything you can't tell me," he prompted quietly when the uneasy silence continued.

"It might change how you think of me."

"Not going to happen. I already know who you are."

The rock-solid surety in his tone eased some of her trepidation. Before she could think it through and come to her senses, she caught the hand he'd tangled in her hair and drew it down over her collarbone. She stopped when their entwined fingers reached the small circle of scar tissue above her left breast. Matt's body went motionless.

"I got this the day he died," she whispered.

He stroked his thumb over the scar. "You think you're responsible for his death." It wasn't a question.

She went still, but couldn't form a response.

"I remember what you said about this scar when you first showed it to me." Matt's voice was a quiet rumble in the dark. "When you were trying to convince me my battle scars shouldn't be hidden." He took their joined hands and laid them against his side, the gnarled ridges of his scars—the result of an explosion in

Afghanistan—hard under her fingers. "You told me some marks deserve to be worn. You consider your scar penance for something, but I doubt it's that straightforward. If war taught me anything, it's that situations are never as black and white as we try to make them." Letting go of her hand, he settled her securely against him again. "Tell me about him. It'll never be easier than here, in the dark."

Spoken by someone who knows, Leigh thought. *You need to be honest with him and it's never going to be easier than right now.* She took a deep breath and forced the words from between her lips. "I'd been a trooper for two years when it happened. It was only weeks after I lost dad, not that it's any excuse. If you can't do the job, you're a danger to yourself and the public, and you shouldn't be there."

"You took some time off?"

"Yes. But sitting at home by myself wasn't making me feel better, so I went back. I needed to keep busy." Having lost his mother in the same horrific car accident that left his father paralyzed from the waist down, she knew Matt understood. "Some people said it was too soon. At the time I was stationed with Field Troop A, on highway patrol. A call came in. Trooper Joel Morgan had pulled over a car with a broken taillight on a rural road. But as he approached the vehicle, the driver took off, hoping to escape while Morgan was out of his cruiser. Afterwards, a search of the car found heroin. That's why they took off. They tried to lose Morgan, but he pursued. I radioed in to assist. But with the two of us after them, they got desperate. They took a corner too fast and lost control. They drove into an oak tree, totaling the car."

Matt winced, but stayed quiet, allowing her to tell her story at her own pace.

"It was obvious they needed medical assistance, so Morgan radioed for an ambulance. I took the passenger side; Morgan took the driver's side. I could see the driver was dead through the window. The autopsy later showed he had a ruptured aorta."

"Gone in less than a minute," Matt said.

"Morgan checked on him anyway. I went to check the passenger. His door was jammed and I had a hard time getting it open. The guy seemed unconscious, maybe dead. But it turns out he was faking it and only had several broken ribs. When I reached in to check his pulse, he went for my gun. I was too focused on helping him, so his attack caught me off guard. We struggled, but even injured, he got my gun and pistol whipped me with it. I went down. Morgan tried to get to me, but he was shot in the neck. Then he turned the gun on me."

She had a flash of lying on the ground, pain lancing through her head, panic radiating as she realized she was going to die. Seeing the muzzle turn toward her and knowing that between her and her father, the Abbotts' four generations in law enforcement would end within a mere matter of weeks. But, unlike her father, there would be no one to mark her passing. Then there was only fiery agony, melting into icy numbness and finally, a blessed blackness.

She surfaced at the warm press of Matt's lips to her forehead, wordlessly drawing her out of the darkness and back to the present. "The only reason I didn't bleed out is that the ambulance was already on its way before I was shot. They were pulling up just as I lost consciousness. But it was too late for Morgan. The shot had severed his jugular."

"You came close yourself. Considering the location of the wound . . ."

"So the surgeon told me. I was the lucky one, but shouldn't have been. Instead, Morgan died, leaving behind a shattered wife and two small children who didn't understand why daddy was never coming home again. No one would have missed me. My family was gone by then."

"I said it earlier and I'll say it again." Matt's voice had a razor-sharp edge to it. "I'm sorry you lost someone, but I'll never be sorry it wasn't you. And from what you've told me, I don't see how it was your fault."

"I forgot for a second that he was a perp. I was only seeing him as a victim at that moment. That rookie mistake cost Morgan his life."

"You're being too hard on yourself. You had an injured man on your hands and you were trying to keep him alive. It's what you needed to do at that moment."

"That opinion is in the minority. The guys in Field Troop A didn't agree with you, by and large. Hell, most of the guys in the unit still don't, including Morrison. He says the only reason I got away with it was because I was the golden child." Frustration and bitterness laced her words for the view she never won anything on her own merit, only by riding her father's coattails. "A lot of the other guys felt I gave up too easily or was stupid to let him get the drop on me."

"Were you formally reprimanded?"

"No."

"Meaning the brass didn't consider you responsible and they had all the evidence in front of them. And it didn't get in your way when you made the transfer to the detective unit. As I said, you weren't responsible. Did some of the officers holding you responsible convince you to transfer out of Field Troop A?"

She gave a small, awkward shrug. "I always wanted into the Detective Unit. It was the life dad lived, and I lived it vicariously through him until he died. It was always the end game. But their attitude might have put on a little extra pressure to get out."

"You called Morgan's name in the nightmare. He was there? In the dream?"

"They all were. I watched Morgan die again. Then Morgan became Tapley, and I was back in the factory trying to keep him alive. But then Tapley's bullet wound morphed into the same wounds as John Hershey." A vision of the nearly-dead victim left by the first killer they'd caught together shimmered into her mind's eye in a morass of bloody organs and shredded tissue. She rubbed a hand over her face and shook her head to clear it. "Too much blood. Too much death. It's all getting mixed up in my head."

"Too much stress and not enough sleep. That's what likely led to that jumble of memories. It was never a good combination for me."

Leigh needed no other explanation. She knew all about Matt's struggles with PTSD after leaving Afghanistan, and his efforts to find a new life and leave his career in medicine behind. Nightmares had plagued him for years. Worse, waking nightmares had been a horrific result of their first case together. Luckily, none of the cases they'd worked since had put him through that particular hell again. But she feared for the next time they had to deal with a freshly mutilated body.

Leigh lay quietly for a moment, concentrating on the steady beat of his heart. "There was one other thing though. Something that never happened in real life, but I'm sure is my subconscious trying to make a point. In the dream, Kepler was in the room inside the abandoned factory with Tapley and me. He just stood in the corner, staring at us." She paused, casting her mind back. "No, that's wrong. Staring at *me*. He never saw Tapley."

Matt's head came off the pillow as if staring at her in the dark. "He wasn't a part of the op today, was he?"

"Not on site. We had so many groups involved; everyone was cherry-picking who they wanted for the actual raid. He was monitoring from Salem, but he sent Riley and me as backup. We weren't involved until today."

Matt's body jerked as connections solidified. "He sent you? The moment things got nasty, he sent you in?"

"Yes."

Leigh didn't need to be a mind reader to know where Matt's mind jumped. She was already there.

Sergeant Kepler. The man who replaced her father after his death. The man she suspected was behind the mysterious deliveries. Packages containing photos of her father's violent death, and, supposedly, from his shadowy life detailing his nefarious dealings. Except Tucker had already proved the photo was faked and police records at the unit had been changed.

Your father wasn't the hero you think he was. He was a dirty cop. Soon the world will know it. And you'll be the one to pay for his crimes.

Someone was trying to smear her father's name. And the more Matt, Tucker, and she worked to find the truth, the more it looked like Kepler was responsible.

"Goddamn it." Matt's voice was tight with anger. "It's been my fear for weeks he might try to kill you to cover things up. Send you out to die in the line of duty because we're getting too close to the truth. That might have been exactly what Kepler intended today. Does Tucker know?"

"I haven't told him. But you don't have to with Tucker. He's likely already connected the dots and will be considering Kepler's motives."

"You mean that Kepler wants you dead?"

"We don't know that."

"No, we don't, but we'd be putting our heads in the sand not to realize there's a possible threat there."

"I know. Tucker's still doing some digging, but if we haven't heard from him in the next couple of days, I'll reach out to him. We need to meet with him again to decide on next steps."

"Sooner rather than later. I don't want Kepler getting the chance to aim another bullet at you."

"Agreed." Rising up on one elbow, Leigh peered at the glowing numbers of the clock on the far beside table. "But in the meantime, we need to get some sleep. It's almost a quarter after four and I need to be in the office first thing."

"I thought you were off."

"I was supposed to be, but no one's off at a time like this." She settled down again, looping one hand over his shoulder and snuggling in. "I'm glad you were here with me tonight."

"Me too." He kissed the crown of her head. "Now put it out of your mind and go to sleep. I'm not going anywhere."

Sleep was a long time coming. Matt slipped off while her brain still whirled and she continued to turn the day's events over in her mind.

It all came down to Kepler. It was time to clear him or bury him.

Before someone buried her.

CHAPTER THREE: OPSEC

OPSEC: Department of Defense acronym for operations security—the process by which an organization categorizes and discloses unclassified information. OPSEC challenges members to look at the organization through the eyes of someone intent on harming its members, resources, or mission.

Monday, December 9, 9:19 a.m.
Boston University, School of Medicine
Boston, Massachusetts

"Matt, can I ask a favor?"

Matt looked up in surprise to find Kiko standing beside his desk. He was so deep into writing a grant proposal to help support their next few years of research at the Old North Church columbarium, he hadn't heard her come in. "Sure. What's up?"

"I don't know what to do about something." She restlessly shifted her weight from foot to foot.

Intrigued, Matt closed his laptop and gave her his full attention. This awkwardness was new for his senior grad student; usually she was the most self-assured student in the room. Of Japanese descent, Kiko carried herself with grace and the strength brought about by years of martial arts training with her *katana*, a traditional Japanese sword.

"What's the problem?" He pressed a little harder when she hesitated. "I can't help if you don't tell me what's going on."

"Do you remember when we were at the conference last summer, how I met that girl doing her Ph.D. at Harvard? Cynthia? The one in Sharpe's lab?"

Trevor Sharpe. The name was like fingernails on a blackboard. Matt liked to think he was easy to get along with in his professional life—he fought for what was his and his students', but he always tried to be collegial and a fair collaborator both inside and outside his field of expertise. But one experience with Trevor Sharpe had forever tainted his opinion of the man.

"I remember," he said, his tone flat.

"Well, day before yesterday, I was at Harvard. Cyn invited me to look at her work. They've been exploring some new technical aspects of 3D computer facial modeling, and she knew I'd be interested. She doubted Sharpe would be pleased about her showing one of your students the tricks of their trade, so we saved it for a Saturday afternoon when he wouldn't be in the lab. He was busy with some sort of Christmas thing at his wife's business."

Matt's gaze drifted to the calendar on the corner of his desk— December 9. He pushed away the thought of how far behind he was in his Christmas shopping.

"When I got there, Cyn was the only person in the lab," Kiko continued. "But when she tried to show me their modeling, she had an issue connecting to the group's server, so she left the lab to reboot it. I was killing time, so I wandered around."

Matt chuckled. "Doing a little spying?"

"I admit I was curious. I've only worked in this forensic anthropology lab. I mean, we've spent a lot of time in Rowe's facilities lately," Kiko said, referring to the Medical Examiner for the Commonwealth of Massachusetts, Dr. Edward Rowe, and the cases they'd worked with him. "But it's not the same thing. So, yeah, I was looking at their work." She glanced around the lab, her gaze travelling from the bone grinder sitting beside the light microscope, to the box of animal bones in the corner that still needed sorting months after it arrived, to the shelf with the antelope and alligator skulls, and finally to the tiny fetal skeleton on the countertop. "Their lab is bigger than ours."

"Of course it is," Matt said, struggling to keep professional jealousy out of his tone. He wasn't sure he managed it. "Sharpe is considered a big deal there."

Kiko contemplated him with a narrowed expression. "And yet you don't think he's a big deal. You've never said why you don't like him."

"I've never said I don't like him."

"That's true. You haven't. But I can see it. You *really* dislike him, enough that he's not a topic of conversation for you, even though he's just across the Charles and is a professional competitor, so to speak. Maybe someday you'll tell us why."

As disconcerting as it was, Matt took it as a positive sign of the group's connectedness that Kiko could see through him so easily. It was one reason they worked well together. "Maybe someday."

Kiko skirted Matt's desk to stand in front of a fully articulated adult skeleton hanging from a stainless-steel stand. A plush Santa hat sat jauntily on its smooth ivory skull. "Anyway, like most anthropology or anatomy labs, they have an anatomical skeleton just like this. In fact, they have several, but one was sort of pushed into a back corner. And I noticed something odd about it." Her voice trailed off as she picked up the skeleton's right hand, and then dropped it, watching it swing back and forth several times.

Matt tipped his chair back, his eyes narrowed on his student. It was unlike Kiko to be so hesitant. She stood stiffly, and when she moved, her usual athletic gait seemed stilted. But he remained quiet, letting her take her time.

She spun around suddenly. "I swear this isn't because of the cases we've worked with Leigh. I'm not looking for victims because I want more criminal work."

Matt bolted upright in his chair. "Victims?"

"The skeleton. I don't think the person died of natural causes."

"Why?"

"Usually we buy anatomical skeletons from scientific suppliers, right? They used to come from India or China, but both those countries have put a stop to exporting human remains, so now it's more a matter of reselling existing specimens or new donations given for research purposes. I don't know where this one came from, but there's something funny about it."

This was like pulling teeth. "Anything specific?"

Kiko didn't answer immediately, but crossed the room to her desk and stopped in front of the Christmas tree beside her laptop. She had brought in the small crooked tree a few days ago, and the students had playfully decorated it with tiny microfuge tubes filled with colored solutions, intricately cut origami pathogens, and an organic chemistry model to crown the top. She ran a finger over the spiky paper glycoproteins surrounding a virus particle. "There was a kerf mark on the hyoid. It's not deep, and if the light hadn't hit it just right, I wouldn't have seen it. But once I did, I used the flashlight app on my cell for a better look. It's there all right."

Matt thought about the small U-shaped bone that hung directly under the lower jaw, just above the Adam's apple in men and in the equivalent position in women. While it didn't articulate with any other bone in the body, it was a muscle and ligament attachment point connecting the soft tissues of the mouth, neck, and upper chest. It was also a common osteological indicator of strangulation because it broke easily under direct pressure. But in this case, if it bore a kerf mark . . .

"What kind of kerf mark?" Matt asked. When her face clouded, he held up a placating hand. "It's not that I don't believe you, I'm just looking for more details."

"Obviously, I didn't have time to unwire the bone and examine at it under the scope, but from a quick look, I'd say a knife, non-serrated. It's on the upper left side, moving diagonally down the anterior surface. It doesn't look like a processing artifact from defleshing the bones."

"That's usually done by bath because they want the bones to be pristine." Matt ran his index finger from the left side of his throat to his right in a slight downward diagonal. "You think the throat was cut?"

Kiko shrugged, both hands spread wide. "Have I totally lost it?"

"You're reading the evidence and using deductive reasoning to extrapolate cause. It's what we do." He reached for his phone.

"What are you doing?"

"Calling Leigh. I need to run this by her."

Kiko tipped her head forward into her hands to cover her face. "She'll think I'm crazy. As it was, I stewed over this all day yesterday trying to talk myself out of talking to you."

Matt paused, one finger hovering over the key to speed dial Leigh. "Do you think you're wrong?"

A quiet sigh. "No. I just wish I'd taken a picture of it. By the time I finished looking at it, Cyn was coming down the hall and I had to move fast so she didn't know I'd been snooping."

"Then calling Leigh is the right thing to do." He dialed her number and waited until she picked up. "Hey, it's me."

There was a smile in her voice. "Hey 'me'."

"How are you feeling today?"

"Better. Thanks for spending so much of the weekend with me and being there when I needed to sound off."

"Happy to. You've certainly done the same for me. Look, this actually isn't a social call. I have a business question for you."

"Police business?" The two words were full of curiosity.

"Yeah. What would need to happen if we think we've found a murder victim, but aren't one hundred percent sure?"

"*What?*" There was a mumbled curse and then a long pause. "Okay, I just pulled over before I drove off the road. What did you find?"

"It wasn't me, it was Kiko, and it might be a suspicious death." He quickly recapped Kiko's tale. "What do you think?"

"First of all, it's not my jurisdiction. That's Middlesex County. You need the Middlesex Detective Unit."

"I don't know the Middlesex Detective Unit. I know you."

An exasperated sigh came through the line. "Truth to be told, you don't know you have a victim, either. You can't call this in yet, Matt. You need to see it. *You*, not one of the students."

"You want me to get into Sharpe's lab?"

"Is that a problem?"

"He's not going to invite me in, let me tell you. We'll have to get in at some point when Sharpe isn't around."

"Can you do it?"

Matt looked up at Kiko, who stood by his desk, staring down at him. "Can we do it? Get in unseen? Leigh says I have to attest to the damage. But if Sharpe sees me, it's game over for our little expedition and possibly the evidence. On top of that, I could be fired from BU and you could be expelled from the program. You need to be sure."

"I'm sure and we can do it. Let me start with a fact-finding mission to find out when the lab might be empty, and we'll give it a try."

"It's a go," Matt said to Leigh. "God help us, we're actually going to break into the research lab of my top competitor. Wish us luck."

CHAPTER FOUR: HUMINT

HUMINT: Central Intelligence Agency acronym for human intelligence—any information that can be gathered from human sources.

Monday, December 9, 4:35 p.m.
Harvard University
Cambridge, Massachusetts

Matt pushed through glass doors and into the foyer of the building housing the Anthropology department, looking for all the world as if he belonged there. "You're sure we're going to be clear?" he asked *sotto voce.*

Kiko scurried to keep up with Matt's longer strides. "Cynthia says they start their lab meeting at four-thirty and usually go for a couple of hours."

Matt shook his head in disgust. "Who starts their lab meeting at four-thirty in the afternoon?"

"Cynthia's theory is Sharpe doesn't want any of his grad students to have an actual life. He makes them work all day and then schedules lab meetings at the end of the workday so it's on their own time. Apparently, originally he wanted to schedule lab meetings on Friday at four-thirty, but someone threatened to take it to Grad Studies, so he moved it to Monday instead."

"Must be a lovely place to work," Matt said dryly, angling for the elevator.

"He's pretty prestigious, so his students are considered lucky by outsiders. But within the inner circle, he's considered a massive egomaniac and everyone hates him. Did you know everything that goes out of that lab has to be analyzed and submitted by him alone?"

Matt stopped dead in his tracks, ignoring the muttered curse of the man who nearly plowed into him from behind. "But that means one person controls all the data coming out of the lab. One person controls the message and potentially steers the results the way he wants instead of how they actually turn out."

"I know." Kiko narrowed her eyes in apparent suspicion. "Cyn didn't come right out and say it, but she sort of implied changes might be made."

"Son of a bitch. Not that I should be surprised, but still." He grasped Kiko's arm and tugged her toward the bank of elevators. "Come on. Now I really, *really* want to burn his ass."

She laughed. "You wanted to before."

"Totally. But now it's going to be an extra pleasure. I *hate* academic dishonesty; it makes the rest of us who work damn hard look bad. Science is about objectivity, not about twisting the results to fit your personal agenda."

Kiko gave him a wide, satisfied smile. "Let's get him then."

They took the elevator to the third floor. "To your left," Kiko murmured as they stepped into the hallway and snaked through the end of the day crowd. "Second door from the end on the right."

"You're sure it'll be unlocked?" Matt lowered his voice to match hers.

"Positive. Because it's a shared space, they keep everything unlocked until six o'clock. After that, security automatically locks the doors. Only registered pass key access until seven the next morning."

Matt kept his head down, resisting the urge to look around like a wide-eyed tourist; he also didn't want to risk being recognized from either his work with Leigh or within his own field. Reaching the door, Matt pushed through first, Kiko behind him. The door closed behind them with a soft *click* and they found themselves inside a large, airy lab.

Matt scanned their surroundings, only relaxing when he knew the space was empty. He chuckled when Kiko did the same.

"Look at us. We'd make lousy spies," he said.

"Give me a *katana* and a matched opponent in a *dojo* any

day," she retorted. "But leave the subterfuge out of it. That's more up Paul's alley."

"Wait until he hears about this. He's going to be beyond ticked we didn't invite him."

Matt scanned the lab again, this time taking in the polished floors, new cabinetry, and long banks of windows letting in the last of the failing twilight. State of the art equipment was scattered around the lab, including a cluster of high-powered desktops with huge monitors, ideal for facial modeling. "Actually, I'm glad Paul's not here. Now he can't complain that we don't have the latest equipment to make his life easier."

"We manage just fine. Nothing wrong with using your brain rather than technology."

Matt tossed her a quick grin. No doubt about it, he loved his students because they were truly good people. He glanced at the clock on the wall—4:39 p.m. *Time to move this along.* "Which skeleton are we looking at?"

"The one in the corner. There, beside the fume hood."

"Right."

They crossed the lab, skirting two other anatomical skeletons—a juvenile and an adult—with almost no notice. Matt assessed the skeleton as they approached, taking in the gross phenotypic markers—medium stature, robust glabella and mental eminence, narrow sub-pubic angle. All typically male attribu—

Matt and Kiko froze as the doorknob squeaked and the door opened several inches. It paused before it swung toward the doorjamb again as voices sounded from the hallway, the words filtering in through the narrow gap.

"I don't have the time now. My students are waiting for me. I forgot the latest analysis I wanted to share with them, so I'm just getting that. I can free up some time for you tomorrow morning if that's convenient."

Matt recognized the voice instantly. "*Sharpe!*" he hissed at Kiko. "*Hide!*"

Kiko dove under a nearby benchtop and curled up between a stack of drawers and a box of lab supplies. Matt cursed his bigger frame; he could never fold up like that. Then he spotted a narrow alcove housing an electrical panel between the wall and the fume hood. Biting back a groan at the effort, he squeezed into the gap. He barely fit, his ski jacket adding unwanted bulk. If Sharpe came too far into the lab and actually looked into the corner, he would catch Matt red-handed. He held his breath and kept his gaze fixed on the far side of the lab.

"That sounds good. Call me tomorrow. I'll be happy to advise you." Sharpe's voice boomed, followed by the sound of the door closing. "Incompetent moron," Sharpe muttered. "Not enough intelligence to fill a teaspoon."

On the far side of the lab, Matt's hackles rose. *There's the attitude we all know and nobody loves.* He squeezed back even further as Sharpe came into view. Matt hadn't seen him for over a year, but he hadn't changed one iota: tall and blond, he kept his hair perfectly coiffed to brush his collar, seemingly casual but perfectly calculated in reality. As always, he was in shape; Matt knew his narcissistic streak wouldn't allow anything else. Today, he went for the yacht club look—pressed khakis, dock shoes, and a designer button-down shirt.

It's all a big act, Trevor. From your research to your image. You're a real-life comic book character.

Sharpe went to a big desk beside one of the wide windows and flipped through papers until he pulled out a specific document. He took an extra moment to page through it, nodded in satisfaction, and then strode out of the lab. The door slammed shut behind him.

Matt let out a relieved breath and inched from his hiding place just enough to catch Kiko's eye. He held up an index finger as he listened to the silence for a full thirty seconds before being satisfied Sharpe was gone for good. "Okay, we're clear," he whispered. "Let's do this and get the hell out."

Kiko crawled out from under the bench, jumped lithely to her feet, and lead the way back into the corner. "Take a look and see what you think. And this time, we'll take pictures."

"Absolutely." He pulled a miniature, powerful flashlight from his jacket pocket and trained it on the small, U-shaped hyoid bone, hard wired to the C-3 vertebra to jut outward just under the mandible. He quickly identified the mark Kiko had described. "Good call. This would have been easy to miss."

"I think a lot of people have missed it up to now. What do you think?"

"Give me a second. That's why I brought this." He pulled a small magnifying glass from another pocket. "If we're going to call this in, I want to be totally sure and we don't have time to take this skeleton apart to look at it microscopically."

"Good thinking."

"If I'm sticking my neck out, I need to be absolutely sure of the details."

Matt held the glass over the hyoid and trained the light on it again, taking in the small slash running diagonally over the bone. The edges of the kerf mark narrowed as it sliced into the bone, the two sides meeting to form a narrow, shallow trench. "On first look, I don't see anything that indicates serrations, although I want to confirm that microscopically."

"But with the placement where it is . . ." Kiko prompted.

"The knife would have cut both the internal and external carotid arteries. Hold this." He handed her the flashlight. "Keep it focused right there." He pulled his cell phone from his pocket, and took a series of pictures, some detail shots, some wide angle. He included several shots of the skeleton's unique serial number for unmistakable identification later. "Okay, let's get out of here."

Matt paused at the door and looked back into the lab, but there was no sign they were ever there. He gave a short nod to Kiko, who opened the door and stepped through, looking like she didn't have a care in the world. He closed the door behind them and followed her down the hallway.

Neither relaxed until they were out of the building, strolling down the sidewalk to Matt's SUV, parked around the corner. The sky was clear, but the afternoon's light snow blew in airy swirls along the sidewalk.

Kiko let out a breath of pure relief, the warm air creating a cloud of mist. "That was a little too close for comfort."

"No kidding. But we got what we needed."

"What do we do now? Leigh can't help us."

"Not when it's a Middlesex case. I'm going to call it in to them as an anonymous tip. If they don't take the bait, we'll have to reveal our expertise and use the pictures to document our claims. But I don't want either of us connected to this case if we can help it. At least not yet."

"What do you mean?" Kiko asked.

"What do you think will happen once the skeleton is taken into custody?"

"It'll go to the state medical examiner's office."

"And then . . .?"

Kiko's face was a study in bafflement until a light bulb virtually flared over her head. Her eyes went wide and then she laughed at her own cluelessness. "Rowe's going to need a forensic anthropology consult. And that will be you."

"Exactly. I want our hands off this case until then. Once we're brought in officially, it will be a different matter." Rounding the corner, he spotted his SUV and quickened his pace. "Until then, we know nothing about this."

"It's going to be weird working with someone besides Leigh."

"I'm not sure how much working we'll be doing. Leigh is the exception, rather than the rule. I've worked with other cops before and it was a very different experience. She considers us a part of her team. Most cops consider scientists to be nothing more than technicians and have very little interaction with them. We'll see how this one goes, but I don't have high hopes." As they approached his vehicle, he unlocked the doors and got in. Settling behind the wheel, Matt scanned the surrounding area. "Now, the bigger challenge. We need to find a pay phone to call this in."

"I'll bet there's one at the supermarket we passed on the way here," Kiko said, fastening her seat belt.

Matt pulled away from the curb, merging into rush hour traffic. "That'll do nicely. I want the call to come from Cambridge and not Boston so there's no trace back to us. Now, let's give Dr.

Sharpe the shock of his life."

"Unless it isn't," Kiko said.

Matt flicked a sideways glance at her. He'd thought the same thing, but, considering his feelings for Sharpe, hadn't wanted to voice it. But Kiko had put it out there for him. "That's right," he agreed. "Unless it isn't."

CHAPTER FIVE: BLACK SWAN

Black Swan: an extremely rare event that exerts disproportionate effect because it cannot be predicted.

Wednesday, December 11, 2:51 p.m.
Boston University, School of Medicine
Boston, Massachusetts

Matt picked up his phone, pleased to see the familiar name displayed on caller ID. "Rowe, this is a surprise." He caught Kiko's eye and gave her a raised eyebrow, *here-we-go* look.

"Lowell, how are things?"

"Good. You?"

"Up to my ears in bureaucratic BS, but you know how that is. Look, a case just came in and I could use your expertise."

Matt purposely played dumb. "Decomposed remains?"

"No, skeletal. But not from Essex. These came in through the Middlesex Unit."

"What's the story behind them?" Matt tipped his desk chair back and grinned at Kiko who settled a hip on the corner of his desk to blatantly listen in on the conversation.

"Middlesex followed up on an anonymous tip. A lab at Harvard supposedly had a skeleton with some suspicious markings. The officer on call, Trooper Jefferson, went in and couldn't make heads or tails of the skeleton, so he took it into custody as evidence. Apparently, the researcher in the lab went ballistic. Dr. Trevor Sharpe. Said he was a forensic anthropologist and he'd know if there was a problem with one of his specimens."

"Only if he took the time to take a good look at it."

"You know Sharpe?" Rowe asked.

"We've met once or twice," Matt said. "We're local and in the same field. You know how you sometimes bump into colleagues at gatherings."

"Sure do. Since the skeleton was in his lab, we can hardly use him as an objective consultant in this case. So I want you."

"I'm happy to help. When do you want me to look at the remains?"

"How about now? Jefferson is still here. When he heard I wanted to transfer the remains, he stayed to maintain chain of custody. I can send both him and the remains over in the van now."

"That works for me. I can meet him in Receiving and transfer the remains to my lab. I'll sign off on any paperwork he needs. Does he know we've worked with law enforcement before?"

"He wasn't wild about the remains leaving this office, so I told him this wasn't your first rodeo with me or with the state police. But you might need to give him a rundown of what you'll be doing before you send him on his way."

Matt stifled an internal groan. *Great. One of* those *cops.* "Let me guess—old school?"

"A little. Some of the older cops think science conjures results out of thin air. It makes them suspicious."

"Awesome." There was no mistaking the dry sarcasm in Matt's tone.

"As I recall, you and Abbott didn't exactly see eye to eye at first, either. He's not a bad cop. Give him a chance to settle in with you. The remains are in x-ray, but they'll be out any minute. I'll have the driver call when they're leaving."

Matt ended the call and turned to his students. "It took a little longer than I expected, but there's our call." He indicated the table in the middle of the room, which currently held the aged remains of a young woman recovered from the charnel house beneath the Old North Church. "Let's pack her away for now. We don't know how long ago this victim died, but we should still move on it ASAP. And heads up—the Middlesex cop is coming with the remains. It sounds like he's an old school kind of guy, so be prepared for anything. At least he didn't dump the remains and run, so that's a good start."

The first five minutes will tell us what we're dealing with.

Wednesday, December 11, 4:04 p.m.
Boston University, School of Medicine
Boston, Massachusetts

"We're here." Matt called as he backed through the lab doorway, guiding a narrow gurney holding a body bag. A morgue tech followed at the other end, and an older man wearing a heavy navy jacket came in last, closing the door behind them.

They wheeled the gurney to the larger lab table. "On three," Matt said, as he and the tech grasped each end of the bag. "One, two, three." They lifted it in unison and carefully lay it down on cold stainless steel. "Thanks. Do you need a hand getting back down to the dock?"

"Appreciate it if you could lend me one of your students for a few minutes," the tech said.

"Sure. Juka?"

Juka looked up from where he stood with Paul, his polar opposite. Juka was solid and stocky with the darker coloring of his Bosnian ancestors, whereas Paul was tall and gangly with nearly Nordic blue eyes and fair skin. The young man gave a single nod—Juka would never waste words when a gesture would do—took Matt's end of the gurney, and maneuvered it out of the lab.

Matt considered the older man. His salt and pepper hair was close-cropped and he was clean-shaven. Ice blue eyes studied him, coolly assessing.

Matt held out his hand. "We didn't have time downstairs for a proper introduction. Trooper Jefferson, I'm Matt Lowell. I'm a forensic anthropologist here at Boston University."

The returning handshake was firm, but perfunctory. "So I hear." The man's deep voice was gravel rough as if he'd just come off a three-day bender and had the migraine to prove it. "Rowe says you're solid."

"High praise from Rowe."

Jefferson's gaze skimmed over the lab, finally coming to rest on the two students standing shoulder to shoulder—Paul, seeming even taller with his spiky blond hair, and Kiko, willowy and graceful, her long black hair twisted into a charmingly messy bun at the nape of her neck.

Paul grinned at him and thrust out a hand. "Hi, I'm Paul," he said enthusiastically.

The cop didn't move to shake hands.

Kiko took the hint and didn't hold out her hand. "Nice to meet you. I'm Kiko."

Jefferson turned back to Matt. "I've never had a case that had nothing but bones. No murder scene, no burial ground, no associated evidence. You'll excuse me if I'm a little skeptical about what you can do."

Matt walked behind Kiko and Paul so he spoke from the perspective of the group. "What *we* can do might surprise you. Skeletal structure can indicate age, sex, and race that can then in turn be used to filter missing person reports. Any signs of previous healed bone injury can help to confirm identification, as can dental work." From his previous quick look at the remains, Matt didn't recall any antemortem healed breaks, but Jefferson didn't need to know that. "Without any other evidence to guide you, victim identification is all you've got and that's exactly where we can help. I'll write you a full report with our findings, but if you'd like to stick around for twenty minutes, I can give you a quick overview to get you started."

Jefferson pushed back his heavy sleeve to reveal a sturdy black watch. He stared at it, considering. "I can give you fifteen."

Matt swallowed the sarcastic response that rose to his lips for a cop who considered he was giving up his precious time for the case. *Clearly, he's not on board. Only way to change his mind is to show him otherwise.*

"Okay, guys, let's see what we've got."

As Kiko and Paul joined him at the table, he unzipped the bag.

"Looks normal to me," Paul said. "Minus the wires and screws holding it together as an anatomical specimen."

"The devil will be in the details on this one. Let's get him out of the bag and onto the table. Kiko, get the camera. We need full pictures before we can start." The door to the lab opened and closed while they were settling the articulated skeleton. Without looking over his shoulder, Matt called, "Juka, come and give us a hand. We're just starting on the remains."

"Look who I found," Juka said.

Matt spun around to find Leigh standing beside Juka just inside the door, snow dusting her shoulders and a soft scarf wound around her neck to peek out from the collar of her wool coat. He was confused for a moment—*why was she here?*—and then memory slammed back into place. "Oh, damn. We were supposed to meet at four."

She arched an eyebrow at him. "Did you forget?"

"Uh . . ."

"He did," Paul interjected freely. "But he has a good reason."

Leigh's gaze trained down to the skeleton on the table and then moved to the stranger in a State Police jacket. "New case?"

"Just in from Rowe's office." Matt crossed the lab to her. "Sorry, I got sidetracked when Rowe called an hour ago and asked for a consult."

"It's all right. If anyone understands, it's me. We can reschedule our plans to go climbing."

"Not a chance. Can we just get started a little later than we initially planned?"

"Sure." She took in the students gathered around the table and her shoulders slumped fractionally. "Want me to get a cup of coffee and come back later?"

He'd been the guy on the outside looking in often enough to know it wasn't a good place to be. More than that, he was well aware Leigh knew all about being on the outside since that was frequently where she stood in her own unit. No way was anyone kicking her out of his lab, a place he wanted her to feel welcome. "Not at all." Taking her arm, he drew her into the group. "Trooper

Jefferson, this is Trooper Leigh Abbott from the Essex Detective Unit. Leigh, this is Trooper Jefferson out of the Middlesex Detective Unit."

Leigh held out her hand. "Trooper Jefferson."

"Trooper Abbott." They shook, but Jefferson's eyes grew speculative as he looked from Leigh to Matt. "Hold on. Abbott and Lowell? Are you the Abbott out of Essex who cracked the Bradford case?"

"The very one."

"Well, I'll be damned." He swung around to Matt. "And that was you working with her. The egghead who found the burial ground and identified how the victims were killed and when."

"The very one," Matt echoed dryly, raising an eyebrow when Paul snickered at the term 'egghead.'

"Huh." Jefferson stared at them thoughtfully, his head absently bobbing up and down as he considered them. "That changes things."

"In what way?" Leigh asked.

"I was a little skeptical Lowell here could add anything to this case considering the evidence. But considering his track record . . ."

"He and his team's track record," Leigh clarified. "Give them some time, they'll find your answers. Mind if I stick around for a bit? I'm off duty, but it's always fascinating to watch them put together an ID from something that looks totally generic to the rest of us."

"Not at all. So, Lowell, what do we have?"

Pleased at the sudden turnaround in opinion, Matt launched into an explanation. "What we have is an articulated skeleton. Now, don't get me wrong, this is a great anatomical teaching tool but for our full analysis, we want to dismantle it so every bone can be examined from every angle. All those wires and nuts and bolts will have to come out. On that note, Juka, grab the toolkit under the balance, please. Kiko, are you done?"

Kiko placed the SLR camera on a nearby benchtop and gave Matt a thumbs-up.

"Taking out that hardware's going to leave holes," Jefferson stated.

"It will. And we'll note each mark in every bone. But those were made postmortem—after death. After the victim was reduced to nothing but skeletal remains. How that happened is something we still need to figure out."

"You mean how the victim became nothing but bones?"

"Yes." Matt pulled on a pair of latex gloves and ran the fingertips of one hand down the long stretch of the right femur. "You see what a nice even ivory color this is? That means the bones weren't buried or, if they were, it was for a short period of time because bones tend to absorb minerals and take on the color of the soil they're buried in." Bending over, he scrutinized the femur. "I don't see any marks that might indicate the flesh was stripped off with a blade. Or that the flesh was removed by carnivores."

"A blade or teeth would leave marks?"

"They would. Bone is hard, but not that hard. Teeth and metal tools will leave slashes and grooves behind. Speaking of which, Juka, find the wire cutters, please."

As Juka opened the toolbox and rooted through the contents, Matt circled the table.

"Usually, we're just looking for cause of death and who was responsible. But in this case, because of the curious displayed nature of the remains, we need to figure out how the body went from fleshed to defleshed in a manner that left the bones basically pristine. Time since death is going to be problematic here. We can't judge weathering of the bones because they've been stored inside. We can't use decomposition stage, because there isn't any flesh. But if we can figure out how long the bones were at Harvard, and how they were defleshed—and therefore how long that would take—I can give you a minimum time since death. A maximum will be pretty much impossible in this case."

"We also need to figure out how the Harvard lab acquired the skeleton in the first place. Assuming the jackass professor didn't do it himself." Jefferson's face wrinkled in disgust.

Matt took in Kiko's amused look. "I hear Dr. Sharpe wasn't too happy about releasing the evidence."

"He was all ego and bluster. *'You can't do this to me! I'm important!'* God, you should have heard him. By the end of it I wanted to flatten him." Jefferson glanced at Leigh. "Sadly, they don't let us do that even when it's deserved. I will have to question him again when he calms down though."

Leigh grinned. "Maybe you should have him brought into the unit. That usually scares most witnesses before you even start. If he's as big an egomaniac as you say, it wouldn't hurt to have him slightly off stride. You might get more out of him."

A sly smile curved Jefferson's lips. "I like the way you think, Abbott. That's a good plan."

"Here you go." Juka handed Matt the wire cutters.

"Rowe said the report came in about a kerf on the hyoid." Matt snipped the two small wires holding the small U-shaped bone to the C-3 vertebra and pulled the metal remnants free. He flipped the hyoid over in his gloved fingers, angling it so the light accentuated the defect in the bone. He held it out toward the officers. "Can you see the kerf mark? Look carefully, it's small."

Leigh leaned in for a better view. "I do, but it's tiny. Hard to believe anyone spotted it." Matt noted she kept her gaze fixed on the bone and away from Kiko. She might know how the skeleton came into their possession, but she wasn't about to let Jefferson know.

Jefferson jabbed a finger at the minute slash in the bone. "With that mark, are you thinking the throat was cut?"

"That's exactly what I'm thinking. But I need to get the bone under the microscope to be able to nail that down."

"You're sure this couldn't be left over from cleaning the bones? You did say a knife would leave a mark."

"I can't say there's no chance whatsoever of that, but it's less likely. When we're preparing a skeleton for examination, either for forensics or for teaching, we go out of our way not to use sharp implements that could leave permanent marks behind. In both cases, you want the bones to remain as pristine as possible. The best way is to use a detergent bath to dissolve the tissues. Either way, the angle of the cut seems wrong to me to be from cleaning, but a closer look will confirm that." He set down the hyoid. "Let's start dismantling. Concentrate on the pelvis first and I'll do the skull. Before Trooper Jefferson walks out of here today, let's give him the basics so he can start looking into missing persons. Avoid using tools of any kind unless absolutely necessary—we want to make sure any tool marks on the bones don't come from us."

Matt and the students moved in, unwinding stubborn screws with fingers, cursing those that didn't budge, wrapping bones with surgical drapes to protect the surface when tools were required. Finally, the last stubborn wire connecting the pelvis to the spine was severed with cutters and they stood back, the floor around them littered with metal wires and connectors, carelessly dropped to keep the table clear of everything but the remains. Matt picked his way through metal flotsam as he circled the table to first examine the skull and then the pelvis, lifting a bone here, turning over another there.

Matt looked up to find Trooper Jefferson staring at him. "Even with the skeleton only partially dismantled, a few things are clear. Both skull and pelvis indicate male, and the pubic symphysis is phase two, suggesting an age range of twenty-five to twenty-nine years. Skull sutures shift that range slightly higher, so we'll go with twenty-five to thirty-two for now, pending additional study. Skull indicates that race is white American. We'll calculate stature, but we're going to have to do better than that to really nail down ID."

"We can pull DNA," Juka suggested. "Teeth are intact and in good condition, so tooth pulp is an option."

"It is," Matt agreed. "But the first thing we do after the rest of the dismantling is to catalog every defect." The collective groan from his students made the corners of his lips twitch. "Yes, I know, there are now a huge number of extra artifacts because of the articulation process, but we need to detail every . . . single . . . one. There are two hundred and six bones; I want notes on all of them. Full gross examination before we move onto the microscopic exam. That won't be until tomorrow."

"When will you get me the details on what weapon might have been involved?" Jefferson asked.

"I'll get to that tomorrow unless something unexpected pops up," Matt said. "We'll do standard scanning electron microscopy, but I want to use digital microscopy as well."

"That's something you've never used before on any of our cases," Leigh said. "What's the difference?"

"Scanning electron microscopy, or SEM, is very useful. It will show us characteristics of the blade used, the direction of travel, and if it was a symmetric or asymmetric blade."

"You're talking about the cutting edge?" Leigh asked

"Yes. How's your algebra?"

"Beyond rusty. How's yours."

"Pretty good. But this is basic. Remember what an isosceles triangle is?"

"That rings a faint bell. That's a triangle that has two identical angles."

"And you said you were rusty. Yes, and that's exactly what some blades look like."

Facing the two officers to include Jefferson in his explanation, Matt made a chopping motion with both hands, the sides of his hands meeting at the bottom of a 'V' shape. "But some blades are more like a right-angled triangle, with a vertical and a horizontal side and one angled side between them." He mimed that blade shape as well, one hand falling vertically and the other sliding diagonally down to meet it.

"As you might imagine, those two blade shapes will make very different defects in the bone. SEM will show us basic aspects of the blade. But with digital microscopy, we can take multiple pictures from different angles, and then the software sews them together and models a single image of the defect."

"That gives you a 3D picture?" Jefferson asked.

"The shape of the blade will only get you so far. But if you know the dimensions of that blade edge, mainly the blade angle, you'll go a long way to being able to convince a jury you've identified the killing weapon."

"But can't you just measure the defect itself to get that information?"

"Not exactly. The problem with living bone is we think of it as a durable solid, but, in reality, it's very elastic. The material bends to absorb the force of an impact. Only when that flexibility is overcome does the material break. In the case of a slash into bone, the bone is forced away from the blade. When the blade is removed, the bone relaxes back into place, leaving a furrow that is actually narrower than the physical blade with a smaller angle. I won't get into the mathematics, but with digital modeling, we can account for both the elasticity and the resistance coefficients, and calculate the angle of the original blade."

"I can't see a lot of force being used for a wound like this," Leigh said. "All you'd be aiming for is soft tissue if you're trying to cut the victim's throat. Hitting the bone would be incidental."

"Which is why the kerf mark is so shallow," Matt said. "But even shallow defects can be used for the calculation. At this point, with no death scene, identification, or soft tissue for trace evidence, that's literally all we have to go on."

"Matt."

His attention was drawn to Kiko, who was drawing something out of a large pocket on the side of the discarded body bag.

She held up a large envelope. "These are probably the x-rays."

"I figured Rowe would send them. Put them up on the light box for us?"

"Sure." Kiko crossed the lab to the large double light box for x-ray films and pulled out several films.

"Did Crime Scene Services process the skeleton as evidence?" Leigh asked Jefferson.

"They did. They swabbed for trace and got a few smudged partial fingerprints, but they weren't hopeful on either score. Not to mention a material like bone is tricky in the first place because it's a textured surface."

"I bet there were too many people handling it," Paul said. "If the perp was stupid enough not to wear gloves, his prints are likely long wiped off, depending on the chain of custody of this skeleton."

"Top of my list, let me assure you," Jefferson said.

"Guys." Kiko's raised voice carried from across the room. She stood staring fixedly at the backlit x-rays, her hands on her hips and her head cocked to one side. "You need to see this."

They crossed to her.

Paul was the first to spot the unexpected evidence. "Whoa. That's an orthopedic implant." He walked back to the skeleton. One that, as least to the naked eye, did not have an implant. "It's *inside* the bone?"

"Let me see that." Matt stepped in front of the light box. The x-ray held an image of the victim's pelvic girdle. A narrow vertical stripe glowed bright white in the upper right femur, with four short horizontal bars sprouting from it. A fifth bar rose diagonally upwards to pierce the head of the femur. "That's a proximal femoral osteotomy. But it's *inside* the medulla."

"English for the cops, please," Leigh said.

"It's an orthopedic implant used for upper femur fractures or for congenital hip deformities like hip dysplasia—where the hip spontaneously dislocates—or *coxa vara*, a deformity where the angle of the femur shaft and head is reduced, leading to a shortened leg and limping. It's not that unusual." Joining Paul at the table, he lifted the right femur and studied it carefully. "What is unusual is that the entire implant is internal to the bone. The bone has completely remodeled around it, essentially encasing it within the bone marrow."

"That's bizarre," Kiko said.

"I've heard of it happening," Matt said, "but I've never actually seen it. The only way this could happen is if the apparatus was implanted in a child and then never removed, giving the bone time to remodel and grow over the titanium."

"I thought they usually removed implants like that," Paul interjected.

"Usually they do, but there are circumstances where they don't, or surgeons who think removing the implant will cause more instability and complications from infection than it's worth. But you know what this means."

"It means we can identify the victim," Kiko said. "Those implants come with serial numbers. Look up the serial number and you'll have a direct connection to the victim and his medical records. We'll have to break the bone to remove the implant though."

"We might be able to saw through the bone to the blade plate and pull the serial number from it. It's usually along the edge of the plate."

"That would be tricky work." Kiko considered the bone in Matt's hands. "How would you do it? Stryker saw?"

"Yes, but it would take a dead steady hand. Up to the job?" Matt nearly laughed when her eyes went wide with shock.

"Me?"

He set the bone down onto stainless steel. "You're the artist. Hands down, you have the best fine motor skills of any of us. And I'll be with you every step of the way."

Her brow furrowed as she gnawed on her lower lip, but she nodded her willingness to try.

"Lowell, are you sure that's a good idea?" Jefferson took a possessive step toward the remains, placing his body protectively between the remains and Kiko. "This is a victim. You don't use victims for teaching newbies."

"I understand your caution, but respectfully disagree. My students aren't 'newbies'. They're trained scientists who are honing their skills. Kiko will start on an animal bone sample as a dry run, but even with only that under her belt, she'll have the finest touch with this. You're in good hands."

"Let me reinforce that statement," Leigh said. "I was leery of them, too, at the beginning. But they're careful and skilled and they won't interfere with your investigation. We've worked four recent cases together, and every one of them was solved successfully because of the work they did. Trust me on this."

There was a long moment while the two officers stared at each other, then Jefferson nodded curtly and stepped away.

Heaving a silent sigh of relief, Matt brought them back on course. "I'll let Rowe know where we are so far, so he's in the loop. He might have other suggestions on how to free the implant. Now, before we wrap for the day, let's see if this gentleman has any other surprises for us."

CHAPTER SIX: ORGANIZATIONAL MEMORY

Organizational Memory: the consolidation of an organization's history and early experiences into a training manual for future members.

Wednesday, December 11, 7:11 p.m.
Boston University Fitness and Recreation Center
Boston, Massachusetts

"Nice." Half way down a staircase that arced around an open rotunda, Leigh paused, admiring the rock wall. Three stories high, the rock wall was enclosed by two sweeping staircases that separated the center atrium from the fitness facilities on the far side. The wall's craggy surface was covered with small colored lumps tagged with a variety of striped tapes. Long lines of nylon rope hung from the top edge, ending in neat coils on the floor.

"Go rent a pair of climbing shoes at the pro shop," Leigh said. "Then we'll see what you're made of."

"Game on, Trooper," Matt said.

She eyed him—in a crimson BU rowing T-shirt, black athletic shorts, and cross trainers, he looked ready to take on whatever she threw his way. "I do love your competitive side."

"You want competitive?" He stepped closer, crowding her as his voice dropped low. "Want to put your money where your mouth is?" He asked, his voice low, and his gaze dropped to her lips.

She waited for his gaze to rise to hers and boldly held eye contact. "You mean a bet? Like your students?"

One side of his lips curved in a sly smile. "Afraid you're going to lose?"

Her eyes narrowed at the challenge. *If you're going to throw down the gauntlet, you better be prepared for the consequences.*

She moved in closer and intimately nudged her hips against his, feeling triumphant at the small catch in his breath. "Not on your life. *You* put your money where your mouth is. What's it worth to you? Ten? Twenty?" She ran her tongue over her lower lip and watched with satisfaction as his pupils dilated. "Or maybe something a little more interesting. How about the loser gets to spend thirty minutes cuffed to my headboard?"

One eyebrow cocked in unmistakable intrigue. "Really?" The word was a low drawl. "I had no idea you were into . . . those sorts of games."

"You never know what will happen when you date a cop. You in?"

"All the way. What's the deciding factor?"

Leigh considered the climbing wall. "That's on you. If you can master a moderate level problem without a fall before we leave, you win. If not . . ."—she ran an index finger with agonizing slowness down his throat—"you're mine."

"Deal." He stepped back, only minimally cooling the heat between them with distance. "Although I'm honestly not sure anyone's really going to lose this bet."

She turned away, but threw a glance over her shoulder at him. "Aren't those the best kind? Now stop wasting time and go get your shoes. I suddenly find I'm in a rush to see if you can do this or not."

His low rumbling laugh rolled to her as he jogged across the hall toward the pro shop. She pushed through the gate of the low divider encircling the padded rubber floor at the foot of the wall. The climbing space was empty except for a single BU fitness center employee sorting through climbing equipment. Sitting on a bench opposite the wall, Leigh studied its setup, noting the different routes traversing different sections of the wall.

Matt came through the gate, holding out a pair of thin, laced shoes with a molded sole and no treads. "Ready."

"Those look good. A nice general-purpose climbing shoe." Leigh pulled out a lighter pair, crossed over the top by Velcro straps. "These are my indoor shoes. They're too thin for outdoor use. It's almost like climbing in your bare feet."

"I didn't know you climb outdoors. You're just full of surprises tonight."

"I like to keep a man on his toes." She strapped on her shoes. "Normally I use a climbing gym in Salem, just for convenience. There are some local places to go bouldering, but for a real climb, the Berkshires are only a few hours away. We could go some time if you're interested."

"Let me win here first. Then I'll wow you in the great outdoors." Matt toed off his cross trainers, pushed them under the bench, and laced on the climbing shoes. He stood up and gave a couple of experimental bounces. "Weird. I've never worn shoes like this before with absolutely no cushion."

"You don't want cushion, you want to feel rock under your toes." She grabbed a bag from the bench and then stood next to him staring up at the wall. "Now, do you want to top rope or boulder?"

"How about you explain the difference." He sent her a sidelong look of calculation. "And no making the hard choice sound easy so I don't have a chance to win."

Coyly, she fanned her fingers across her collarbone. "Would I do that?" She batted her eyelashes and then grinned when he burst out laughing. She grabbed his arm and tugged him toward the wall. "Here's the deal. Top roping is when you wear a harness and tie onto one of the ropes hanging from the ceiling. Or . . ." Leigh pointed to the black dotted line painted twelve feet off the ground along the width of the wall. "See that line? That's the bouldering line. Below it, you can free climb. No ropes, no harness, just you and the wall."

"That sounds like more fun to me. Ropes are for sissies."

"Then my cuffs will be right up your alley." She moved away, smiling at the thought of him slack jawed behind her at the suggestion. She stopped to look up the section that bowed out from the main wall, curving into an arch that bent backwards to the floor. She waited until she felt him behind her. "Bouldering isn't as easy as it looks. It requires a huge amount of upper body strength to fight gravity. And if you fall, you go all the way down. The big mats on the floor are called 'crash mats' for a reason."

"Have you done it before?"

"Lots of times."

"Then show me. Nothing I like better than date night with a crash mat." He leaned in, his breath feathering hotly over her ear as he murmured, "Except the thought of you in those cuffs. And nothing else."

Something clutched low in her belly as her mind went places not meant for a public space. She pushed the image away and cleared her throat.

"Over here then." She led him to the bottom of the wall. "Okay, the two-minute primer on climbing." Reaching into the bag, she pulled out a white ball encased in mesh. "Chalk keeps your hands from getting sweaty and minimizes slip."

She passed the ball back and forth between her cupped hands a few times before handing it to him. As he did the same, she rubbed her hands together, coating them in chalk.

"A couple of basic climbing rules. First, try to keep your arms straight when you climb. If you hold a position with your biceps flexed, you'll tire early and might not make it halfway up the wall you're climbing. You want to hang from your fingers and leave your weight shifted to your shoulders.

"Next, keep your center of gravity near the wall." Grasping two holds, Leigh stepped up onto two others. She rotated sideways on the balls of her feet, swinging her hips toward the wall. "If I'm reaching for a hold with my right hand, I'll move like this so my right side is against the wall." She repeated the motion, swiveling one hundred and eighty degrees the other direction. "Or like this if I'm reaching with my left hand." She hopped down to the ground. "Now, when you step onto a hold, you want to step onto your toes, not the instep or heel because being on your toes gives you those extra inches that might be the only way to reach the next handhold."

"Sounds straightforward. Let's give it a try." Matt stepped toward the wall and laid a hand on a curved hold.

She slapped a palm to his chest. "Not so fast, eager beaver. You also need to know how to fall correctly. First off, when you get to the twelve-foot line, you have to jump down. You want to fall onto one of the crash mats, landing with your knees bent and then rolling backwards onto your back, protecting your neck and head. And when we climb together, we'll spot each other. So when you're climbing, I'll be behind you like this . . ." She stepped back and raised both hands over her head, spread shoulder width apart, fingers splayed. "When I'm spotting you, I'll keep my hands in range of your shoulders. A woman's center of gravity is lower than a man's, so when you're spotting me stay in range of my hips. Now, do you want to watch me try it?"

"Sure."

"Let's start with something basic." She walked to the vertical wall and stepped onto the crash mat, her feet sinking into the softness. "See how the hand holds have different colored tapes tagging them? Those are routes to follow." She pointed to a navy tape with a thin light blue line running down the middle. Her finger then followed the upward rising pattern of blue on blue ribbons. "In bouldering, each route is called a 'problem'. I'll start with this blue problem. Ready?"

Matt raised his hands, holding them a foot away from her hips. "Ready."

Bracing the toes of her left foot on a hold, Leigh pushed off the floor, easily reaching up for a handhold with her right hand as her right foot found a hold and her body swung to align her right hip with the wall. From then on, it was only about twenty seconds as she easily scaled the wall, quickly evaluating each position and smoothly moving to it, transferring her weight from foot to foot and stabilizing her balance with her hands. When she reached the top, she glanced down to find Matt's gaze glued to her hips. "I'm up here you know." Releasing one hold, she pointed at her eyes and then waited as his rose to hers. "Did you watch the actual climbing?"

"You bet. But I'm spotting you just as instructed." He grinned. "You can't blame me for enjoying the view at the same time."

"Step back before you regret enjoying it quite so closely." She waited until he moved slightly away, then simply pushed off the rock. Air whipped cleanly by, and then she landed on the mat, cushioning her fall with bent knees and letting inertia roll her backwards onto her back, her knees tucked against her chest.

"Nice." Matt grinned down at her and held out his hand. She slapped her palm against his forearm and gripped tightly as he hauled her up. "I don't think I'll be that fast."

"I'm used to the strategy that goes into figuring out which hold to go for next. You'll want to take a little longer to sort that out and to manage your balance, but you'll do fine. Give it a try." She assessed the wall. "Start easy and go with a V1 problem. See the green tag? Follow that one."

Standing back, she watched Matt plan his attack, his gaze running higher and higher as he tracked the holds. Only once he had his path sketched out did he step up and grasp a handhold. Looking down, he set his foot onto a hold, shifting position a bit before deciding he was satisfied and pushed up onto it. He quickly found the second foothold.

Leigh stood behind him, her hands spread behind his shoulders. "You need to reach to the left for the next handhold, so swing to the wall to your left and reach up for a more natural extension. Right, just like that. Good." It took him two minutes to climb to the same height, but he worked steadily. Once his foot slipped, but his hands held tight and he relaxed to hang a bit while he slid his foot back into place. Finally, he reached the top and she stepped back, giving him room to fall onto the mat. He rolled off the mat as if he'd been bouldering for years.

"That was a blast." He flexed his hands. "But I can see this is where I'm going to get tired. The constant gripping."

"Most beginners find they fatigue quickly, especially in the hands and forearms. Don't overdo it. You want to stop before failure occurs." She considered the underside of the arch, studded with colored holds. *This could be where she'd win the bet.* "Want to try something a bit more challenging?" She sent him a sly look. "Do you dare?"

His eyes went to slits. "You bet I do. What are you thinking? Upside down on the arch?"

"That's actually not the hard part. The hard part is getting from the horizontal wall face to the vertical wall face. It really tests your upper body strength."

"I'm game. Show me, then let me try."

Leigh re-chalked her hands; sweaty palms on this kind of climb were an instant ticket to the crash mat. She climbed the interior arch wall, handling the curve to the ceiling easily. From that point on, as she moved toward the edge, it was all about three points of contact at all times and the fastest of hand hold switches.

As she approached the edge, she eyed the change in angles as the holds disappeared up the vertical wall above the arch. This one was going to be tough. And blind. She eyed the double thick crash mats, knowing they were stacked there because this was the place where most falls occurred.

But she'd seen the long hold with a flat top when she'd assessed the wall. She took a deep breath, selected a nearby pinch hold, and moved. She pivoted her body, then, closing her eyes, she extended her leg, feeling for the hold just around the vertical edge. Her toes hooked over the edge, then she slipped her second foot around to join the first. A quick change in hand holds at the edge and then she flipped her feet off the hold to hang free. Using nothing but upper body strength, she painstakingly pulled herself up by only her hands until she could get a foot into place. From there, she easily scaled the arch to the flat top running alongside the black dotted line. She pulled to her feet and looked down at Matt, breathing hard. Grinning at her, he gave her a slow clap. Laughing, she hopped off the platform, hitting the crash mat and rolling easily to her feet.

"That looked tough," Matt said. "And totally dependent on upper body strength."

"It is tough. Still think you're up to it?" She let her gaze drift down his body. "Considering what's at stake, and all."

"Damn straight. Where do I start?"

"Why don't you try climbing the inner wall and managing the angle change to inside the arch? Let's go with the purple and red problem this time. It looks straightforward. Chalk your hands first."

She waited while he prepared and then started slowly climbing the wall. When he came to where he was maneuvering to a position hanging from the archway roof, she moved back from the spotting position. At that point, if he went down, it was better to have nothing but soft mat underneath. If he managed this the first time without a fall, she'd be damned impressed.

She could see the fall about ten seconds before he went down. In an attempt to find a better hold, he'd crossed one arm over the other. Now to retract it and grab a fresh hold, he'd be left dangling from only three points of contact far too long for a new climber yet to develop the required hand strength. "Careful. Switch your right hand to the purple hold over your head before you lose your—"

But it was already too late, and Matt was falling to land eight feet below on the thick crash mats. The bags wheezed as he hit and sank in before bouncing slightly. He lay still for a few seconds before propping himself on his elbows.

"Still think ropes are for sissies?" she asked, once it was clear nothing was wounded but his pride.

"Sure do. This thing hasn't whipped me yet. It just got in the first point. I'm not out of the game with it or with you." He held out his arm and she hoisted him to his feet.

"Want to go back to the vertical wall?" she asked.

"No way in hell. I'm just getting a sense of how this works. Time to get back on the horse."

They climbed for longer than Leigh expected he'd be able to manage, but finally she could see the strain in Matt's arms. As he was about to reach for the chalk bag, she caught his arm. "Let's call it quits for today. You've done great, but you're starting to tire. Better stop now before you have another fall; it might not be so graceful next time."

"Because that fall was the epitome of grace. I admit my arms are getting tired. I suspect I'm going to wake up tomorrow with a few strained muscles."

"That's certainly how I felt after the first time you took me rowing. But the more you do it, the easier it gets."

When she turned away, he caught her arm and spun her against him. "So . . . ?" His eyes gleamed as he stared down at her. "Did I win? Be honest now."

For a second she considered lying, but knew she couldn't do it. "I may regret this, but yes, you won. Truthfully, I'm impressed. You picked it up faster than I expected."

His breath whispered over her mouth a fraction of a second before his lips. "You won't regret it, I promise." He slipped his fingers through hers and tugged her toward the bench and their bags.

She took the towel he handed her and wiped most of the chalk off her hands before digging into her bag to check her cell phone for messages. But when she saw the call log, her heart skipped a beat and most of the color drained out of the evening, leaving her in murky shades of grey. She looked up to find him watching her, his sharpened expression telling her he knew something was wrong before she even spoke. "Tucker called."

"Did he say what it was about?"

"Didn't leave a message, but he did leave a follow-up text." She quickly scanned the message. "He wants to come over tonight. He doesn't say why. But that was half an hour ago, so now it might be too late for him." Her eyes scanned the climbing wall. "Besides, we had a deal. We had . . . plans."

"Those plans won't be any fun if you're not in the mood. And understandably, you're not anymore. Text him back. We can meet him at your place in less than an hour."

She sent the message, then looked up. "More bad news, you think?"

"No, I think we've already hit rock bottom. We already suspect the worst possible outcome for you. He's either going to confirm it or shake that possibility loose. Either way, it's another step forward. Do we have time to grab a quick shower before heading to your place?"

The fact he didn't question that he was both wanted and needed smoothed some of Leigh's rough edges. Matt had made it clear often that they were a team. And they would do this together to the very end, no matter what that end was. "As long as we're quick."

As they passed through the gate, Leigh glanced back at the rock wall—a fun bet and a good workout, but still an artificial stand-in for real adventure. "Someday, I'll take you to the Berkshires and we'll do this for real. There's nothing like the feel of actual rock under your fingers and a deadly drop onto jagged boulders below to give you a kick of adrenaline. You'll love it."

CHAPTER SEVEN:
CALLING IN THE PICKETS

Calling in the Pickets: combining military forces into a single group before battle.

Wednesday, December 11, 9:33 p.m.
Abbott Residence
Salem, Massachusetts

Leigh pulled the Crown Vic to the curb in front of her two-hundred-year-old house on the edge of the historic Chestnut Street neighborhood. The simple two-story colonial was a traditional New England clapboard, painted in warm beige and trimmed with white. The rich burgundy front door and red Christmas berries, pine branches, and birch sticks bursting from twin urns flanking each side added a festive touch of seasonal color.

She climbed out of the car as Matt parked his SUV behind her. Pulling her collar closer around her ears against the biting wind, she scanned up and down the street. "I think we beat him," she said as Matt climbed out.

"Lucky for us, Tucker must be running a few minutes late. Come on, let's get inside. My hair is still damp and it's starting to freeze."

He pushed open the gate and they jogged up the front walk. Leigh fumbled for her keys in gloved fingers made clumsy by the cold. She managed to work the key into the lock and then they burst through the door into the warm quiet of home.

Matt bent down and unlaced his heavy boots. "Winter's coming on a little too fast to suit me. It felt like fall only a few weeks ago."

Leigh tossed her gloves between an antique oil lamp and a miniature grapevine reindeer on the narrow entry table. "I'll put on a pot of coffee. Can you start a fire? I'll meet you in the living room."

The crackle of flame and the warm smell of wood smoke met Leigh when she came in a few minutes later bearing a wooden tray with a sugar bowl, a small jug of cream, and an array of pewter spoons. From the corner by the window, the white lights of her Christmas tree threw a warm glow over the room. Leigh set the tray down on the coffee table as several heavy knocks sounded at the front door. "That's timing."

Matt pulled out of a comfortable sprawl to push off the couch. "I'll get it."

As he passed, she threaded her arm through his. "We'll get it."

When they reached the entrance, Matt stepped back, gesturing for her to do the honors. She pulled open the door to find Rob Tucker, engulfed in a hooded ski jacket nearly twice his size, standing on her stoop. "Tucker, thanks for coming out again."

"Not a problem." Tucker's voice came from the shaded inner recesses of the hood. "We need to move on a few things."

"You've got something new?"

"I do. And I'll be happy to share it with you, assuming I can come inside and not freeze to death on your front step."

Leigh belatedly realized she was blocking his way in. She stepped aside, nearly bumping into Matt who stood behind her. "Of course, come in." When Tucker stepped through the door, she moved to close it, but Tucker shot out a gloved hand, holding it open.

Confused, she met his eyes.

"I brought someone with me," he said simply and pushed the door open wider, revealing a second man on the front walk. Tall and hatless despite the weather, his cleanly shaved head exposed to the biting wind, he studied the tableau inside the house with dark, unfathomable eyes.

Shock slammed into Leigh, her pulse rate spiking as ice

sluiced through her veins. "What have you done?" The words came out on a whisper, barely slipping past the panic rising in tangled coils up her throat. But her gaze remained locked on Sergeant Daniel Kepler—her superior officer and the man possibly responsible for months of fear and anxiety. The man who sent her out on an op only days before that might have ended her life just as it had ended Tapley's.

Matt stepped partly in front of her to block her as if anticipating an attack. "What the hell is this, Tucker? We trusted you."

Tucker shoved back his hood to show his face. He held up both hands, as if both to placate and prove he was harmless. "You *can* trust me."

"Then why is he here?" His voice was a low growl.

"Because it was time to bring him into this." Tucker swung around to face Leigh. "Give me a chance to explain, Abbott. Give *him* a chance to defend himself."

Leigh's mind was racing with connections. Herself to her father. Her father to Kepler. Kepler to herself. A bloody triangle of death and jeopardy.

But as she stared at a man she'd known for years, and trusted until just a few weeks ago, something settled inside her. The surety of a decision made. It was time to close the circle for good. No more hiding. It would never be safer for her than now, with Matt at her side and Tucker as her backup.

She grabbed Matt's arm, tugging him back a step. "Let him in."

He didn't budge, taking a moment to study her face. Apparently satisfied with what he saw, he stepped out of the way to stand behind her. But the weight of his hand settled at the small of her back. Ready to catch her if needed.

He stood for her more often than she liked. Not this time. This time she would stand on her own. "Come in, Sergeant."

Kepler gave her a curt nod and stepped onto the front step and then into the house. Leigh took their coats, indicated the living room, and then left them to bring in the coffee.

Matt followed her into the kitchen. "What do you think Tucker is up to?" he whispered as she pulled thick stoneware mugs down from the cupboard.

"I have no idea. But it's time we found out."

She turned away, but he caught her by the shoulders and angled her toward him. "Are you okay with this? We can stop it right now."

"No, we can't. We're past the point of no return. It's time to find out if he's involved. And you know what? I'm okay with it. As you said, it's time to bring this out into the light. I'm done skulking in the shadows and I'm done with my subconscious ruining my sleep while it tries to work out this whole scenario in my dreams. I haven't done anything wrong and neither did my father. It's time to make that clear."

He studied her for a moment, and then pressed his lips to her forehead. When he pulled back, he was smiling, though worry still touched his eyes. "That's my girl. Let's go get him."

They carried filled mugs into the living room, passed them out, and then waited while everyone fixed their own coffee. Leigh watched the men as they moved in silence, not meeting each other's eyes, as if everyone was waiting for the other shoe to drop. A veneer of civility, of being normal, when God knew it was anything but.

Tucker dumped half the sugar bowl into his coffee, and half-heartedly stirred the sludge at the bottom of his cup before he took a long sip and wrapped his fingers around the mug's warmth. "I kind of feel like I owe you an explanation."

"You think?" Sarcasm was thick as tar in Matt's tone.

Perched beside him on the edge of the sofa, Leigh touched his knee, catching his eye to make sure he understood her message to stand down. The set of his jaw went mulish, but he sat back against the cushions with his coffee in hand, taking himself out of the circle, but his eyes stayed watchful.

"I'd certainly like an explanation," she said to Tucker.

Tucker hunched down in the chair, his feet propped on the edge of her coffee table, his usual position in what had become his place in her living room. His bright red hair was in disarray as usual and he was sporting his uniform of a casual shirt and baggy jeans. Today's shirt proclaimed 'Nerd? I prefer the term intellectual badass.' "To be fair, Sergeant Kepler doesn't know why he's here."

That caught her off guard, and her head whipped toward Kepler. Still in the unit uniform of a suit and tie, he sat in the armchair opposite Tucker, his black coffee untouched on the table. Unlike the jiggling foot that belied Tucker's casual slouch, Kepler sat motionless, his ever-watchful eyes appearing to take in every nuance. It was one of the things that made him such a high caliber leader. He saw things others missed, especially in his own people. Until her foundation was shaken a few weeks ago, Leigh had held him in the highest regard. "You don't?"

"Tucker told me one of my officers was in trouble and asked if I trusted him to show me. He didn't say what it was about and he didn't say it was you."

His eyes narrowed on her and Meg felt like a tiny bug in a jar under the weight of Kepler's searching stare.

"Are you in trouble?" Kepler asked.

"I don't know how to answer that." She swung around to Tucker. "You're sure about this?"

"I'm sure. I found some new information today that convinced me it was time to bring Sergeant Kepler on board. Things aren't as they seem, Abbott. We've seen layers of that through this whole affair, but now there's more. Since the sergeant is implicated, I thought it was only fair to bring him into the conversation. But I didn't want to do it in the office. Until we really find out what's going on, we need to keep this off the radar. Now, do you want to explain it or should I?"

"I think you better because I don't know where you're going with this."

"Once again driving the hard bargain." Tucker pulled himself upright in the chair, and dropped his stockinged feet from the coffee table to the floor. He set down his coffee cup and reached for a bag Leigh hadn't noticed before. He rooted through it, then pulled out a file folder. "It started when this was delivered to Abbott two months ago." He pulled out a color photo from the folder, and paused briefly to look at Leigh, as if suddenly unsure.

She knew what was in that picture. Knew the horror of it. Relived it in her nightmares in the dark when her guard was down. She nodded at Tucker, giving him the go ahead.

Tucker tossed the photo face up onto the table. It slid across to Kepler, who picked it up slowly, as if he'd suddenly aged thirty years in the space of time it took for paper to glide over wood. Then his gaze snapped to Leigh.

The memory was there in his eyes. As the officer investigating the death of Sergeant Nathaniel Abbott, Leigh's father and Kepler's superior officer, he'd never forgotten the death scene in that photo: the body sprawled face down in the snow, blood a gruesome halo around what was left of the head, blood and brains splattered against a nearby wall, his gun thrown feet away, released by lax fingers and propelled by the force of his spinning body.

But she saw something else in his eyes—shock. He hadn't seen that photo since he'd closed the case and had likely worked for years to forget it as much as humanly possible. Leigh looked at Tucker, who simply tilted his head and returned her fixed stare. She could practically hear his sarcastic tone in her head. *See?*

"What the hell is this?" Kepler's words were clipped, with fury layered over disbelief.

"That was delivered to me at the unit in October," Leigh said. "In an unmarked envelope with no fingerprints and no DNA. The return address was Boston PD headquarters. While it was postmarked Boston, I don't believe for an instant BPD had anything to do with this. That's a red herring. And if you look on the back . . ."

Kepler flipped over the photo to read the words burned into Leigh's memory: *Your father wasn't the hero you think he was. He was a dirty cop. Soon the world will know it. And you'll be the one to pay for his crimes.* "That's bullshit. Nate Abbott wasn't a dirty cop." He set the photo down on the table, facedown, hiding the blood and gore from everyone's eyes. But Leigh knew he really did it for her.

"We know that," Tucker said. "But someone is trying to throw mud on him anyway. As evidenced by what came the following week." He removed from the file a cell phone log and a second photo of two men standing under the glow of a neon light that read *Bruno's Tavern*. He passed them to Kepler. "The call log supposedly belonged to Nate Abbott's phone. The three highlighted lines are for a single number suspected at the time to belong to a known drug dealer. But it's not a real log, obtained by a subpoena; it's fake. However, the number is real; it was associated with one of those burner phones drug dealers use for doing business for a short while and then toss so there's no way to track them. The photo itself shows what looks like a meet or a drug buy. All of this is obviously meant to imply that Nate Abbott had ties to local drug rings."

"Not a chance." Kepler discarded the photo and log on the coffee table, his careless motion telegraphing his disgust. "I knew Nate, and he'd never be involved in anything like that. He hated the drug trade for what it did to young people and families. Hated watching the body count rise because of it."

"That's exactly what I said." Leigh picked up the photo of the meet and studied the now-familiar figures. "It had been just Matt and I trying to sort through this, but at that point we knew we needed help, so we brought in Tucker. He digitally analyzed the photo and could tell immediately that my father was added to the picture, replacing the person who was originally standing there." She dropped it onto the table. "Dad was never there. Someone was setting him up to take the fall."

"This is the original content of the picture." Tucker pulled out a large glossy photograph and passed it across to Kepler. "The man we can see in profile didn't give us much to go on, but I extrapolated his face and produced a 3D image I could run through facial recognition. It came back as Thomas Dawlin, a known drug dealer and petty criminal. Unfortunately for us, Dawlin was gunned down a few weeks before Nate was killed."

"Convenient for whoever is setting all this up," Kepler commented. "If you got lucky enough to ID the man in the photo—"

"That would be skill, not luck," Tucker interjected pointedly.

"—then you'd hit a wall as soon as you got his name," Kepler continued, as if Tucker had never spoken. He turned the photo around to reveal a figure in the place where Nate Abbott had previously stood. He tapped the head of a figure whose face was mostly shadowed beneath the fur trimmed hood of a dark parka; only his chin and lower lip were revealed. "What about this person? It doesn't look like there's enough information to even tell if it's a man or a woman."

"My educated estimate is it's a man," Matt said. He'd been holding back, staying out of the circle as the cops talked. But now he leaned in, joining the conversation. "The bone structure of the chin looks masculine to me. It's not much information to go on, but my money is on it being a man under that hood." He glanced at Tucker. "There's no way to lighten the picture to see if there's any other features we can play with?"

"I tried. It was a night shot, the face was shaded and it was from a crappy security camera. There's nothing to lighten because the camera basically didn't record any information in that area."

Kepler's head whipped up at the mention of the camera. "What security camera?"

Leigh leaned back against the arm of the sofa, casually crossing her legs. "Go on, Tucker. Tell Sergeant Kepler about your field trip." She took a slow sip of coffee, staring at him expectantly.

Tucker sent her a narrowed-eye glare before answering his sergeant. "The picture had to come from somewhere. The time stamp in the photo implied it was from a security cam. We knew the probable location from the neon sign. I extrapolated where the camera had to be located to get that shot and went to check it out."

There was a moment of silence before Kepler spoke. "You went out into the field? A computer geek who spends his time hunched over a keyboard?"

Tucker threw up his hands in frustration. "Why is this such a big deal for everyone? You'd think I wasn't able to tie my own shoes or safely cross the street by myself. You know, even us computer geeks can be fully functioning adults." Lips twisted, he fixed his eyes on the ceiling as if praying for patience. "Anyway . . . The camera was on a convenience store in North Salem, run by this little old guy who's likely the founder and president of the New England Paranoid Squad. Because the bar across the street was a hotbed of criminal activity—much of it drug-related—the Salem PD boys were constantly coming in to get copies of his security footage, which conveniently captured the bar's front door along with Mr. Paranoid's parking lot. The guy happily handed the tapes over, but only after he made copies for himself. He still had those copies and I managed to talk him out of them as a short-term loan. I think he's hoping to end up on TV as a local hero or something. Anyway, based on the time stamp on the original photo Abbott received, I tracked down the actual frame it came from. That's what you're holding."

Kepler laid the photo on the table. "Okay, so we've got two deliveries received by Abbott pointing the finger at her father. We agree it's bullshit. So where do I come into the picture?"

"Right here." Tucker pulled several more files out of the bag. "This was the third delivery."

"The one that came here to her house," Matt pointed out.

That caught Kepler's attention. "It came here? To a cop's unlisted address?"

Leigh nodded. "Same packaging, same handwriting, same lack of fingerprints and DNA. But yes, it was delivered here a few weeks ago, in the middle of the Ward case."

Tucker opened one of the files to reveal a Salem Police Department case file for a standard drug bust. The only abnormality was that all the personal information had been redacted—the names and addresses were blacked out. "We have two case files like this. Nothing too interesting here. A scum bag drug dealer arrested for pushing heroin and coke." He closed the file and picked up the second. "Then there's this one, a couple of Salem State students arrested for having a little weed. Same sanitized style. In fact, they both look like they came through Freedom of Information Act requests."

"If that's true, then there should be records of the requests," Kepler said.

"There should be," Tucker agreed. "But there aren't. So either there was a request and it's been removed, or the file was obtained through internal means, copied, and then manually redacted to look like a FOIA request. That's another loose thread. Now, the first two cases are out of Salem PD and I haven't found any connection between them yet. But this is where things got . . . uh . . . interesting." He opened the third file, a thicker one, angling it so only he could see the contents.

Kepler's reaction to the death photo weighed heavily in his favor as far as Leigh was concerned, but this was the bigger test. His reaction to this file would cement her opinion of his involvement. Kepler stared at Tucker's bent head. Tucker seemed oblivious to the moment, but Leigh was able to read him better now; his paper rustling and finger tapping betrayed his nervous state. This was it—they were either going to make a very dangerous enemy or find a powerful ally in their attempt to end this investigation.

"This is the case of a drug bust that also took into possession a number of illegal firearms. It was in Salem, but due to the nature of the case, it wasn't just worked by Salem PD. An eight-year-old boy was killed when a stray bullet from the shootout went through his apartment wall and struck him in the head. He died instantly. That meant the case was shared with us."

If it was possible, Kepler had gone more still than before, a deep furrow across his forehead. His eyes were fixed not on Tucker, but on the file in his hands. "Are you talking about the Hanson case? Kevin Hanson, who died at his own dinner table?" His gaze shot to Leigh. "That was my case."

The knot that had been tangled in Leigh's gut for months loosened its stranglehold at Kepler's expression. "You don't know anything about this, do you?"

"Of course I don't." Temper frayed his words. "But now I want to know a hell of a lot more."

"Tucker, how did you figure it out?" Leigh asked. "Two weeks ago, we were discussing how dangerous it would be to have a commanding officer being responsible for this, but you've done a one-eighty on this. Correctly, it seems. What tipped you off?"

"I'll get to that shortly, but let's just say for now that it was enough for me to connect the dots." Tucker handed Kepler another file. "Sir, look at this. It's been redacted of personal witness information, just like the other two cases, but there's a difference. Your name isn't anywhere in this paperwork. Trooper Robert Mercer is listed as the investigating officer."

"Mercer? He died years ago."

"But not before this case. If you look at the case file in house, it also has his name on it. And not whited out and written over. Someone took the time to rewrite the *entire* file. If it was your case, then this file should be in your handwriting. It's not."

Kepler studied the first page. "Definitely not. And, yes, it should be. You don't remember the details of every case you work, that's why case files are so detailed, but some of them stay with you. Child deaths always do. I remember this case and I know all the paperwork for our unit was filed by me. But I don't recognize this handwriting." He thumbed through the paperwork in a *whir* of paper. "This is no small file, either."

"Nor should it be, considering the case," Leigh said.

"What about the electronic files?" Kepler asked. "Who's listed as the investigating officer?"

"It's Mercer in every instance."

"So we've been hacked? From inside or out?"

"I can't answer that yet, sir. But I'm looking into it and have some promising leads. I hope to have answers there soon."

Kepler sagged back into the armchair, loosening his tie and blowing out a long breath. "Putting aside the fact that you suspected a superior officer of sending you threatening notes on the QT"—He flicked a narrowed glance at Leigh that had the hair on the back of her neck standing straight up—"what made you connect me to the case if the in-house file, the mailed file, and the electronic version all list Mercer as the investigating officer?"

"That was actually my father's doing," Leigh said.

"Your father's doing? From the grave?"

Leigh winced at Kepler's sharp retort. *He's pissed that we suspected him. But he's keeping his temper . . . mostly.* "I have Dad's remaining possessions. One of those things was his old computer. Dad used to work on cases at home some nights while I was still living with him."

Kepler's eyebrow shot up.

"I know, I know, we're not supposed to work on confidential material at home, which is basically every case we have, but you know and I know sometimes we can't just walk out at the end of shift and leave something unfinished. I had Tucker review Dad's hard drive to see if there was anything there to help us. He found a bunch of files, and one was the details pertaining to this case since he was the supervising officer. It clearly outlined that you were the investigating officer."

Kepler's cold stare made her want to squirm in discomfort. Enough. It was time to defend herself.

"Sir, put yourself in my position. Imagine for months you've been getting information about your father being dirty and all along you've wondered if it might be someone within your own unit, simply because of the nature of the first delivery, the crime scene shot. You know as well as I do that officers have access to old files without any paper trail so long as they don't sign out the evidence. I would have been an idiot not to consider my own colleagues. Then when your name came up, and it looked like you might have changed records to officially remove yourself from the case . . . well, it looked bad."

"Who have you told about this?" Kepler asked.

"We're the only ones who know. There wasn't enough evidence to take this to Harper, and Tucker wanted more time to look into things." She turned back to Tucker. "Okay, spill. What new evidence do you have?

Tucker took a long pull from his mug. "We were left with some loose ends after this last delivery. First was whether the sergeant was involved, but we were also missing information. Where did the copy of the meet photo come from? We know where I got our version of it—directly from Mr. Paranoid himself—but I asked him if anyone else had come looking for old tapes, and he said the local boys only ever came looking for recent footage. I took a chance and asked if he had any recent break-ins, but he hadn't."

"You were actually thinking someone broke in, stole the tape, copied it, and somehow put it back unnoticed?" Matt asked.

"Yeah, I know, it would be an astronomical long shot, but I had to ask. Laying it all out, some things become clear. Let's look at it a piece at a time. The original picture—clearly it's a case file picture. No press photographer would have been allowed access that close, especially to a fallen officer. We know for certain that photo still exists in the office case file."

"What about digital versions?" Kepler asked. "We've been doing digital photography since two-thousand-and-five. If we're looking at a potential hack to change the case database, then they could have gotten access to the photograph at the same time."

"That's exactly what I think happened." Tucker turned to Leigh. "I think that first delivery was supposed to shake you but good."

Leigh laughed darkly, a sound void of all humor. "Mission accomplished."

"Not only the visual but the statement on the back. Whoever sent it knew you'd identify it as a crime scene photo, especially someone who was there that night and knew you were on scene and had to be physically held behind the tape."

Kepler winced. When he glanced at Leigh, regret was etched in his expression.

"You did what you had to do to preserve your crime scene," she said. "At that point, you had your eye already fixed on finding him justice."

"Some justice," Kepler muttered. "The perp was already dead by Nate's own hand, but he didn't live long enough to know his bullet found its mark."

"But no matter how shaken you were to have your own sergeant lying dead at your feet, you had the presence of mind to handle the scene properly. I didn't see that at the time, I was too much in shock then, but I see it now."

Kepler gave her a nearly imperceptible nod, appearing to accept her unspoken apology.

"So there you were," Tucker continued. "You had the first delivery in hand, and were already suspecting it might be someone in your own unit. As best I can tell, whoever is sending this stuff never thought you'd take action, but thought you'd try to bury the whole thing to save your father's good name. He tried to add extra leverage by saying you'd pay for your father's crimes. If saving your father's good name wasn't enough incentive, he thought saving your own would be the extra push you needed. I think he fully expected you to cover your own ass and to keep it to yourself, working totally off radar."

"Which makes me wonder if whoever is responsible for this knows Leigh at all, if that's what he really thought would happen." Matt propped his elbows on his knees. "If he thought she was going to curl helplessly into a ball, he got totally the opposite reaction. Sure, it knocked her off her feet for a few hours, that would happen to any of us, but she's a fighter. She pulled it together and brought the whole thing to me and we started working through it together."

"And then Matt convinced me we needed help and suggested Tucker, knowing he was responsible for many of the best connections in the Bradford case."

"And then there were three," Tucker quipped. "The additional deliveries were meant to cement Nate's guilt but were clumsily done. Maybe they were rushed. We don't know what the guy's agenda or timeline is—or even if it's a guy, but let's just say it's 'him' for the sake of argument—but instead of convincing us Nate is guilty, he's done nothing except convince us of his innocence."

"Then there are all the dead ends," Matt said. "There's no way that's a coincidence. We've got a dead dealer and two dead Essex police officers. We can't get anything from them."

"Then there's your involvement." Leigh pointed an index finger at Kepler. "Was that to throw us off the trail, to shake me up more, or was that totally inadvertent? Was the point that you became involved, or was it more a matter of looking for the right case to tie into all this and you just happened to be connected to it? We don't work basic drug cases—that's usually handled locally until it reaches the level of the *Chacal* bust and it's a multi-agency action. Actually, when you look at it from this side of these smaller cases, maybe you weren't meant to be included. The case you were involved in was attributed to someone else, someone we can't talk to. If it hadn't been for Dad's drive, we never would have known you were associated with it. Maybe the point was to include Mercer, not to exclude you."

"But he changed the files, or had them changed. He knew I was originally involved. All it would have taken was a careless word to me, or someone else with a long memory and it was blown." Kepler took in the photos and case files spread over the table. "What I keep coming back to is why implicate Nate? There's been no big bust to connect him to this years later. What don't we know?"

"You think this is because of something that has yet to break? It's all a setup?"

"It makes me wonder. So far, there doesn't seem to be a rhyme or reason to it. But someone's gone to all this effort. It's not just for kicks."

"My feelings exactly," said Tucker. "So my theory was to follow the evidence. Too many hands could've gotten a hold of the crime scene picture in house and there's no way to track who last reviewed the file. The cell phone log is faked. The case files are faked to look like FOIA files, which anyone can ask for. But the tapes . . . the tapes are the first real direct line that leads *out* of the Essex Detective Unit."

"But that line leads directly to Salem PD," Leigh said. "Are you implying it's someone there who is responsible?"

"Well, let's just put it this way—the photo had to come from visual material of some kind," Tucker stated. "And we know for a fact it was from an old-fashioned VHS tape, and not from a digital source. While I can't discount that a copy hasn't been made, I can tell you the original tape is exactly where it should be in the evidence room on Margin Street. I can also tell you there's a blip in their evidence access records. Everything is smooth as glass up to about four months ago. Then unexpectedly, for the space of several days, there are no records whatsoever. Then back to multiple daily entries. Now, I don't know about their evidence room, but I know for a fact there isn't a single day that goes by without new evidence being submitted or old evidence being signed out of ours. Color me suspicious, but that set off alarm bells for me in a big way."

Leigh stared at him, nonplussed. "You hacked the Salem Police Department? No, wait." She threw up a hand to stop his response. "Maybe it would be better if you didn't answer that question in front of a co-worker and your superior officer."

"Luckily enough, your superior officer finds himself temporarily deaf for a few minutes," Kepler said dryly. "When you hacked in, could you tell what happened to those details?"

"It looks like the entries were removed after the fact by someone in-house based on the IP address. That's when my attention shifted from our house to Salem's. Abbott, I think this is where it's coming from."

"But why would they want to smear Dad's name like that? Dad had a great relationship with the Salem cops whenever he worked with them."

"I don't know, but the criminal drug trade funnels through that department. They get the perps, they get the take from the drug busts. Maybe . . ."

"Maybe the dirty cop is there and he's trying to deflect it your way," Matt finished for him.

"That's a serious accusation," Kepler cautioned. "If we're going to go after a Salem cop, we'd better be one hundred and ten percent sure of ourselves."

Shock jerked through Leigh, surprising her with its intensity.

"*We?* Are you with us, sir?"

"One of my officers is threatened, the unit geek is walking a very thin line and is in it up to his ears, and a man I respected and considered a mentor is being smeared. You're not getting rid of me now, Abbott. I'm in it with you until we wrap this. I'll also be there when you take this to Harper, because you know very well that if we're going to accuse another cop of wrongdoing—and we're going to have to—you'll want me with you as backup."

A lump lodged in Leigh's throat while some of the strain lifted from her. Tonight they'd laid their cards on the table and joined forces in a way that brought the whole group extra strength, committed in their common goal to clear the name of a good man. "Thank you, sir." The words were husky, even to her own ears.

"I love it when a plan comes together." Tucker grinned and leaned forward conspiratorially. "Okay, team. So where do we go next?"

CHAPTER EIGHT: SURVIVAL KNIFE

Survival Knife: a knife intended for basic use in the wilderness. Survival knives are used for field dressing, skinning, butchering, and occasional combat.

Friday, December 13, 1:22 p.m.
Boston University, School of Medicine
Boston, Massachusetts

Leigh peered through the window in the heavy metal door, trying to catch a view of the occupants inside before she barged in with her news. The call had come through an hour earlier; as a result, she felt lighter than she had in days. Perhaps she hadn't been honest with herself before, but now she could be—the thought of someone else working with her team felt wrong. Even though Matt tried to include her, she'd felt like an intruder.

Not anymore.

Matt and his students were grouped around a large microscope on the far side of the lab. Leigh squinted at the equipment, sure she'd never seen the large color monitor or tall scope before. She swiped her security card and pushed through the door. Four heads swiveled in unison at the sound of the door opening.

"Hey," she said in greeting. "If you're in the middle of something, don't let me interrupt."

Seated on a rolling lab stool, Matt spun away from the scope. "Hey." He checked his watch.

To her amusement, she could see him furiously running through appointments in his head, thinking he'd missed something again. She couldn't hold back a laugh at his obvious confusion and let him off easy.

"No, you didn't forget something. This time, I'm here on

business."

"Business? You've got a case that needs a consultation?"

She walked to the table where the Harvard skeleton was laid out in neat anatomical order. Now completely dismantled, each bone was pierced by holes made for the wires and screws, and the right femur had a straight-sided half-inch gouge down to the silver implant that dully glinted in the overhead light. "Sure do." She touched her fingers to the metal surface, knowing better than to touch the evidence. "This one."

Matt pulled off his gloves as he stood and discarded them to cross toward her. "What do you mean?"

"Rowe called me a few hours ago saying he had an ID based on the serial number on the implant." She studied the gap in the bone. "Nice job there, by the way. Very neat."

"Thanks," Kiko said. "I was so nervous about it. I thought my hands were going to shake too much. But after a few false starts, I settled into it."

"It was worth the damage to the bone to get the number. It led Rowe to an ID. And that's where things get tricky because the vic was last registered living in Wenham."

"I don't get it," Paul said. "How does that make things tricky?"

"For jurisdiction," Leigh explained. "We don't know where the victim was killed, or where he was processed to skeletal remains, so to speak, assuming it was done artificially. The victim was discovered at Harvard, but, currently, that's not a crime scene because of the nature of the remains."

"You're sure you can't call it a crime scene, just once to Sharpe's face?" Matt asked. His face was schooled into neutral lines, but the playful gleam in his eye gave him away.

Leigh slyly cocked an eyebrow at him. "Want to be there when I do?"

"God, yes." He grinned. "I'd pay good money to see that. He'd go crazy if you tried to shut down his lab."

"I'll be sure to call you then if that becomes a possibility. Anyway . . . Rowe called D.A. Saxon and presented the case to him to ask how he wanted to handle it: leave the case in Middlesex or bring it to Essex. Normally cases have cut and dried jurisdiction—if the crime scene is in Middlesex, it stays in Middlesex—but in this case, there was nothing concrete linking it to Middlesex, so Saxon wanted to bring it to Essex. He called the Middlesex D.A. and they worked it out. Apparently, Jefferson was cool with it and called Kepler to suggest he assign the case to me since I was already familiar with it. Kepler had no problems with that." She met Matt's eyes briefly, seeing the flash of memory of the night before last. "And here we are, back together again."

"Woot!" Paul crowed as he and Juka high-fived.

Juka had the grace to look slightly embarrassed at their enthusiasm, but Paul just grinned.

"Nothing against Jefferson," Paul said. "But working with him just didn't have the same vibe, you know? You get us, and don't think we're nothing but a bunch of geeks."

"You *are* a bunch of geeks," Leigh said dryly.

Paul brushed non-existent lint off his sleeve before he cracked a smile. "Well, yeah, but you know we're more than just that."

"True." Leigh turned to Matt. "Rowe sent over everything he had, and even though I knew in rough terms where you were, I took the time to review before coming into Boston. I'm up to date on the newest developments. Where are you now?"

Matt swung toward the microscope. "We're working on cause of death. You remember we talked about digital 3D microscopy to look at the kerf mark left behind by the knife? That's in progress. We sent the bone off to the scanning electron microscope earlier today, and now we're looking at the wound for more specific weapon measurements."

"How did SEM go? Were you able to visualize all the details you need?" Leigh asked.

"Yes. While this digital scope can magnify up to two hundred times, the SEM goes up to five hundred thousand times magnification. That allows us to visualize the surface of the kerf mark at the level of only a few hundred microns—that's millionths of a meter"—Matt gave Leigh a pointed look—"if you don't speak geek."

Paul hooted while Matt only grinned.

"From that, we can identify details that will allow us to match the killing weapon, if it can be found," Matt continued. "It will also tell us exactly how the knife moved through the bone. But let's back up so you understand how the victim died."

"You can confirm cause of death?" Leigh asked.

"We had a solid idea before, but after today we can confirm it. Now, as you've probably seen during your career, knife wounds can come in different forms: stabbing—which causes punctures, slicing—which causes incisions, and chopping—which causes notches or clefts."

A slideshow of victims slipped through Leigh's mind. She'd seen too many of these deaths, either self-inflicted or at the hands of someone else. "Oh yeah, I've seen them. I have to admit, though, they've always been on fleshed bodies."

"In the case of remains that are so decomposed the tissue no longer has any structure, or when there's nothing left but skeletal components, you have to let the bones tell you exactly what happened. In this case, after a thorough inspection, we can tell you it really does come down to this one bone."

Leigh eyed the U-shaped bone under the bright light of the microscope. "The hyoid."

"Right. Remember when you looked at it before—it appears to be just a small incision in the bone. The borders of the incision look clean and there are no fractures around it."

"Would you see fractures around a knife wound? Wouldn't that require a huge amount of force?"

"It would. And it tends to be something we see around punctures from stab wounds; something that has a lot of force behind it concentrated into a small area. But an incision like this is incidental and only grazes the cortical surface of the bone. Now, looking at the line and the width of the incision also tells us a few things. In this case, the line is straight, so no hesitation from the perp during the kill. If the blade had wobbled when it sliced through, there would be a wider kerf mark, or at least one with different widths along the incision line."

"It looks to me like a straight line. So the killer was fast and sure."

"He was. It's a very professional job."

That was an angle Leigh hadn't considered before. "Professional. As in a hit?"

"Not saying that. Just saying this is someone who was familiar with a knife in his hand. Kiko, can you finish the shots on the digital scope while we walk Leigh through the SEM data?"

Kiko claimed Matt's abandoned chair. "Will do. We only need a few more, and then I'll run the extrapolation. Hopefully I'll have it finished by the time you're done."

"Great. Juka, will you walk us through the SEM analysis?" Matt asked.

Juka bowed his head and moved to the computer on the opposite bench while Matt, Leigh, and Paul grouped around him. Matt nudged Leigh closer so she had a clear view of the monitor.

"We ran the bone through the scanning electron microscope after we sputter-coated it with gold as the conducting material to improve our signal-to-noise ratio," Juka said. "Normally, we would first ensure the sample was totally desiccated, but, in this case, that wasn't a concern."

Leigh opened her mouth to ask what a 'signal-to-noise ratio' was, but then thought the better of it. She preferred to skip the brainiac lecture this time and head straight for the finish line. "What were the results?"

Juka brought up the first picture. It was in fine-grained black and white, the craggy landscape of the surface of the bone transected by an angled gash. "What we're looking at is the superior surface of the hyoid, on the greater horn, moving toward the lesser horn." He formed a 'U' with the thumb and index finger of his left hand. "This is the rough shape of the hyoid. The bone is thicker at the base of the 'U'; that's called the body." He indicated the webbing of skin that joined his thumb to his index finger. "The bone then narrows and angles up toward the back end of the 'U'. Those sections are the greater horns. There are small ridges where the body and greater horn meet on each side and those are called the lesser horns. The defect transects the bone from the middle of the greater horn to the lesser horn in a downward diagonal. Like this." He touched the tip of a finger to the first knuckle on his thumb and ran it on a downward diagonal to the second knuckle. "But the knife edge is not straight on. It's angled upward." He pointed at the monitor. "We can see that angle here."

"It was like this." Paul held the edge of his right hand against his neck, just under his left ear. "Assuming the killer used the knife like this, then depending on his height or the position of the victim, the blade would not be exactly perpendicular to the bone." He angled the heel of his hand down, titling the 'blade' on an upward angle. "So you'd naturally get this."

"It took some repeated tweaking, but we managed to get shots down the kerf itself. But before we look at that specifically, you can see from this smaller magnification the classic signs of a knife kerf—a narrow, shallow cut with a 'V' shaped cross-section with little bone wastage or chipping at the surface of the defect. Now, when we get into the defect itself and look at the walls of the kerf . . ." Juka pulled up a new picture, one that showed a magnified surface with pronounced ridges and several continual lines dragged across the surface of the bone. "Do you see these lines?" He pointed to the white streaks running through the bone. "Those are striations and are caused by minute defects in the blade, usually through the manufacturing process. In knife wounds, those striations run perpendicular to the kerf floor, as you see here."

This was something Leigh was familiar with. "Those striations look like the kind you'd see on a bullet. Those are a result of the manufacturing process as well, but allow us to exactly match bullets to the gun they were fired from." Bracing her hand on the desk, she leaned in further for a better look before looking over her shoulder at Matt. "Could we do that? Could we match the blade, if we can find it, to the striations in the bone?"

"We could certainly give it a try. We're not that experienced in that kind of comparison though. I could see if we could find someone who is."

"No, no, we don't need that." Leigh straightened, for the first time feeling the thrill of the chase in this case. "I have a contact at the Sudbury crime lab. He's their ballistics expert. If he can match bullet striations, maybe he could match knife striations. You'd just have to give him some samples to work on."

"Find me what you think is the killing weapon and I can get him bone samples and electron micrographs to work with."

"Sounds good." Leigh turned back to the monitor. "What else does this show us?" she asked Juka.

"A few things. For instance, we now know for sure the knife moved from the posterior to the anterior—from back to front." Juka pointed to several ragged sections that had separated from the surface of the bone on three sides, leaving a single attachment point. "You see these? These are called 'lifts'. As the knife moves through the bone, it puts pressure on the surface and produces these lifts in the opposite direction. In this image, the edges of the lifts are on the right side, so the knife was moving from right to left, or, when you look at the bone itself, from back to front."

"From under the ear toward the front of the neck," Paul clarified.

"Now we know the angle of the cut, the angle of the blade, and the direction of the slice," Leigh summarized. "Nicely done."

"And there's one other thing," Juka said. "We can prove the victim was alive at the time his throat was cut."

"How on earth can you tell that from a slice through the bone?"

"You have to remember that bone isn't just minerals; it's living tissue. And living tissue is moist and flexible when it's alive and dries out after death." He brought up another shot of the kerf mark. A heavy ridge marked the edge of the furrow. Normal bone ran toward the ridge, but a small depressed valley separated the upper surface of the bone from the edge of the defect. "You see this surface here?" Juka pointed to the surface of the bone. "That's the periosteum, a layer of connective tissue that covers bones. It got cut as well when the blade passed through the bone.

But do you see how this layer has pulled back leaving a gap"—he pointed to the dip between the periosteum and the kerf edge— "here? That's what happens when the bone is living at the time of wound creation. Had the victim been dead and the bones and tissues drying and no longer elastic, like if the mark was made while processing the bones, then there would be no gap. Thus, the wound was inflicted perimortem, not postmortem."

"Excellent. Now give me the knife characteristics and we'll be all set."

Matt glanced at Kiko and the graphics displayed on her monitor. "We're just about there. What I can also add is that we're looking at a non-serrated knife. The microscopic striations in the kerf are what we'd expect from a smooth blade. If the blade was serrated, we'd be seeing a lot more bone damage. And I think Kiko's finished, so we may have more for you."

"I am." Kiko waved them over. "This will give you something to go on for the weapon. We've mapped the entire length of the cut mark, but it's easier to see it in a smaller representative section." She indicated a three-dimensional image of the surface of the bone, flowing horizontally, then dipping into a deep V-shaped trough in the middle that ended on a narrow plateau before rising again to the surface. "As you can see, this is a nice cross section of the kerf, showing the 'V' shape of the defect. Previously published studies show data correlating the angle of the knife blade, the force, the kerf angle and the bone elasticity coefficient. Without getting into a lot of boring, complicated math, I can tell you the force applied to the blade changed during the knife stroke—there was more force applied at the beginning of the cut and the force lessened slightly as the blade swept forward. I can also tell you you're looking for a blade with an angle of thirty to thirty-two degrees. Now, I did a really quick and dirty web search while I was waiting for the information to come back, and it seems that things like kitchen knives have a blade angle in the low to mid-twenty-degree range. When you get closer to thirty, you're looking at hunting knives. Over thirty degrees implies a military knife." She looked up at Matt. "You did say the cut looked professional. Not necessarily a hit then, but maybe someone in the military? Or ex-military?"

"Combat knife skills are one of the things you learn in training," Matt said. "You never knew what you'd need in battle and we'd carry as much as we could with us. If you run out of ammunition, you'd at least still have your knife for self-defense. Or any other time you needed a blade. Yeah . . . the guy could be ex-military."

"We'll definitely have to consider it," Leigh said, nodding in agreement.

"Now I've got a question," Kiko said. "I know all this science is useful, but we're missing something here. You came here because they'd ID'd the vic. We've been so focused on the cause of death we've skipped ahead of the fact that someone died. Who was he?"

"His name was Brent Pratt and while we're not sure when he died, if he was alive today, he'd be twenty-eight years old. He was born and grew up in Hamilton, but moved to nearby Wenham when he was twenty. His parents still live at the last address we have on record for him, but that was seven years ago from his last valid driver's license."

"Seven years?" Kiko exchanged a look with Juka and Paul. "That makes sense because that's when he became old enough to drink. You can use your driver's license as proof of age, so a lot of kids early renew at twenty-one. But a license is only good for five years. Why did he let his lapse?"

"Because shortly before he should have renewed it, his parents asked him to leave their house and he was out on the streets."

"Harsh," Paul muttered.

"Yes, but from the police records he gave them cause. From the time he was twenty-two, you can see the downward spiral. He got sucked into the North Shore heroin culture. Multiple charges in Wenham and Hamilton, occasional bookings at first, then coming closer together. After twenty-six, there's only one drug charge, but not in Essex county. It's out in Springfield. The man in the mug shot looks very different from the man from Wenham on the old driver's license. Homelessness destroyed him, broke him. Then after his arrest in Springfield . . . nothing. Now that I'm up to speed, I'm headed to Wenham to break the news to the Pratts."

"I suspect they gave up hope on their son years ago," Matt said. "Maybe even assumed he was already dead. Want me to come with you? We don't have a lot of details yet on cause of death, but I might be able to answer their questions. More than that, I'd like to meet them. With our other victims, I felt some sort of connection, you know? We recovered the body, or excavated their graves. But this one . . ." His gaze tracked to the sterile bones on the table. "The remains still just feel like a lab specimen at this point. There's no human factor. I'd like to put more than just a face to this victim."

"I know what you mean. So, yes, you can come with me, but the usual rules apply: let me take the lead and don't volunteer information unless you get the go ahead."

"I can do that." He turned to his students. "We'll be gone for the rest of the afternoon. Finish up here and then call it quits for the day. We've had a busy week."

"Do you want us in tomorrow?" Juka asked.

"Not sure yet. Let me see where we stand after talking to the parents and I'll let you know." Outside the window, dark clouds moved sluggishly over the city and out over open water. "It looks like it's going to snow, maybe before we make it to Essex."

"We have your SUV if we really need it," Leigh said. "But last I heard, we're only supposed to get a couple of inches. It's certainly cold enough for it."

Paul walked to the window by his work station, overlooking Albany Street. "Supposedly this cold snap is going to lead into some kick ass Nor'easter just before Christmas. The forecasters are talking a foot or more of snow. That could toast a lot of people's plans for the holiday."

"I'll believe it when I see it," Matt said. "They usually can't get two days from now right, much less more than a week from now. They're probably just trying to boost ratings with talk of another 'snowpocalypse'."

"Weather forecasters do love to jump on any kind of nasty weather like it's a high-speed train, and then blow it all out of proportion," Kiko said with a snort. "If they're calling for twelve inches, I'm betting it's two."

A calculated gleam sparkled in Paul's eye. "You're on. Ten inches."

"I'll take six," Juka chimed in.

"Five bucks?" Kiko suggested.

"Deal," the men chorused.

"Last time I saw this," Leigh said, "you boys didn't do so well. I recall Kiko cleaning up when you bet on who stopped Bradford."

"Ah yes." Kiko grinned, rubbing her hands together gleefully. "That was a nice win. It paid to bet on both of you."

"As I recall, Juka won the next round." Chuckling, Matt slipped out of his lab coat. "They do this about once a month— find something to bet on and lay five dollars on the line. The theory is by the end of the year, they'll all break even."

"Hey, nothing wrong with a little good-natured competition in the lab," Paul protested.

"I'm not saying there's anything wrong with it. I'm just thinking I should be taking a cut from all these bets since it's always happening in my lab."

"Not a chance," Paul protested. "You want to make money, you have to play." He elbowed Juka. "If we can talk him into betting, maybe we can raise the stakes. You know these profs and all the money they make."

Matt laughed. "More than a grad student, I'll grant you that. But not nearly as much as you think." He hung up his lab coat on a peg by his desk and finger-hooked his ski jacket off the back of his chair. "Okay, let's go meet the Pratts."

CHAPTER NINE: FIELD-EXPEDIENT DIRECTION FINDING

Field-Expedient Direction Finding: real-time navigation without compass or map using the sun, moon, shadows, stars, or an analog watch.

Friday, December 13, 5:45 p.m.
Pratt Residence
Wenham, Massachusetts

Leigh sat down on the sofa in the formal living room, and Matt settled beside her. The Pratts—Kyle, still dressed in his suit and tie from the office, and Maggie, in neat slacks and a blouse—took the opposite loveseat. They sat stiffly, but held hands, presenting a united front.

They've probably been expecting this visit for years.

The couple looked like they belonged here in this upper middle-class house and neighborhood. The comparison to Haverhill couldn't be starker—Haverhill with its high poverty rate and largely non-white population, versus Wenham which was ninety-eight percent white, with a high per capita income and a one percent poverty rate. And yet, Brent Pratt had left Wenham for the Haverhills of the world.

The Pratts' affluent lifestyle probably gave Brent the means to experiment with drugs, but when it became a problem, they didn't know how to handle it and sent him away, hoping he'd straighten out and come home. In the end, they lost him forever.

This was without a doubt the part of her job Leigh disliked the most. "Mr. and Mrs. Pratt, I'm sorry to drop in on you like this, but—"

"It's Brent, isn't it?" Kyle interrupted, his eyes flat with resignation. "We've waited for news of him forever. Please . . . just tell us."

"Your son's remains were recovered a few days ago," Leigh said in a gentle voice, then paused to give them a moment to absorb the news. But they remained stoic, frozen, neither comforting the other beyond their clasped hands. "This isn't a surprise for you," Leigh stated after another few beats of silence.

Kyle shook his head. "As I said, we've been waiting a long time. And we knew it would either be Brent arriving, or someone else bearing bad news. Was it a drug overdose?"

"The evidence points to murder."

This got a reaction as Kyle's hand twitched in his wife's while Maggie shuddered.

"A drug-related killing?" Kyle asked, his voice thick.

"We don't know. It's early in the case. His skeleton was found in a university teaching lab."

Maggie's gaze met Leigh's. The pain shadowed there was a punch to the gut. Expecting bad news was one thing, actually hearing it was another.

"I don't understand. How did he get there? And as a skeleton?" she asked.

"Those are just two of the questions we're asking," Leigh said.

"But you know it was murder?" Kyle asked.

Leigh nodded to Matt to jump in.

"Yes. I'm a forensic anthropologist. It's my job to determine this type of information from human remains." Matt paused, indecision flashing briefly over his face. "Your son's throat was cut."

Maggie gasped, a hand flying to her mouth and tears in her eyes. "Did he suffer?"

Matt shook his head. "He died quickly." He threw a quick glance at Leigh, silently passing the ball back to her.

"Mr. and Mrs. Pratt, we have some significant challenges ahead of us in this case." Leigh kept her tone matter-of-fact, knowing sympathy, while kind, often caused the grieving to break down faster. While there would be time for that, she needed answers first to set the team on their path. "Because of the nature of your son's remains, we don't know exactly when he died. We also don't know where he died or who might be responsible. So the very best way of grounding our search is to start at the beginning. I know this is a difficult time, but if we could ask you a few questions . . ." Leigh trailed off, allowing them a moment to regroup.

"Of course. How can we help?" Kyle's eyes were dry, but his voice was rough, as if fighting tears.

"When was the last time you saw Brent?"

"That would have been two years ago," Maggie said. "Brent . . . he had trouble with drugs. He was a good student in high school. Maybe not straight A's, but definitely a B+ student. He was on the debate team, and the track and field team. He had a steady girlfriend. But then he went away to college."

"Endicott College in Boston," Kyle said. "For business. That was when things started to go wrong."

"He was young," Maggie said. "Away from his small town for the first time, and just feeling his way."

Kyle pulled his hand from his wife's, breaking the wall of their united front. "That's what you said when he kept asking for money. When he stopped coming home for visits. When the first warnings about his academic standing came in. We can't keep making excuses for him. At a certain point, he had to be responsible for his actions. He was a grown man."

Maggie paled, her lips folding into a seam of misery as she seemed to collapse inward.

Kyle blew out a long breath and took his wife's hand again, holding it, lifeless and stiff, in both of his. But it was Leigh's gaze he met. "We've gone around and around on this before. It's useless and gets us nowhere. We're both responsible for taking too long to figure out Brent was in trouble. By the time we realized what was happening, it was already too late and we'd lost him. He was a heroin addict. He'd stopped going to classes and he'd spent the money we sent him, not on books and transit passes, but on drugs. We brought him home, tried to get him clean. But the damage was already done."

"Did you take him for treatment?" Matt asked. "Methadone?"

"Yes. And at first it seemed to work. He did four weeks in-patient rehab. When he came home, he talked about returning to school at the start of the next year. But even with the outpatient treatments to ease his cravings, it didn't last and he slid back into old habits. We cut him off from any money, so he started stealing. First from us, and then from others."

"Addictions like that are powerful," Matt said. "Some have more difficulty overcoming it than others."

"He tried in the beginning." Maggie's voice trembled, but she gamely continued. "When he first came home, he and I spent many hours talking about his hopes and dreams for the future. He was so sorry he'd failed us." Her voice went throaty, tears shading her words. "He cried and I held him like when he was a little boy. But we weren't enough for him."

"You're not being fair to yourselves, Mrs. Pratt." Leigh reached out to touch the other woman's arm, both to comfort and connect. "You couldn't fight this battle for him. You gave him every opportunity to get better. It's not your fault he didn't."

"Or perhaps, couldn't," Matt said. "He might not have been able to overcome his own biochemistry. Maybe he was already feeling guilty and didn't want you to know he'd failed you a second time. It was easier to slink away than face what he perceived would be your disapproval, even if it never existed. At times like that, an addict is his own worst enemy."

"That part is certainly true," Kyle said. "Things came to a head one night two years ago when someone drove by the house and shot out our living room window. Here. In *Wenham*."

It was clear from his disapproving tone that while other communities might consider this a normal activity, such a thing would never be allowed on Wenham's hallowed streets.

"We told him he had to leave before he put our lives and the lives of those around us at any more risk," Kyle continued.

"We told him we'd be here waiting for him when he got clean and was ready to come home," Maggie said. "We told him we'd always be here." She broke down, sliding her fingers from her husband's grip to bury her face in her hands.

"He left the house that night and we never saw him again." Kyle's voice was flat, void of expression. "For weeks we were on edge. Every time the phone rang, or a knock sounded at the door, we'd jump, sure it was Brent." He looked across the room toward the framed photo of a dark haired teenage boy, dressed in a track uniform, his face red and shiny with exertion, grinning widely and waving a gold medal at the camera. When he spoke again, his voice was nearly a whisper. "But it never was."

"Mr. Pratt." Leigh waited patiently while stunned eyes slowly focused on her. "You don't know where he went after he left? You didn't hear from him by phone, or through mutual acquaintances?"

"No, never."

Damn. His police record is probably a better recent history than his parents' knowledge.

"Can I ask about your son's implant?" Matt asked.

Maggie's raised her head from her hands, her face streaked by silent tears that continued to fall. "His implant?"

"The one in his hip. When we examined your son's x-rays, we found radiographic evidence of an implant. It was the serial number on the implant that led us to the identification and to you."

"Brent was born with one leg shorter than the other." Maggie patted her right thigh. "It seemed to take longer for Brent to walk than the baby books suggested, and then when he did, he always seemed unsteady. When he got a little older, he walked with a limp. We asked the doctor about it and he sent us for x-rays. He told us Brent had something called *coxa vara*, meaning the hip joint was angled wrong, causing that leg to be shorter. Brent had surgery when he was six. They broke the hip and realigned it using a plate and screws at the proper angle. It was called a val . . . a valgus . . ."

"A valgus osteotomy," Matt supplied.

She nodded. "It was a miracle for Brent. Once he healed from the surgery and went through physio, he was able to walk and then run like a normal child." She furiously blinked and backhanded one damp cheek. "He joined the track and field team. He was good at track and field. He could hardly run before."

"Your surgeon never recommended removing the plate and screws?"

"He mentioned the possibility at the beginning. But he left them in since the implant didn't cause Brent any pain. That was fine with us. Brent was so active, we didn't like the thought of putting him through surgery a second time. And it never bothered him, so I think we made the right choice."

"Mr. and Mrs. Pratt, thank you for seeing us." Leigh pulled a card from her blazer pocket and handed it across to Maggie. "My numbers are on this card. If you think of anything else, please don't hesitate to call. Even if you think it's something small and insignificant, someone Brent mentioned or someone he knew in rehab, please let us know."

Back in the car, shivering in the cold, Leigh cranked up the heat. Christmas carols burst jauntily from the radio and she dialed them down, their cheeriness jarring her dark mood. "I don't think Brent's parents will be able to help us."

Matt put on his seatbelt and then blew on his hands for warmth. "I agree. They're just too far out of the picture. And the people he interacted with, the drug dealers and other underworld types, they're on a different planet compared to those nice people. What's next, assuming this was a dead end?"

"It gave us some idea of who our victim was, but even that's not entirely accurate because it's not a recent picture. I want to go back to his police records. Let's find his latest arrest and start from there with his last known location. We'll trace his steps from that point forward. And, at the same time, the next person I have in my sights is Trevor Sharpe."

Matt nonchalantly crossed his arms over his chest. "Really?"

"You know, you look casual, but the rapacious gleam in your eye says you're all over this idea."

He grinned. "Of course, I am."

"Yeah, I got that. You can't sit in on this, you know. You're too connected to Sharpe and have too much background with him." She gave him a feral smile. "But if you're really nice to me over the next few days, I might let you observe."

"You name it. Your car detailed? Your walk shoveled? Maybe breakfast in bed?" The gleam went sharp. "Maybe some fun before breakfast?"

"All of the above works for me." She pulled away from the curb. "You give it your best shot and I'll let you know if you've done enough to win my favor."

CHAPTER TEN: SORTIE

Sortie: a sudden assault by a group of soldiers who abandon a defensive position to attack an enemy.

Monday, December 16, 9:39 a.m.
Essex Detective Unit
Salem, Massachusetts

Leave it to Sharpe to arrive late to a police interview regarding a murder investigation. Anyone else would be terrified enough to come early; he makes the investigating officer wait.

Matt looked at his watch for the third time in as many minutes. He stood in Observation waiting for Leigh to bring Sharpe into Interview, and still the room on the other side of the mirrored glass was empty. Matt leaned against the wall beside the window frame, trying to quench his growing irritation. *Everything about the man sets you off. Why would this little inconsiderate act be any different?* He tipped his head back against the wall and closed his eyes, trying to settle his impatience.

His eyes flew open when he heard the interview room door open.

"After you, Mr. Sharpe," Leigh said.

"That's Dr. Sharpe, Trooper," he said, clearly offended.

Matt pushed off the wall and whipped around in time to see Leigh duck her head. "My apologies, Dr. Sharpe. Can I get you a cup of coffee?"

Sharpe's lips formed the slightest of grimaces. "No, thank you. But I will take a bottle of water."

"Of course. I'll be right back. Make yourself comfortable." Leigh slipped out the door.

"Make yourself comfortable," Sharpe mimicked under his

breath to the empty room. "As if that could be possible here." He took a seat in one of the four chairs and folded his hands on the surface of the table.

The door to Observation opened. Matt turned to find Leigh leaning on the jamb, one eyebrow arched. "Can you hear it?" she asked.

He cocked his head questioningly. "Hear what?"

"The 'little lady' that practically follows every sentence when he speaks to me?"

Matt swallowed a bark of laughter, cautious of sound traveling into the other room. "Caught that, did you?"

"Arrogant jackass. Involved in this case or not, I already don't like him."

"Amen to that." He stared through the glass at Sharpe's hawkish profile.

Leigh joined him at the window. "Someday you'll have to tell me why you hate him so much."

"It isn't relevant to this situation at all or I'd have brought it up already, but I'll tell you later today as thanks for this treat. It's the least you deserve for setting this up."

"Deal. Now, I'm going to go find him a bottle of water. Preferably somewhere on the far side of town so it takes a while and is warm when I get back. Notice he didn't ask for a glass of water? It's almost like he doesn't trust it to be to his standards of cleanliness."

"Notice he didn't show up on time?"

"Sure did. And he didn't even apologize. Kind of makes me not want to rush things for him this morning."

"Let him cool his heels for a few minutes. Maybe it will tone down his attitude. By the way, nice docile lady cop routine you've got going so far. I assume you'll let the tiger out to play soon?"

"With great pleasure. Okay, time to get started. Enjoy the show." She slipped out the door and closed it with a soft *click*.

Over the next ten minutes, Sharpe grew more and more restless. He sat quietly at first, but then abruptly slid back his chair with an impatient grunt and pushed to his feet. He stalked around the room a few times before he came to stand at the glass.

Matt's heart rate kicked as Sharpe stood opposite him, squinting as if trying to see through the glass to who might be on the other side. He leaned in, as if he could see something and Matt squelched the urge to step back a pace in defense of being caught spying. *You don't know I'm here. And even if you do, you can't do anything about it. You have no power here.* He took in Sharpe's irritated expression through the glass and grinned. *And the best cop in this unit is about to give you a run for your money.*

Right on cue, Leigh entered the room with a bottle of water and a file folder. "Sorry, that took so long. I couldn't find any bottled water at first." She looked a bit sheepish and kept her eyes downcast. "And what I could find isn't chilled."

Again, Sharpe's reaction was subtle, but Matt caught his narrowed eyes in distaste for a split second before it vanished.

"That's all right, my dear," Sharpe said magnanimously. "I appreciate the effort. Now, what can I do to help you in this investigation? It doesn't look good for one's reputation to have this sort of thing happening in one's own lab."

Matt admired Leigh for maintaining her slightly dim expression when, in reality, he knew Sharpe's superiority would disgust her.

"One wouldn't want that, would one?" she said sweetly.

"I'm not sure where one of my people went wrong to bring in such a specimen, but I'd like to get to the bottom of it as much as you. What do you need from me? I am at your disposal."

Matt braced his hands on the windowsill, his knuckles going white as he gripped tight. *You bastard. You don't hesitate to toss one of your underlings under the bus. Have you conveniently forgotten it's your lab and you're responsible for* everything *going on there?*

"As head of the lab, I assumed you oversaw every aspect of the work." Leigh posed the question politely, with just the tiniest bit of naiveté. "It would certainly be a credit to you if you could manage that in your busy schedule."

"In a perfect world with copious spare time that's exactly how it's done. But when you reach my level—"

Matt choked back the growl building in his throat.

"—you don't have time for minutiae like that. That's why I delegate others to be responsible for various aspects of running the lab."

"And, in this case, someone else was responsible for ordering in the skeleton."

"Yes. I can go through my records and see if I can track down when that particular skeleton was acquired. You may not realize it, not having been to my lab, but I have several and—"

"That won't be necessary." The pleasant tone of voice was abruptly gone, and the real Leigh was back. She opened the file folder and pulled out a sheaf of papers, pushing them across the table. "I asked your purchasing department for some assistance and found they were most helpful. Your order was placed in January of this year and fulfilled in April. In fact, because of the amount of the order, extra approval was required. The order was placed in your name and was signed by you with one-up approval. Beyond that, there is no evidence anyone else was involved in this order. Certainly not one of your subordinates."

Sharpe drew back, his eyes wide. "You went over my head to trace the order?"

Leigh sat back, casually resting her forearms on the arms of the chair. "Of course I did."

"You had no right to—"

"I had every right, *Dr.* Sharpe. Your lab is considered a crime scene and you are one of the possible suspects."

"I'm *what?*"

Matt noticed with interest that his lab being labeled a crime scene didn't seem to bother him nearly as much as the being personally under suspicion.

"A suspect, Dr. Sharpe. You were responsible for bringing a *murder victim* into your lab and propping him in the corner until someone with a sharper eye than yours noticed the damage. Because you clearly didn't."

"Who noticed the damage?"

"The call came in anonymously from a payphone near Harvard. We have no way to trace the caller, but since access to your lab is limited, if it were me, I'd be tempted to look closely at my own people. You know, to see if it was in someone's interest to bring this to the attention of the police."

Colour suffused Sharpe's face, but he blustered on. "Who are you working with? Because I'd like to examine his credentials. Perhaps I can suggest someone certified by the American Board of Forensic Anthropologists. There aren't many of us, you know."

A wide smile curved Leigh's lips. "Then you'll be glad to know I'm working with one of you."

"Who?" Sharpe demanded.

Matt leaned forward with anticipation. This was going to be good.

"Dr. Matthew Lowell of Boston Univer—"

Sharpe's bark of laughter cut her off. "Lowell? He's hardly noteworthy. How many publications does he have?"

At least I deserve every one of mine.

"I don't care how many publications he has," Leigh retorted. "He's Board certified, as you suggested. And he's a damned good scientist. You don't happen to remember a rather high-profile serial killer from this past fall? Neil Bradford?"

"Of course I do. But . . ." Sharpe's gaze narrowed on Leigh's face. "That was Lowell?"

"I couldn't have solved the case without him. When bones are involved, he's my go-to consultant." Leigh braced both hands on the table and leaned in to get right into Sharpe's face. "So when he tells me your skeleton is a local boy out of Wenham who had his throat brutally cut, and then bled out, I believe him."

Sharpe's eyes nearly bugged out of his head.

"Furthermore, I don't have a death scene, so that makes your lab my only crime scene. I'm tempted to lock the place down until this investigation is over."

"You can't do that," Sharpe spluttered, his face flushing with color. "We do crucial research in that lab."

"I can do whatever I need to in order to solve this case. And if that means shutting you down, then I will." Leigh backed off and settled into her chair. "And I'm sure that would mean a stop to whatever research you and your students are pursuing. But a man died and ended up unnoticed in your lab, so that takes priority. Of course, if you were willing to help me, I might reconsider."

"Lowell must love this," Sharpe muttered.

"What was that? Sorry, I didn't catch it."

Sharpe scowled and looked away. "Never mind." He took several deep breaths, as if to gather his composure.

Leigh glanced toward Matt behind the glass. Her expression never changed, but the *Gotcha!* gleam in her eyes made him smile.

"Now, Dr. Sharpe. I'd like you to tell me how this order got placed, apparently with your name on it, but without your knowledge?"

Sharpe heaved a sigh and looked back to her. "I will endeavor to explain. I'm a busy man, obviously. My services are in high demand, thus I pre-approve a bunch of blank purchase orders. Orders are placed as needed by my staff."

"Even a skeleton worth thousands of dollars?"

Sharpe shrugged. "Of course. The university courses I instruct require anatomical models."

Leigh retrieved the paperwork from across the table. "According to this purchase requisition, you bought the skeleton from Paleo Natural Systems Inc. in Boston. Human anatomical skeletons are the most expensive item they carry. Why not just use a plastic replica to save time and money?"

Behind the glass, Matt winced. Spoken by someone who didn't fully understand the fine art of human anatomy.

Sharpe's lip curled. "You don't use mass-produced plastic. Companies that produce those aim for the average in everything. There is beauty in the uniqueness of the human form that is lost otherwise. The only way to teach students, including medical students, is to show them the real thing—specimens."

"Back to Paleo Natural Systems then. Have you dealt with

them before?"

"They are our usual supply source and have never given us reason to complain. Of course, they've never previously sold us a murder victim."

"Not that you know of," Leigh said dryly. "They're next on my list to question." She closed the file and tapped it once on the tabletop to stack the pages. "Thank you for your time, Dr. Sharpe. We're done . . . for now."

"You still think I'm responsible?"

"I honestly don't know. You may have knowingly brought a murder victim into your laboratory. To say you didn't means you didn't know what you had in your own lab and shows an unfortunate lack of responsibility. Dr. Lowell spotted the defect on first glance. So either you knew about it because you put it there yourself"—she ignored Sharpe's cry of dissent and continued—"or you're so disconnected with what actually goes on in your lab, you don't notice when the remains of a murder victim are mounted only a few feet from your desk. You'll remain on my list of suspects for now." She stood and walked to the door where she opened it to hold it wide. "Please remain available. No traveling for any reason."

"You can't dictate what I do with my life."

"Actually, I can. For now, I'll take your word for it. If at any time I suspect you're a flight risk, I'd be happy to host you as a guest of the Commonwealth until we sort through this. Good day, Dr. Sharpe."

He rose to his feet and stalked past her, taking great care to cut a wide swath around her as he exited the interview room.

Leigh looked toward the two-way mirror. "Good riddance to you too," she said, shaking her head in disgust.

———

Monday, December 16, 10:28 a.m.
Essex Detective Unit
Salem, Massachusetts

Leigh passed Matt a cup of coffee and watched with amusement while he took a sip. *Wait for it . . .* His eyes widened, and he forced the bitter brew down with a shudder.

"My God, how have I managed to escape this swill during our previous four cases?" Matt took another sniff. "It's horrible, not to mention caustic as hell. You could strip paint with it."

"I warned you about the coffee, though it's no different than other cop shop coffee. They're all deadly. Someday we'll investigate the death of one of our own and this will be the reason." She tapped her coffee cup to his. "Bottoms up." She took a healthy swallow, and then laughed at his horrified expression. "Really, you get used to it."

"You've been getting used to it for what? Three years? Four? I'm on my first day. Let me ease into it." He placed his cup on the coffee room counter and backed away as if it was a coiled rattlesnake.

Leigh leaned against the counter, his horror over something so trivial making her feel lighter than she had all morning. "Okay, if you're not going to drink your coffee, then you can talk while I drink mine. You already know I'm not the President of the Trevor Sharpe Fan Club, but I want to know why you aren't. You're colleagues. I could understand some healthy competition but I've known for years you flat out hate him. It's how I used him to blackmail you into our first case."

"We haven't known each other for years, so how could you possibly know that?"

"Remember I first met you three years ago when you taught our 'Murder School' course on the recovery of human remains for the troopers transferring from the Field Troops to the Detective Units. After one of the classes, I overheard you talking to a Boston PD officer who wanted a consult with either you or Sharpe. You told him to deal with Sharpe if he thought Sharpe was the expert, but you didn't like him or trust him. If I remember correctly, you said something about not being willing to send a student you disliked to work with him."

Matt shook his head at her in amusement. "So that's how you got me on board. You knew I didn't like him and you used it as leverage. You dropped that little bomb and then nearly walked out of the Old North."

"You nearly let me. But enough about my wiles and how I got you on board"—she winked at him—"what created the animosity in the first place?"

Matt lifted her cup from her hands, sniffed at it, took a tentative tiny sip, grimaced, and returned it to her. "Just checking. Still horrible. I don't need caffeine that badly." He pulled up one of the chairs, turned it around, and straddled it backward, looking up at Leigh. "My issues with Sharpe go back more than a few years and while I wasn't actually a witness to what happened, Greg, one of my Ph.D. colleagues, was. Sharpe and Greg both did their Masters of Science degrees at the University of North Carolina - Charlotte. It's a recognized forensic anthropology training program. His supervisor, Dr. David Ellison, was very well respected and seen as a real up-and-comer, someone with the chops to start his own body farm someday. When I did my Ph.D. at the University of Tennessee at Knoxville, it was the only body farm in the country and had been for two decades. Lots of other schools were vying for the chance to establish the next one."

"Why such a big gap between the Knoxville body farm and whatever farm opened next?"

"Western Carolina, twenty-five years later. The biggest issue is always the smell, with circling carrion birds coming in a close second. You know what decomp smells like. Would you like to sit out on your patio and, instead of roses, you smell that anytime the temperature is above freezing?"

Leigh wrinkled her nose in disgust. "Definitely not."

"Exactly. Site selection is always key when you're looking to establish something like this. But running a site is a different matter. That takes ethics and sensitivity and often a fine hand with both the community and the media. Ellison was that kind of man."

"I'm getting a bad feeling about this. You keep mentioning him in the past tense."

"Unfortunately, it's not a happy story. Anyway, Sharpe was seen as the rising star of Ellison's group. He could not only do the science and do it well, but he had a way of working the people around him. Greg thought Ellison intended to take Sharpe with him when he left to start a new body farm. But then they published a paper on a new technique for analyzing soil components in burials to more specifically pinpoint time since death of skeletonized remains."

"I can see how that would be useful. Not knowing that information has certainly been a problem for us in the past."

In her mind's eye, Leigh could see them as they'd been mere months before. Still practically strangers, they'd faced off toe-to-toe in Matt's lab, surrounded by his baffled students as they sniped at each other, Leigh pressuring Matt for a time since death estimate so she could proceed with her missing persons search.

"I'm not asking you to open a vein and write it in blood."

"You're pushing."

He tried to turn away from her then, to give them both the breather they very much needed, but she wasn't having it. In desperation, she grabbed him, yanking him back around to face her. "Don't turn away from me. I need something to go on. Give me something."

They'd nearly come to blows over Matt's unwillingness to guess at the time since death.

"Time-out." Matt's softly spoken words brought her back to him. She blinked down at him to see him watching her, a smile curving his lips. He knew exactly where her mind had been.

She chuckled. "Time-out, indeed. But given we were having that argument in the first place, clearly whatever that technique was didn't hold water or you'd have used it."

Matt grinned. "Got it in one. The paper was peer reviewed and published in *The Journal of Forensic Sciences* and it doesn't get much bigger than that for us. But then people tried unsuccessfully to replicate the results in the field. Then they tried it with burials of known timeline and it flat out didn't work. According to Greg, Ellison suspected Sharpe fabricated some of the results to flesh out the story."

"Why would he do that? Wouldn't he know someone would want to test his technique?"

"You'd think. But to have a paper published in *The Journal of Forensic Sciences* while still doing your Masters—it's practically unheard of. Sharpe was blazing trails and always had his eye on whatever would give him the most glory. And he was happy to step over, or on people to do it. In this case, he stepped on Ellison because when push comes to shove, the person who is responsible for a paper is the last name on the list of authors. That's the guy who ran the project and who funded it. When the data couldn't be replicated, the paper was retracted." Matt shook his head, his jaw tight.

Leigh stared at him blankly, confused. Why all the fuss about a correction? "I'm missing something. They retracted the paper. They took it back essentially?"

"Yes."

"What's the big deal?"

"Spoken like someone outside the field. In science, trust is everything. The peers who review your data can't be there when you do every experiment, so they have to trust your data is honest. Same for your readers. The first time that trust is broken, your career is over. If it's proven you can't be trusted with the data in one paper, everyone will suspect everything you've ever published, and no one will ever trust you for any new data from that point on. If you can't publish, you can't apply for grants. With no money, you have nothing to do and no academic institution wants you." Matt heaved a sympathetic sigh. "Ellison didn't do the work himself, but he signed off on it and was responsible for it. So it was his career, not Sharpe's, which ended. And no one remembered the little grad student who actually did the damage."

"Except those of you with a connection to him." She took a sip of her cooling coffee and asked the question that had been tickling the back of her brain since Matt started his story. "What happened to Ellison?"

"He lost everything. Any opportunity to establish his own facility. A chance for tenure at the university. The university kept him on while he still had grant funds, but when those dried up, he was done." Matt's gaze slid to the floor as if struggling with the next part. "They found him hanging in his garage. He lived alone, and it had been days since anyone had seen him, so one of his colleagues went looking for him. He couldn't live with the shame of his life and what might have been, so he killed himself." The eyes that rose to hers were full of sadness for a life senselessly lost.

"And Sharpe moved on, scot-free."

Matt bared his teeth in an unconscious show of rage. "Sharpe moved on all right. He finished his Masters with a new advisor and then did his Ph.D. at the University of Hawaii West O'ahu so he could partner with JPAC/CIL—the Joint POW/MIA Accounting Command Central Identification Lab. That's where he really built up his reputation."

"And then from there he went to Harvard." Leigh dumped the dregs of her coffee down the sink and rinsed out her cup. "Is that the first time you met him?"

"No, we met at a couple of conferences before that. It's true I already knew of him before then, but I think I'd have disliked him and his condescending attitude without knowing his backstory."

"You're very different people. Sharpe seems to play everyone around him. With you, what you see is what you get." She ran her fingers lightly over his shoulder, a brief display of affection in a place where no affection was allowed. "Thanks for that."

He flashed her a smile. "You're welcome. Now what?"

"I need to check out Paleo Natural Systems in Boston." She paused, studying him intently.

"What?"

"It might actually be useful for you to come with me. This

whole anatomical specimen thing is more up your alley than mine."

"I've purchased a few in my time, yes."

"Up for a field trip?"

He pushed back from the chair and stood. "With you? Always."

CHAPTER ELEVEN: FIELD DRESSING

Field Dressing: hunters' term for the gutting of a freshly killed animal to ensure proper preservation of the meat.

Wednesday, December 18, 11:45 a.m.
Paleo Natural Systems Inc.
Boston, Massachusetts

The bell on the frame jangled as Leigh stepped through the door Matt held open. They blew into the warm shop on a gust of icy wind that whipped Leigh's hair into a wild tangle around her face until the door slammed shut behind them. She brushed the strands out of her eyes and then stopped dead to take in the eye-popping displays that made up Paleo Natural Systems Inc.

An array of Lucite blocks containing insects of every color and size imaginable crowded one of the nearby tables. Wooden glass-fronted cabinets stocked everything from hand-crafted gemstone jewelry to antique bone saws, fossils, and small mammal skeletons under glass domes. A nearby table was jammed with a selection of apothecary jars of various shapes and sizes, many sealed with ground glass stoppers. On the far side of the room, two full-sized human replicas stood, one half skeletal and half muscular systems, the other half muscular and half intact skin. Horned antelope skulls hugged the walls between framed butterflies and poster reproductions of eighteenth century anatomy sketches.

"Wow," Leigh breathed.

"You can say that again. I've ordered from here before, but we had everything delivered. I've never actually been in the store." Matt walked to a table and selected a little bag of sugar cube skulls out of a basket. "This would be the perfect gift for Paul and his coffee."

"You could Christmas shop for all your students here. But you'll have to come back another day to do that. Let's see if we can find the manager."

Leigh wound around a display of human bones interspersed with intact skulls, a few quills, some antique surgical clamps, and a vintage anatomy text open to a page diagramming the nervous system. A small bell lay on the front desk next to the register and she touched it lightly. A high chime vibrated through the room.

"Hang on, be right out!" The voice came from behind a black cloth curtain to the left of the register. Seconds later, an older, balding man appeared wearing a shirt several sizes too small. At first glance, Leigh feared for the buttons straining against his girth and wondered if the projectiles might be dangerous. He brushed grime and cobwebs off his long sleeves. "Sorry about that. I'm unpacking some new items." He gave another brush. "Well, new to me. The older the better as far as I'm concerned. Can I help you?"

"I hope so." Leigh leaned on the glass counter casually, giving the air of an intimate little chat. "I'm looking for the manager."

"You've found him. Owner, manager, shop boy, cleaning staff, you name it, I'm it. This is my place."

"You have some amazing things."

"Thank you. The store front stocks mostly natural history items. Some of those I get from local collectors, artisans, or hunters. As you can see I also work with artists who do biological models for my more commercial trade—medical professionals and schools. Some I buy ahead of time, some I commission."

"I've purchased some items from you in the past," Matt interjected, holding out his hand. "Dr. Matt Lowell, Boston University. You've supplied some of the skeletal components I use when teaching. Mister . . ."

"Harris. Vic Harris." He shook Matt's hand. "A pleasure. What brings you into the shop? Most of my academic business is done online or by telephone using my online catalogs."

"Actually, I'm the one you're doing business with today." Leigh pulled out her badge, and laid it down on the glass-topped cabinet as Harris stared at it in surprise.

"I don't understand. I didn't call the police. I haven't had any trouble."

"But we have. We'd like you to trace a sale for us."

Harris's brow furrowed and he anxiously rubbed one hand over his belly. "I'm not sure I can. Some of my sellers ask for confidentiality. Hunters and the like, if you get my meaning."

"They're hunting out of season?"

"I don't ask questions. We do a cash deal and everyone goes away happy."

"But you still keep records."

"Of course, I do. I run a legitimate business and I declare everything business-related and can support all of it."

"I respect your dedication to running a legitimate business." *Time to pull out the big guns.* "Mr. Harris, I see this going one of two ways. You can voluntarily share the information we're looking for. Or, I can come back tomorrow with a warrant, in which case you'll have to turn the information over to me at that time. If we find the information is missing, lost, or destroyed, I'll have to inform the IRS"—color leached slowly from Harris's shiny face— "and they'll come in to do a full audit. Quite possibly going back years."

"You wouldn't."

"That would only be if you weren't keeping the proper records you say you are. If everything is in place, then there won't be an issue."

Harris's eyes narrowed on her briefly as if calculating his next move. Then his shoulder slumped. "What do you want to know?"

"I appreciate your assistance." Leigh pulled the folded paperwork from inside her winter coat. "It's this sale to Harvard University."

Harris slipped on a pair of reading glasses and took the paperwork to squint down the order. His gaze landed on the item description and lingered a little too long for Leigh's taste. "Ah . . . yes. I remember this one."

"Who was the buyer?"

"Well, according to this bill of sale, a Dr. Sharpe at Harvard, but if memory serves, it was a woman who placed the order by phone. Hold on. Let me look at my records and I'll get you the details you need." He handed back the paperwork and disappeared behind the curtain.

Matt braced an elbow on the counter and sidled closer, a sly smile curving his lips. "You're good," he said under his breath.

Leigh flicked him a sideways glance. "I couldn't risk him destroying any paperwork before we came back tomorrow. On top of that, he knows something," she said, her voice as low as his.

"Why do you say that?"

"Did you see how long he looked at the item description? He was stalling for time. Also, that order was placed nearly a year ago and he remembers a woman calling it in? Either he doesn't get many orders so each one is memorable—"

"Highly doubtful."

"—or that particular order or type of order is unforgettable."

"My money is on that particular order." Matt selected a tiny pewter skull charm from a basket and turned it over in his fingers. "What Sharpe said about it being hard to get real anatomical skeletons, full skeletons specifically, is dead on. Nowadays, you can still get specimens, but often they're previously imported skeletons that are changing ownership. It can easily take three or four years to get one; they're so scarce to come by."

"Three or four years? Interesting this order was filled in only a couple of months."

"Yeah, I thought so too."

Leigh heard a scuff behind the curtain and laid her hand over Matt's arm, a warning that Harris was returning. He straightened, feigning interest in a selection of amber pendants at the end of the counter.

Harris cradled a large open binder in his arms. He laid it down on the counter and then spun it to face Leigh. "This is it here. Purchased in March from Del Gerrit."

"Where did Mr. Gerrit obtain this skeleton?" Leigh asked.

Harris pushed his sagging glasses further up his nose below a forehead now showing small beads of sweat. "I don't ask. My business only concerns the item coming into my hands. I don't ask where it came from. My discretion keeps sellers coming back."

"Was Mr. Gerrit a repeat seller?"

"Yes, though this was the first human skeleton he'd sold me. Usually it was animal skulls—deer, wolf, fox. On occasion he brought in a taxidermied and mounted head—a buck or a bear."

"So he was familiar with taxidermy?" Matt asked.

"It isn't his livelihood, more something he does on occasion if he's running low on funds. He's a seasonal worker. Works on the Boston Harbor Islands ferry boats during the summer, but once the weather turns, he goes to his land out west. That's when he does his hunting, in the late fall."

"And butchering?" Matt asked. "Is he the eat-what-you-kill type?"

"Oh, you bet. He's a proponent of living off the land."

"How far out west is his land?" Leigh asked. Brent Pratt's last known location at this point was Springfield and that was certainly well west of Boston.

"Not exactly sure. Somewhere in the Berkshires, I think." He rubbed one hand over his damp forehead. "As I said, I don't ask questions."

"You don't have an address for Mr. Gerrit?"

"No. He usually contacts me when he has something. We agree on a time for him to come in and I have cash on hand to purchase his item if I can sell it."

"You don't buy everything he brings in?"

"No." Harris waved a hand at the wall displaying animal skulls. "I typically don't buy if I don't think I can move it quickly—unless it's a really unique piece."

"Like a human skeleton," Leigh prompted.

"I always have buyers lined up for something like that."

"If you have a list of potential buyers, how do you decide who gets it? First come, first served? Whoever can pay the most? The most prestigious? The best customer?"

Harris flushed to the roots of his thinning hair. "My

customers understand that a rare item can be expensive—"

"So the highest bidder," Matt finished for him. "Which in this case was Harvard University."

"And you didn't ask for details as to where the skeleton came from?" Leigh pushed again.

"No. He brought it in, I made sure all two hundred and six bones were present and I paid him for it."

"Hold on." Leigh held up a hand to stop Harris. "It came as a pile of bones? *You* put the skeleton together?"

"Sure. Sometimes they come already assembled—"

"Articulated," Matt mumbled under his breath.

"But sometimes I put them together myself," Harris continued. "I have other models to work from, so I can see how it's done."

"Did you have it authenticated after you . . . *assembled* it?" Matt asked.

"Authenticated? Why would I do that?"

"Because you were selling it to a prestigious university. Or maybe just to maintain your own reputation." Matt turned to Leigh. "You have to be careful with anatomical specimens. Because they're hard to come by, sometimes you see inconsistencies: a female head paired with a male postcranial skeleton, the skull of a teenager paired with the pelvis and pubic symphysis of a fifty-year-old." He raised a hand, fingers splayed. "Two left hands on one set of remains. Sometimes when a full skeleton couldn't be obtained, someone will try to cobble together a complete set of bones, not having enough skill to be able to age or sex the bones to reasonably match them."

Leigh's mouth dropped open as the thought occurred to her. She gathered herself to speak when Matt cut her off. "Already done. It all matched. I would have told you otherwise."

Leigh blew out a pent-up breath. "Of course you would. Sorry, that possibility didn't occur to me until you mentioned it. But I should have known better." She crowded into Harris's personal space. *Time to turn the screws.* "When Mr. Gerrit brought you the skeleton, were you aware it was a murder victim?"

Harris went pasty white, his lips working like a fish out of water. "A *what?*" The words were strangled.

"A murder victim," Leigh repeated.

"No. *NO.* I would never... I wouldn't have..." Harris stopped his babbling, visibly gathering himself. "How would you know that?"

"The evidence was there on the bones," Matt said. "It was subtle, so subtle you missed it, or so we have to assume.... But it's there."

Harris's complexion was easing toward grey now and he swayed on his feet. "I touched... drilled holes in..."

Matt pushed past Leigh to dart behind the counter. He pulled up a stool, pressed Harris down onto it, and then pushed his head between his knees before he looked up at Leigh and shrugged.

He didn't need to say what he was thinking; they were already on the same page. No way did Harris know about the origins of the skeleton. His reaction appeared genuine, no doubt about it. Mr. Harris was a dead end.

But now they had a name: Del Gerrit.

Time to pay Mr. Gerrit a visit... once they figured out where to find him.

CHAPTER TWELVE: BLUE FALCON

Blue Falcon: a team member whose improper actions cause other members of his unit to be punished.

Thursday, December 19, 8:48 a.m.
Springfield Police Department, Strategic Impact Unit
Springfield, Massachusetts

"I appreciate you taking the time to see us, Captain Wallace." Leigh preceded Matt into the office and took one of the seats Wallace indicated as he closed the door behind them, shutting out the noise of the narcotics and vice bullpen beyond. A city of over 150,000, Springfield was the third largest city in Massachusetts and one of only three cities—along with Boston and Worcester—to have its own homicide division. But today, Leigh focused her attention on Brent Pratt and his drug convictions.

"Always happy to help out the state police." Wallace sat down at his desk, his back to the narrow window overlooking the snow-dusted Armory Square and Springfield Technical Community College. "You could have called and saved yourself a trip."

"I need to visit someone in the area anyway," Leigh said. "I'm investigating the death of Brent Pratt. Your boys arrested him a few times on drug charges. I'd like to look at his records."

"Name doesn't sound familiar, but let me look him up." Wallace rose from his chair. "We could search electronically, but we still keep paper files so that might be the easiest way to see the whole picture if he's got multiple arrests. 'Pratt' with two 't's?"

"Yes. And thanks."

"Back in a minute."

True to his word, he returned in only a matter of minutes, a brown file folder open in his hands. He was scanning down the pages as he came through the door. "Looks like your boy had a heroin problem."

"That part I knew. His parents put him through rehab, but it didn't take."

"What's your interest in Pratt?"

"He turned up as a skeleton in a Harvard research lab."

Wallace froze halfway into his chair, his gaze shooting from the file to Leigh. "He . . ." Wallace squinted at her as if he'd heard her wrong. "A skeleton?"

"An anonymous call came in to 911, reporting a possible murder victim in a Harvard research lab. Dr. Lowell"— Leigh indicated Matt with an outstretched palm—"was called in to consult."

"The forensic study of bones is my specialty," Matt clarified. "I examine skeletonized or badly decomposed remains in order to determine victim age, sex, and race when no ID is associated with the remains."

Wallace settled into his chair. "Handy. That would go a long way toward victim identification."

"It does. In this case, I was also able to provide cause of death—the victim's throat had been cut with a hunting or military-style knife. Now, normally victim ID wouldn't come together this fast, but this particular victim had a titanium implant from surgery to repair a congenital defect we could trace directly through the serial number to Pratt."

"Amazing. But how did the skeleton end up in a research lab?"

"It was sold to a natural history dealer earlier this year by a Del Gerrit, who, according to the shop owner, came from 'somewhere in the Berkshires'." Leigh smiled when Wallace rolled his eyes at the vague identifier. "Now, there's a Delany Gerrit who lives in Amherst, but that's the only 'Del' Gerrit I could find."

"Amherst? That's only about thirty minutes north of here. Not exactly the Berkshires, but close enough to you east coasters."

"That's next on our list of places to visit. So . . ." She stared intently at the file. "Your files seem to be the last written record of Brent Pratt's location. His parents hadn't seen or heard from him in two years."

"Bank accounts? Credit cards? Driver's license?" Wallace asked.

"No luck. Even our crack computer genius was stymied."

Leigh stood in Rob Tucker's shoebox of an office, watching over his shoulder as he ran search after search.

"I'm telling you, Abbott, this guy doesn't exist by current standards."

"No paycheck? No credit card or Internet spending? No welfare claims?"

"Nothing. You said he was kicked out. This kind of thing isn't that unusual for the street crowd. They turn tricks or they panhandle for cash. They buy drugs and booze with that money. Maybe a little food, but drugs and booze are considered higher up the chain. They turn another trick and the cycle continues as they live hand to mouth. They change cities by hitchhiking or trading sex for a lift. As you might imagine, they're even harder to trace when they move around. You said this guy started in Wenham, but had arrests in Springfield? Well, he had to get from point A to point B somehow. But he didn't leave any trace of himself behind when he did."

"Damn. Would there be another agency who could track him better? Have better resources than . . ." Leigh's voice trailed off as Tucker twisted in his chair to pin her with a piercing stare from under bushy red eyebrows.

"And here I thought I had you trained better than that. You know if I can't find him, no one can. I've already used all the systems they would."

"Apparently I lost my mind for a second there." She rapped two knuckles against her temple. "Well, thanks for trying. Clearly it can't be done by any human means."

"His driver's license is expired, he hasn't used his social security number in years, and he doesn't appear to have a home address," Leigh said to Wallace. "All this compounds the fact that while Dr. Lowell has identified how Pratt died, he can't nail down when he died due to indoor storage of the remains. As a result, your files are the last official record of Pratt's location. And the last evidence of proof of life."

"Then let's see what we can do to help you out." Wallace paged through the file. "Most of what we have here is run-of-the-mill. Arrested twice for possession."

"Did he do time?"

"Got intermediate sanctions the first time because he didn't have a record. Community service, drug testing, and so on. The second time . . ." Wallace flipped through a number of pages before he stopped with a low whistle. "Well, look at that. The second time, he traded information to get the charges dropped. He would have known that he would have jail time for sure on a second identical offense."

Leigh sensed interest in Wallace's tone and scooted forward in her chair in anticipation. "What kind of information?"

"The name of the man supposedly supplying heroin for him and a large number of teens in the area." Wallace lay down the folder. "We *hate* perps who deal to kids. Nothing gets our attention faster."

"You cut Pratt a deal? You dropped his drug charges if he rolled on his supplier?"

"Exactly. And guess who that supplier was?"

The reason for Wallace's whistle snapped into place in Leigh's head. "Let me guess. Delany Gerrit?"

"One and the same."

"When was this?"

"April of last year."

Matt tapped Leigh's forearm. "If it was Gerrit and he was guilty of dealing, wouldn't he have been put away for more than a few months? Because he was certainly around the following March to sell the skeleton to Harris."

"If he'd been convicted of trafficking heroin, the minimum mandatory sentence in Massachusetts is seven years." Leigh turned back to Wallace. "So what happened?"

Wallace was already out of his chair. "Let me check the files out in the bullpen. Be right back."

"There's no way this is a coincidence," Matt said. "Pratt sells

Gerrit down the river and Gerrit kills him for his trouble? Doesn't that kind of seem like overkill?"

"It does if you consider it doesn't look like Gerrit was convicted." She sat back in her chair, and drummed her fingers on the arm. "We must be missing a piece of the puzzle."

"Maybe Gerrit also cut a deal?"

"Maybe, but it would have to be a hell of a deal to get from trafficking to something significantly more minor like straight possession that would carry a maximum sentence of six months for our timeline to work."

Wallace came through the door. "Okay, I've got what happened." He pushed the door shut with his foot and circled his desk to sit down. He spread the folder wide on his desk. "Pratt fingered Gerrit on heroin distribution." He glanced at Matt. "That's 'trafficking' in official circles. We got a warrant to search his premises in Amherst, but came up empty." He flipped another page, and scanned it from top to bottom. "Looks like this guy was doing his best to live totally off the grid."

"From what we learned in Boston, he was a seasonal worker on the Boston Harbor Ferry, and only lived at home during the off season."

"I don't think the ferry runs before May," Matt said. "The search would have been while he was living at home in Amherst."

"Home at Amherst was what many would consider roughing it. The guy ran his own generator, used well water, grew some of his own food. But nowhere was there any indication of drugs. We even took the dogs through the place and they came up empty."

"So he got off scot-free," Matt said. "And that means we're still missing a piece of the puzzle."

"I'm not sure 'scot-free' quite covers it. A large amount of cash was found at his place and seized."

Leigh gave a small internal groan. She knew where this was going.

"Wait." Matt held up a silencing hand. "I don't understand. You didn't find anything at his place to indicate he was part of the drug trade. You only had one guilty guy's word for it and he might have said anything to get out of a jail sentence. Why would you seize anything?"

"We may not have found any drugs on site, but maybe that's because it's not where he stored them. Or maybe he was out of his current stock because he just sold everything. Either way, having that amount of money on hand was suspicious, so we seized it as part of the investigation. It's evidence."

"It's evidence," Matt repeated. "Meaning you still have it?"

"Looks like it."

"That's not right." Matt's voice took on a hard edge. "You can't just take someone's livelihood when you have no evidence they've committed a crime."

Leigh looked from Matt's flushed face to Wallace's hard return stare. She laid a hand over Matt's forearm. "Actually, they can. It's called civil asset forfeiture. Police have the right to seize property during the investigation of a crime. To get that property back, the owner has to prove he and the property weren't involved in that crime." She gave his arm a warning squeeze and met his eyes. *Back off. We need Wallace on our side and you're pissing him off.* She understood how he felt because she didn't agree with the practice either, but knew it was often used by struggling police departments as a way to bring in extra cash for their activities. She carefully kept her voice neutral as she continued, "It's a legal seizure."

"I see." Matt's words were as stiff as the arm under her hand.

"This actually puts a fresh spin on several aspects of the case," Leigh interjected, purposely pulling Wallace's attention away from Matt.

Wallace relaxed slightly at Leigh's business-like tone. "In what way?"

"We're looking for why Gerrit might have killed Pratt, assuming that's how he came into possession of his remains. But if he was living off the grid, he might not keep his money in a bank. He might literally keep it under the mattress. When he lost it all during the search and seizure, he could very well have taken revenge. Even if you guys didn't tell him who named him as their dealer, he still could have found out. News like that gets around. And then he might have taken his rage out on Pratt in the worst way possible."

"You said you identified a hunting or military knife as the murder weapon?" Wallace asked.

"Yes. And from the defect left in the bone, this was someone who was used to a knife in his hand. The slash was exact and sure. A skilled hunter fits that profile." Matt glanced at Leigh. "This is all lining up."

"It is. We definitely need to get out to Gerrit's place." She pulled her notepad from her jacket pocket and rattled off an address. "Is that the address you searched?"

"It sure is. Do you need me to send someone with you as backup?"

"We're good, thanks. If we need additional support, I'll let you know." She stood and held out her hand across the desk. "I appreciate the information, Captain. Could I get copies of those reports? You could email them to me."

"Be happy to." Wallace accepted Leigh's card and slipped it into his breast pocket. "I'll make sure it's in your inbox by the time you make it back to Salem." He crossed the room and opened the door. "Good luck in Amherst. Hopefully you'll track Gerrit down."

"It's December and it sounds like he doesn't like to be out in public," Leigh said. "Where else would he be?"

CHAPTER THIRTEEN: BOUGHT THE FARM

Bought the Farm: was killed, usually by accident or military action.

Thursday, December 19, 10:10 a.m.
Gerrit Residence
Amherst, Massachusetts

Leigh slowly drove up the snow-covered drive, easing the car between tall, scraggly cedars that lined the bumpy gravel lane.

Matt peered through the windshield. "Majorly overgrown here. But if he was aiming for privacy, he got it."

" 'Majorly overgrown' is an understatement. These aren't young cedars, either. They must have taken twenty years to get this big. And from the shape of them, it looks like no one has taken care of the place for a while."

"Maybe Gerrit wants to discourage visitors." Matt studied the house coming into view as they rounded a curve. "Or maybe you're right and no one is taking care of it. The house is a dump."

The tiny bungalow at the end of the driveway had seen better days. A screened porch ran the length of the front of the house, but sections of screen drooped or hung like jaggedly ripped flags, leaving the porch open to the elements. Dirty beige paint peeled from wood siding that rose above bare concrete blocks, and the roof was patched in several places that peeked through a sun-warmed layer of snow. The windows were dark, curtains pulled tightly shut to block out the light and keep the cold at bay. The tailgate of an old rusted pickup truck was just visible beyond the house, parked in front of a carport that leaned precariously to one side. The snow was pristine around the truck; clearly it had not been moved recently. Behind the house, the slopes and peak of Mount Norwottuck rose over a thousand feet into the sky.

"The whole place feels abandoned," Matt said. "No tire tracks or foot prints. No sign of life."

"No mailbox. Not at the street like the other houses nor at the house itself. No evidence of a mailman driving up to the house to leave anything, either. No newspapers. No flyers stuck through the door handle. It's like no one knows anyone lives here."

"Maybe the Springfield cops seized the mailbox, too." Matt couldn't keep the sour sarcasm from his tone.

Leigh eased her foot from the gas so they were only coasting as she gave him a long sideways look. "About that. You can't go after a cop in his own house about his practices. Especially when we need his help. You have to play the game or you risk getting shut out. You risk getting *me* shut out and that could derail our case."

Matt hunched lower in his seat. She was right; he couldn't be the one responsible for a killer getting away. Still, he needed to defend himself, even if only a little and only to her. "I'm a scientist. We don't like games. We like everything straight up and all our cards out on the table."

"You'd make a lousy cop."

"Actually, I'd make a great cop because that's how cops should be." Matt studied the way her sharp green eyes assessed the house. "That's how you are. You don't play games; you're a straight shooter and you don't like politicking."

Leigh gave him a conciliatory nod. "I really don't. And I'd certainly fight against something in the unit that didn't sit well with me. But I can't push my point of view like that in some other cop's house because I carry no weight there, and the only person who'll get burned is my victim."

"So you play the game for them. The ones that end up on my table. Or Rowe's."

"Always. In this case, Gerrit may or may not be totally innocent of any heroin charges, but he still won't get his money back. After they didn't find any definitive evidence, even though Gerrit may have been dealing drugs to boost his income, they probably just let the whole thing go, just making a note in a file to watch Gerrit for suspicious activity. They probably saw it as win-win. Not only did the Commonwealth not have to pay to incarcerate Pratt, but the department got a hefty payout. I don't like civil forfeiture, but the cops are simply working inside the law as written. Do I think it's honest? No, because it goes against being assumed innocent until proven guilty. In this case the guilt is assumed with no evidence to support it, but no charge to come from it. Can I change it during this particular case? No. So I do what it takes for Brent Pratt's killer to be found."

Matt let out a long, frustrated breath. "Okay, I hear you. Sometimes you have to give up the battle to win the war."

"Gritting your teeth the whole time." Leigh stopped in front of the house, eying the patchy snow on the roof. "I'd like to check the weather for this area during the past week. If it's like Essex County, we haven't seen anything more than a small flurry in over a week."

"Looks like they've seen enough sun to melt some of the snow off the roof. And yet the truck is still covered. Maybe Gerrit doesn't get out much? If he's living off the grid like Wallace said, he might be mostly self-sufficient here without needing weekly trips for groceries."

"Only one way to find out." Leigh opened the door, and a biting gust of wind blew in to ruffle Matt's hair with icy fingers.

He climbed out of the Crown Vic and followed her solitary boot prints up to the front door. Jamming his bare hands in his pockets, Matt cursed himself for leaving his gloves in his SUV. He stood behind Leigh as she rapped one black-gloved hand on the scarred wooden door.

Silence.

"Maybe he's gone away for the Christmas holidays?" Matt suggested.

"His truck is still here, so that's a little less likely unless someone picked him up before the last snow fall." Leigh waited another minute and then pounded on the door. "Mr. Gerrit? It's the Massachusetts State Police. We have some questions for you. Please open the door."

But the only sound was the sorrowful whine of the wind.

Leigh tried the door with a gloved hand. "Locked. Let's check around the back for another door. And check the windows as we go. See if we can get a look inside."

They circled the house, stopping at each window to peek between the drawn curtains. Finally, near the back corner of the house, they found one window with an inch-wide gap between the drapes. Matt peered into the gloom. The narrow gap let in only the weakest of watery winter light, falling over a dusty, battered tabletop and down onto rough wood planking. A long knife with a wooden grip lay beside a rectangular block. He spotted the end of a handle—of a hammer or a hatchet—disappearing into the cloak of darkness. "Looks like a kitchen or a work table. Well used and fairly scarred. There's a carving knife of some kind and a sharpening stone on the table." He stepped aside to let her lean into the glass.

"Looks deserted. And for a considerable period of time. Check out the dust." She moved away, taking several steps back to stare up at the roof before she closed her eyes. "Do you hear that?"

Matt stilled, straining to hear something. Anything. "Hear what?"

"Exactly. Nothing. Keep in mind it's December and less than thirty degrees. If he's off the grid then he's not running a natural gas furnace connected to the town utilities, but he's either burning wood or propane, or he's running a generator. There's certainly no smoke coming from the chimney."

"And there's no generator running," Matt added. "You can't mistake that kind of racket. Deserted is right."

"Let's try the back door. But I don't have cause to enter the residence without a warrant. He's clearly a suspect in Pratt's death, so I could get one, but it won't be today."

They rounded the corner to the back door. Leigh knocked again, calling out her designation, and then tried the handle. Also locked. She turned, gloved hands on hips, to survey the land behind the house. "There's the carport and another couple of outbuildings. Let's check them out."

They found the truck parked twenty feet behind the house, blocking their view of the inside of the tilted carport. Leigh circled the hood of the truck, but Matt crouched down beside the front left wheel. Snow was drifted against it, but when he brushed it away, bright orange rust and flaking metal were visible between the spokes of the battered hubcap. "This truck hasn't moved in weeks."

Leigh's voice floated over the roof of the truck. "Why do you say that?"

Matt pushed to his feet. "The brakes are badly rusted, and likely seized. This thing isn't going anywhere without some serious work done first." He scanned the back of the truck which was full of various pieces of junk—broken chairs, empty crates, and some electronics that looked like they were scavenged for parts. "I think this is more of a storage unit now, rather than a moving vehicle. Maybe it doesn't even run." He rounded the back of the pickup to find Leigh standing with her head bent. "What have you got?"

She stepped sideways to let him see. "Found the generator. But clearly it hasn't been run in a while, either." The generator was positioned close to the entrance of the carport, covered in several inches of snow. Leigh brushed a layer of snow from the top, leaving a brittle crust on the exposed outer edge. "Looks like a good unit, though. Sufficient to power the house."

A large, dented gas can sat behind the generator. Matt nudged it with his boot. It tipped slightly, then settled again into a small snowdrift with a quiet *slosh*. "There's gas for the generator, so he could be running it."

"The question is—why isn't he?"

Matt scanned the carport, which was mostly full of stacked wood. A tool bench at the back held saws and several large axes. A fat stump surrounded by splinters of wood stood nearby, clearly the platform for splitting tree trunks into firewood. "He's got enough wood to fire his wood-burning stove for the winter. Yet, as you said, no smoke."

"There's a shed out back and what looks like a chicken coop.

Let's check them out."

Snow squeaking under their boots, they wound through bare trees, branches creaking menacingly overhead. A shower of snow sprinkled down on them from above and Matt gazed upward, expecting to see a squirrel, but even the wildlife had quit this lonely land.

Matt bunched his bare hands into fists inside his jacket pockets and hunched his shoulders against the cold, inching the collar of his jacket up around his throat. "I keep waiting for the other shoe to drop."

Leigh's brow furrowed. "What do you mean?"

"This is way too easy. We find the ID of the vic, which leads directly to our killer? Our cases are never this easy."

"I'm not sure I'd call finding Pratt's remains easy. It was a total fluke Kiko was on site and noticed that tiny defect."

"Okay, you've got me there, but after that, it's been straight connections. We're never that lucky."

"You're waiting for the other shoe to drop. Aren't you Mr. Glass-Half-Empty today."

Matt's cheeks warmed self-consciously and he half shrugged, aiming for nonchalance. "Wallace and his asset forfeiture pissed me off, I guess."

She chuckled. "Yeah, I got that." She pointed a gloved finger at the shed. "You go that way; I'll take the coop." She broke away and trudged further into the trees as he approached the shed. It was hand constructed of wooden boards, weathered, and warped, allowing snow to blow through the thin gaps and into the darkness inside. There were no windows, and the single door was padlocked, the lock rusted with age and disuse. Matt wrapped his fingers around the icy metal and gave it a strong tug, but it didn't budge. He brushed his wet hand off on his jeans and circled the building, looking for any loose boards or gaps big enough to see through, but the shed was impenetrable. "Nothing here," he called. "Locked up tight."

"Nothing here, either." Leigh's voice was muffled from inside the small wooden structure, then she stepped through the open doorway. "Door was ajar, but there's nothing inside. Feathers, hay, rolls of chicken wire, evidence it was once in use, but not anymore." She crossed to him. "We can check some of the back property, but after that, we're out of options until I can get a warrant."

"I don't think he's here, but no point in not covering all our bases while we're on site. I'll go this way"—Matt pointed to the east—"if you want to take the other direction."

"Yell if you find something." Leigh pulled out her cell phone. "Five bars. I wasn't sure I'd have a signal. We're way out of town."

Matt looked up toward towering Mount Norwottuck, rising majestically behind Gerrit's property. Bare limbed trees gave way to conifers on the upper slopes. "You can't see it from here, but when we were on our way up, I noticed the cell towers on the top. They're all over this range of mountains to make sure there's full coverage in the valleys. This may be the best reception you have in the whole state."

"Good to know. If you can't call out, then phone me. I'm not sure about property lines and where it goes from his land to Department of Conservation and Recreation land, so don't go more than about a couple hundred feet for now. If you don't find anything, circle back and I'll meet you here."

"If I run across a fallout shelter, I'm *not* going in," Matt quipped. He grinned as he caught the roll of Leigh's eyes just before she turned away.

Matt trudged into the thicker snow behind the shed. The property ran for several hundred yards before the base of the mountain sloped upward. He made a mental note to remember this location in the summer; it would be a great place to hike in warmer weather. He and Leigh could bring Teak, his father's Belgian Malinois service dog, who would love some of the lower, manageable, hiking trails.

But for now, balmy summer weather seemed an eternity away. He brought his hands to his mouth, and wrapped them around each other and cupped them over his lips to blow into them. The warm air set his skin tingling so he slid his hands into his jeans pockets to warm them against his thighs.

Matt had been wandering in a slow arc for over ten minutes when it happened. He was actively scanning the area around him as well as up into the far reaches of the property, but there was no sign of man or building. The quick flash of a deer running through the trees caught his attention in the distance just as he moved to step over a snow-covered log blocking his path. Distracted, he didn't lift his boot high enough and it caught on the rough wood. He had just enough time to yank his hands from his pockets as he toppled with startling speed toward the rock-hard, frozen ground. His palms slammed against the icy dirt, small rocks, and twigs digging cruelly into his skin. Air whooshed from his lungs as the rest of him hit the ground, his fall only slightly braced by his hands.

He lay there for a few seconds, one boot still hooked over the log, snow a cold smear against his cheek, and his bare hands slowly freezing against the icy ground. With a mumbled curse at his own stupidity, Matt unhooked his foot and gave the log a satisfying little kick in the process, and pushed to his knees, jarred bones protesting each motion. "It's get up or freeze to death," he chided himself. "So get up."

He surged to his feet and stumbled slightly as he caught his balance. Looking down, he brushed at the clumps of snow ground into every crevice of his ski jacket, but the snow didn't want to budge. He cast a last narrowed glare at the log that felled him, and then trudged toward the house.

He took three full steps before his brain registered what he'd seen and he slammed to a halt. He slowly turned to look back at the log. "Damn." He fished for his phone, fumbling it in frozen fingers as he pulled it from his pocket, and dialed Leigh.

She answered on the third ring. "I'm coming up empty. You?"

"I just found the other shoe."

"What?"

Matt walked back to the 'log', wondering how he could have ever mistaken it for a piece of wood. Even through the blanket of snow, dead-white skin tipped with frost, matted hair, and rough clothing were visible. He hadn't seen the dead man because he'd only been looking for life. "I can't see everything because of the snow cover, but I have a dead male, looks to be in his mid to late thirties. From the driver's license photo you showed me, it's Del Gerrit."

"Where are you?" Leigh's tone was urgent and the sound of rapid footfalls filled the background.

Matt looked up at the sun, trying to gauge his location. "Roughly due south of the house. At the base of the mountain. Watch for my jacket, it should stand out against the snow and I'll keep my eyes peeled for you."

"Can you tell if it's natural causes?"

Matt squatted down beside the corpse and scanned the visible sections for any sign of trauma. "He's rolled over on his stomach and wearing a winter coat, so I can't see down to flesh. Sorry, I just can't tell without touching the body." At that thought, he winced, thinking of the kick he'd given the 'log'.

"And you know better than to touch it."

Leigh's voice coming down the line made him wince again, but that conversation could wait for when they were both warm and dry. Maybe after a couple of glasses of wine to soften the blow.

"On the bright side," she continued, "now I don't need a warrant to search the house."

"You don't?"

"It's a crime scene now, so I can enter without one."

"You'll need a locksmith to get through the door."

"That can be arranged. Right after I report in, and then call Rowe."

"Tell him there isn't anything for him to do here, so this time he can send one of the techs. This guy is going to need time to defrost before Rowe can do a damned thing. We want him if he's available, but we don't want to waste his precious time."

With a last glance at the dead man, he stood and turned away from death and toward life, visible in the distance, striding directly for him in hiking boots and that look of determination he knew so well.

CHAPTER FOURTEEN: SHTF

SHTF: survivalist acronym for "Shit Hits The Fan"—a catastrophic event or natural disaster that results in a breakdown of the social order and large numbers of refugees. Although widespread in effect, SHTF events are generally temporary in nature. Hurricane Katrina is an example of SHTF.

Friday, December 20, 9:22 a.m.
Office of the Chief Medical Examiner
Boston, Massachusetts

Shoulder to shoulder, Matt and Leigh pushed through the swinging steel doors and into Rowe's brilliantly lit autopsy suite.

The big man looked up as he finished knotting the last tie of his surgical gown. "You're early. I don't even have your man on the table yet." Rowe looked expectantly behind them, at the doors slowly swinging to a stop. "No students today?"

Not long ago, no one wanted Matt's students under foot; now everyone questioned their absence. "I sent them to the Old North. I know once the twenty-third rolls around, they'll be scarce until the New Year, so I'm squeezing a few more work hours out of them this week."

"Slave driver," Leigh murmured under her breath, then rocked back and forth on her feet, staring innocently at the ceiling while miming a whistle.

"Damn straight." Rowe clapped Matt on the shoulder. "Grad students try to get away with anything they can, even yours, who are the most on-point I've ever seen."

"They wanted to come, but they also have goals to hit. Especially Paul. He has a committee meeting the first week after the Christmas break. There's nothing worse than sitting in front of your committee and explaining why you didn't meet your assigned goals. It's lit quite a fire under him lately."

Leigh's smiled slipped, worry clouding her green eyes. "And I've been taking up the team's time. Is that a problem?"

"Nah." The concern in her eyes dissipated at his easy smile. "I won't let him get into trouble. He's almost there; he just needs a little push to stay on track. Kiko and Juka know it too, so they're making sure he gets there."

"One for all and all for one, eh?" Rowe pulled on latex gloves. "I like the way you run your lab."

"I can't take credit for everything. I'm lucky I have three students who get along like thieves and have a vested interest in helping each other." He turned to Leigh. "And you. It makes my life much easier."

"Still, there's something to be said about leading by example." Rowe swung around at the sound of a gurney banging through the back door of the suite. "Ah, here's our client. As I'm sure you both suspected, fingerprints confirm this is Delany Gerrit."

Matt approached the gurney, but stood well clear as the tech and Rowe lifted the body onto the autopsy table under the bright lights. Unlike most corpses, this body had no flexibility whatsoever and was stiff between their gloved hands. "I have to admit I wondered how you could defrost him so quickly." He scanned the body, still frozen as it had fallen in the wood, arms at its sides, head turned, one cheek abnormally flattened as if an invisible hand pressed against it. The starkly pale skin was marbled with vivid shades of red. "But he's still frozen."

Rowe carefully slipped a head support under the skull to steady the body. "Yeah, that's going to take more than a day. With a case like this, where a body is frozen, we want to avoid warming quickly or we risk liquefying the internal organs. Some leave the body at room temperature for this. I prefer slowly bringing the body to four degrees Celsius in cold storage. Putrefaction doesn't happen below five degrees, so it better maintains the body. However, with an adult body mass, defrosting can take at least four or five days. Maybe more depending on the original body temperature."

"You can't autopsy for four or five days?" Leigh's words were measured, but the dismay she tried to stifle still snuck through at the edges.

"Not without risk of missing something that might make or break a case. But don't worry, Abbott, I've got your back. That's why I called you in. I'm not doing any cutting today, but that doesn't mean I can't tell you a lot already." He motioned the tech away with a flick of his hand. "Thanks, Doug. I'll let you know when we're done."

"Yes, sir." The tech disappeared through the back door.

Matt circled the table, assessing the victim. "You're going to have to watch your timing once the body is defrosted. The usual decomp time schedules will be accelerated."

"That's been my experience in the past."

"Why would it be faster?" Leigh asked.

"Cellular damage," Rowe said, as if it was all the explanation required.

When Leigh looked at Rowe in confusion, Matt clarified. "A human body begins to freeze at less than a degree below freezing. As body temp drops further, ice crystals form in the cells of the tissues. That tears a lot of cells apart. So when those tissues defrost, the cells are already essentially broken down, their contents spewed into the tissue itself, exposing intact areas of tissue to proteases and other enzymes earlier than under normal decomp processes. Freezing also breaks down the barriers for the gut bacteria that do a lot of decomp damage normally." Matt pulled on a pair of gloves. "Here's a good example." He ran a finger down the exposed left arm lying over the sheet-draped torso. "See how the veins in the arm are bright red, standing out against the white skin? That's because the red blood cells in the vessels have exploded and ejected their contents into the vein. The same thing happens with somatic . . . uh . . . body cells, but you don't see the results as clearly."

"Is there going to be lasting damage done to the body from freezing? The kind of lasting damage that could confuse cause of death?" Leigh took a cautious step toward the body.

"You can come closer." Rowe waved her in. "I know you don't like autopsies, but there isn't much smell at this point because the tissues are frozen. And, in answer to your question, yes, there is lasting damage, but nothing that will interfere with determination of cause of death. Cryogenic damage is mostly at the microscopic level. It's definitely won't affect this." He tugged down the drape covering the body and exposed the torso. "This is what I wanted you to see."

Matt whistled and moved in closer. A straight-edged wound gaped in the abdomen, just under the sternum. Several other smaller wounds pierced the right side.

Leigh stepped next to the table. "Look at the lack of finesse." She glanced up at Matt. "Think about the tiny kerf mark on Pratt's hyoid. That was a mark of precision. This looks like a careless carving. Hit somewhere around the stomach and hope for the best."

"It might look that way, but I'm not sure that's actually the case." Matt circled the table to view the gash from the other side. "This one single strike could actually be very effective. If it hit either the celiac or hepatic arteries, he'd have bled out fairly quickly. A stab to the heart would kill faster, but then you'd have to get through all those ribs, so your chances of failure are much higher. This is actually a relatively safe way to do maximum damage with a single strike, if you have a long and sharp enough weapon. Perhaps these smaller strikes were to disarm or simply to disable, so the primary blow could be properly targeted. But to do this on purpose, the killer would definitely need to have some knowledge of anatomy."

"I'll be able to confirm the details for you early next week," Rowe said, "but I knew this would be enough to get you started."

"Will you be able to determine the type of weapon?" Matt studied the wound edges. "This is where the microscopic damage may be a problem. Where you'd normally be able to determine a wound track with clean delineation, this is going to be mushy at the margins."

"I'll do my best for you. I should be able to give you an

approximate length of the blade from the depth of the wound, give or take how far into the soft tissue the hilt went. There's no bruising at the entry site implying hilt pressure, but I should be able to give you a minimum blade length. It might also be good if there is bone damage for you to look at, Lowell, but I don't think we'll see it unless it's vertebral."

"Which might still be useful if the knife strike dead-ends there. Could tell us if it were a single or double-bladed knife. That's the kind of detail you may lose when the body defrosts."

"I'm afraid so." Rowe walked to a nearby light box. Tiered rib bones floated above the curve of hips. "What I can tell you is there's no metal left in the body. The tip didn't break off during the attack, so there won't be any evidence there. Was there any evidence on site?"

"Not where the body was found. But the house and other buildings on the property are on my dance card for today," Leigh said. "I didn't have time to search the house yesterday because I was running around making arrangements to keep this victim part of my case. Technically, it's part of Hampshire County but I talked to D.A. Saxon and he cut a deal with the Hampshire D.A. as this death is clearly connected to the Pratt case." She winced. "I think he's beginning to be a little less than amused that I keep bringing out of county victims into Essex's purview. At the same time, he understands how this case is stitching together over a wider swath than usual. But we need to get to the bottom of this before this case gets bigger. Now, any idea about time of death?"

Rowe frowned down at the victim. "That's going to be hard to nail down exactly, but I can give you a rough estimate. There's virtually no decomposition, so he was frozen almost immediately. If he was killed last winter, the body would have decomposed during the summer after thawing. Had it happened in the early fall, the body would have partially putrefied before freezing. Check your temperature charts, but my memory says it's been around or below freezing for about the last three or four weeks. That's the likely window of this death. The skin is somewhat weathered, so I put death at the far end of the time scale on a preliminary estimate. I'll have confirmed temperatures and dates by the time of the autopsy, so the definitive information will be in my report."

"Three or four weeks is a damned big window for trying to nail down the killer's whereabouts," Matt said. "Are we safe in assuming this was the crime scene and the vic died where he was stabbed?"

"Leaves under the body were soaked in blood," Leigh said. "The techs who picked up the body transferred it and kept it face down, but he was wearing a winter coat, which could indicate that he was outside at the time of death. It's possible he was killed inside and moved outside, but our search of the house today will probably confirm there is no crime scene inside. It's more likely he was killed where we found him, but we'll make sure there isn't any other possible location on the property."

"The coat was unzipped," Rowe supplied. "Granted, if it was a big enough and sharp enough knife, that wouldn't have stopped the killer, but a closed zipper might have partially deflected the blow. Your vic was out there for a reason, but from the open coat, he may have left the house in a hurry or wasn't planning on being outside very long."

"He took the time to lock up the house though," Matt said. "We know that from yesterday. Unless the killer did it after Gerrit was dead."

"The crime techs did full photos of the area and we'll have another look at it today"—Leigh glanced at Matt—"but unfortunately, you falling over him and then scrambling to your feet might have disturbed some of the evidence."

"Which reminds me." Rowe pulled off his gloves and walked to a nearby counter, picking up photos and leafing through them. He pulled one out and passed it to Matt. "Is that your boot print? It was the one thing on the body we couldn't identify."

Matt's heart sank. So much for a couple of glasses of wine. There was no denying the tread mark impressed in the snow-covered fabric of the heavy winter coat. "Yeah, that's me."

Leigh took the print from his hands, stared at it for a minute before she pinned him with a sub-arctic glare that chilled him nearly as much as the man on the table. "You *kicked* my victim?"

"Not on purpose." Heat warmed his cheeks and Matt suspected he was turning embarrassingly red. "I thought it was a log, and I was annoyed I wasn't paying attention and I'd gotten a face full of snow when I fell over it. I . . . gave it a little tap of frustration when I got up." When her unflinching stare continued, he lifted both hands in surrender. "Guilty as charged, Trooper, but not intentional. You know me better than that."

Leigh heaved a sigh and rolled her eyes. "Did it do any damage to the vic?"

"None," Rowe assured her. "He was frozen solid and it would have taken more force than a 'tap' to do any damage. It'll have no bearing on the case."

The stiffness in her shoulders relaxed somewhat. "Good. Okay, so we're headed back to the scene now. We're looking for a knife and anything that might help pin down when he was last alive."

"We're also looking for anything to connect Gerrit solidly to Pratt and what happened to him. Can we get into that shed now?" Matt asked. "It was locked tight, no windows, so who knows what's in there."

"I have a locksmith on standby. We'll go through the house first, but then I'll get Crime Scene Services to process it fully. We'll get the shed opened up and that processed as well."

Matt looked forward to a chance to redeem himself with this vic. "Then let's get started."

CHAPTER FIFTEEN: BIVOUAC

Bivouac: a temporary or casual shelter.

Friday, December 20, 12:32 p.m.
Gerrit Residence
Amherst, Massachusetts

Leigh removed the police lock from Gerrit's front door and pushed it open, light spilling into the darkness within. On first glance, the interior of the house looked just as sadly abandoned as the exterior. She reached around the corner and ran her fingertips over the wall until she found the light switch and flipped it on.

Nothing.

"He's not on the grid, remember?" Matt's voice came from behind her. "And the generator's not on. Want me to give it a try?"

Leigh swiveled to face him, standing on the porch in hiking boots and a ski jacket, both of which were purchased for style and not their originally intended usage. "You scientists aren't exactly the 'roughing it' type. Sure you can do it?"

Gloved hands falling to his hips, Matt leveled a nonplussed stare at her. "If you're going to pigeonhole me, at least put me in the right slot. I was a Marine, remember? There were times when 'roughing it' would have been a luxury."

"Okay, soldier. Go get me some power so I can see what we're doing in here."

The glare fell away so quickly she knew he was kidding. He cemented it by giving her a wink and a snappy salute before he jogged down the steps, around the corner of the house, and out of sight.

Ignoring the cold, Leigh left the front door open as she moved from window to window pulling open the heavy drapes with gloved hands to let in the weak winter sunlight. Shivering, she finally closed the door and scanned the gloomy front room. It was a small, sparse combined living and eating area with a worn couch and chair flanking a faded area rug on one side of the room, and several rickety spindle-back chairs surrounding an ancient wood table on the other. A darkened frosted-glass light fixture hung overhead and she hoped Matt had luck with the generator or else they'd be searching the dim room with flashlights. As if hearing her thoughts, a roar came from outside and the overhead light flickered on and slowly grew brighter.

Less than a minute later Matt came through the front door, stamping the snow from his boots. "See? Not so hard after all. The generator was a little stubborn at first—it's damned cold and clearly it's been weeks since it was run—but it finally started." He did a slow turn, taking in his surroundings. "Kept things a little Spartan, didn't he? This place looks like it was owned by someone who just moved away from home and could only afford a few second-hand items. No decorating, no knickknacks."

"He was a guy living on his own. How many knickknacks would he have?"

"I know I'm not on my own, but Dad and I decorate in our own way. Interesting pieces picked up on travels. Maybe not 'art' in every sense of the word, but stuff hung on the walls. Some things passed down through generations of the family."

"Your house is masculine, and while it's clear no woman lives there, it's still very comfortable. Lived in. That's what this place is lacking: it doesn't feel lived in. Where's the detritus that comes from normal life? Where are the empty pop cans or the TV remote?"

"Where's the TV," Matt interjected.

"Exactly. Or the bills that need paying, scattered on the dining room table? Granted, if he was truly off the grid, he might not have had a TV or bills to pay if he paid cash for everything he bought." As she talked, Leigh moved down the hall, Matt behind her. She stepped into the next open doorway and flipped on the light to discover the kitchen beyond. Scanning the room, she frowned. The floor was a nondescript beige linoleum that still managed to clash—*How could a color that bland clash with anything?*—with the nineteen seventies' avocado green stove and fridge. The counters had little on them: several mismatched canisters, a deeply grooved cutting board, and a small number of cheap kitchen utensils standing handle-down in a heavy earthenware holder. The table they'd seen through the window yesterday was on the far side of the room. After stuffing her winter gloves into her jacket pockets, Leigh pulled on a pair of latex gloves as she crossed the room. "This is the first sign of life." She picked up the wooden-handled knife from beside the sharpening stone and the hatchet. "Looks like it's seen quite a lot of life actually." She angled the knife more into the light. "When I saw it yesterday, I thought the handle was made of bleached wood, but it's not. Is that bone?"

Matt pulled on his own gloves and carefully took the wickedly sharp blade from her hands. He ran one thumb over the dark vertical grooves in the buff colored handle. "No, not bone. This is antler, probably deer. Looks well used." He ran one finger along the flat of the blade. "See how it curves in a bit from the handle? That's wear on the metal from sharpening over the years. This thing has seen some serious use. It's an antique, maybe a family heirloom, but it wasn't treated like an antique. It was used as a tool."

"Could it have killed Pratt?"

"I thought you'd come around to that," Matt said. "Maybe. Certainly it's a better candidate than that hatchet there, which absolutely didn't do the job. But I'd have to do some tests with it and run kerf mark comparisons." He rotated the edge toward him and studied it. "My first reaction says this isn't the murder weapon. It's an older weapon, well worn, and it doesn't have the kind of blade angle we're looking for. It's too narrow. But let's run it anyway. You'll want your guys to test for the presence of human blood, but I'd be surprised if they found any." He picked up a heavy leather sheath, darkened with age and weathering. "Better check this too, as blood may be smeared inside."

"Considering we think Pratt was murdered last spring, it's more than likely he used the knife again after the killing. Butcher a few deer with it and you'd obliterate any traces of human blood." Leigh pulled several evidence bags from the messenger bag slung across her body. One at a time, she opened each bag wide so Matt could drop the knife into one and the sheath into the other. She sealed the bags, and then wrote the details of date, time and her name on them to maintain chain of evidence. "But we'll try anyway." She slipped the evidence into her bag and surveyed the rest of the kitchen.

Leigh crossed to the sink. "No dirty dishes." She opened a cabinet to find only a few meager dishes inside. "There are a few clean ones, but not really enough to live on." She opened drawers and pushed through the scattered contents with an index finger before she moved on to the next one. "Aside from the knife, it's like no one really lived here."

Matt opened the door of a tall, narrow pantry. "This guy was a survivalist, right?"

"So we're told."

He stepped back, holding the door wide open so Leigh could see the nearly-barren shelves inside. "Then where are the stocks of food for when the world ends? Or water? Forget about living here. No one planned on hunkering down here, which is a more important point considering that personality type."

"That's for sure." Leigh crossed the room, eyeing the few remaining cans and condiments critically. "I'm feeling a huge disconnect. We know what we've been told about the man, but we're just not seeing it in how he lived."

"Could we be missing something? Maybe this isn't his spot to hole up? Maybe he's got the basement set up as a shelter," Matt suggested.

"I think it's an idea worth exploring. Let's finish this floor first. We need to check the closets and the hallway for attic access, assuming there is access to it." She led the way out of the kitchen. There were three doors down the hall, so she angled toward the closest one. "Then we need to check out the basement. We've covered the outside already; there weren't any storm cellar doors, or any other apparent basement access from outside."

"If he was holing up because it was the end of the world, maybe he didn't want the outside world having access."

"Maybe. It's just such a weird mindset. I'm having trouble wrapping my head around it."

They found themselves in a small bedroom. A single bed stood against the far wall beside a tall, narrow five-drawer dresser. A simple, shabby quilt covered the bed and only dust graced the top of the dresser.

"You mean 'the world is going to hell in a hand basket, so I'm just going to hide in here by myself'? That mindset?" Matt pulled open a drawer, perused the inside, and moved on to the next.

Leigh went for the closet. She opened the door to find a yawning empty space beyond. "Yeah."

"That's because it's the last thing you'd do. You'd be out there, doing whatever needed to be done. When trouble hits, you don't hide; you go out and face it. So it doesn't sit right with you." He closed the last drawer. "These are mostly empty."

"Maybe there's a difference between someone who's living off the grid and just wants to live his own life in peace versus someone who hides away at the first sign of trouble. It takes a certain amount of courage to give up the conveniences of modern life and decide to do it all on your own."

"Some would see it as courage. Some would see it as cowardice. As not being able to handle the world and function as a rational and useful member of society." Matt shrugged. "There's no black and white definition for this. It would depend on the individual and why they choose to live this way."

"I guess. Let's try the next room."

The bathroom revealed nothing special—it too looked rarely used—so they moved on to the last room at the end of the hall. Leigh paused in the doorway, one hand resting on the frame. "Okay, this room at least looks like someone stayed here occasionally." If a house this small could have a master bedroom, this was it, although that was being generous. A double bed, a low, wide dresser with a hutch-style mirror framed with old-fashioned lilies etched into the corners. The room was as sparsely decorated as the rest of the house, but the faded comforter looked soft and cozy. Leigh ran her fingertips through the dust covering the dresser, leaving small trails behind. "Bet this was his parents' room."

"Why do you say that?" Matt's voice was muffled as he bent over and checked the space under the bed.

"The mirror. The lilies are a feminine touch. I bet this was the family house and the room down the hall was his. When his parents died, he moved in here, but kept the furniture as it was. But if he was having trouble making ends meet, maybe he had to sell off some of their stuff so this is what's left." She opened a drawer. "A few clothes here, all belonging to a man. Still not much." She closed the drawer, opened the next, and absently pushed through socks until her fingers touched something hard and cold. She brushed aside a pair of hand knitted work socks to find a pocketknife. "Look at this. It's like he was hiding it here."

Matt closed the closet door and moved toward her. "What is it?"

"A Swiss Army knock-off. Not a great one, flimsy, not many attachments." Squinting with the effort, she found the tiny groove in the metal with her thumbnail and pried out a small, slightly dull blade. "This has seen better days too, but a cleaning and a sharpening could go a long way." She turned the knife over. "You think if . . ." Her voice trailed off as her heart rate kicked into overdrive. She angled the knife into the light to better see the shallow engraving on the side, to make sure she wasn't imagining anything. There was no mistaking the initials: BP. "Can you see the engraving?"

Matt cupped his hand under hers and turned it so the light struck the metal at the right angle. Then he whistled. "Definitely not his initials. Brent Pratt, perhaps?"

"You have to wonder. What if he killed Pratt here and then got rid of the evidence? Or almost all of it. He's a survivalist. Would he get rid of something that might ultimately be useful? I don't think so."

Matt released her hand. "But at the same time, it's here with a bunch of stuff that isn't used much, as opposed to with his 'stash', wherever that is, which likely has all the good stuff. It's a backup tool, just in case. One a sensible survivalist is reluctant to discard."

"If so, then he's given us a connection back to Pratt, just to nail the coffin shut, so to speak."

"Will you take the knife to Pratt's parents to see if they can identify it?"

"Definitely." She watched him walk to the window and pull the dark curtains wide to stare thoughtfully out into the back forty. "What are you thinking?"

"That the pen knife really solidifies Gerrit's connection to Pratt. But in all the time we've spent here, there's been no evidence Pratt was either killed or skeletonized here. However, I have a theory."

Leigh sat on the edge of the bed. From this angle, Matt's profile was backlit by the afternoon light, clearly demarcating the planes of his face. "Spill."

"What if Pratt was killed out there." Matt tapped the glass with a gloved finger. "Somewhere out in the woods like the animals Gerrit hunted. Still on the property, but out where no one was an eye witness."

"That would explain how Pratt died. But that doesn't explain how he was skeletonized without a scratch."

"I have a theory about that, too." Matt faced her. "Normally, we deflesh bones by boiling them in detergent. It would take quite a while to deflesh a fully fleshed body. Multiple water changes, loads of stink."

"You think he boiled the body here?" She looked down the hall in the direction of the kitchen. "On the stove?"

"Not at all. Not enough power in that stove to do the job and that kind of smell would be nearly impossible to hide. No, I have something else in mind. We think he was killed in the mid to late spring, right? What if Gerrit let nature do the job for him?"

"Natural putrefaction?"

"Yes, but not in the way you think. Remember all the time I spent on those body farms? We did experiments where we left bodies out for predators to see what tooth marks in bone from specific animals looked like. These bones are pristine, so we know that's not how they were stripped. But another way to strip a body quickly is with bugs. And at that time of year, bugs would be out and about. Or, better yet, he might have used dermestid beetles, which I happen to know you can order over the internet because they are such efficient flesh strippers."

Leigh blinked at him in surprise. "They sell live bugs over the internet?"

"Sure. People who do taxidermy use them, so you can order a colony of mixed adults and larvae from a taxidermy supply company and they'll do the dirty work for you. Or if Gerrit wanted to use cash, he could order a colony from a local supply company."

Leigh shuddered as the mental picture of a body covered in wriggling fat white larvae filled her mind's eye.

"Or you can always buy them on eBay."

"The wonders of modern life. How quickly would they strip a body?"

"Two weeks, right down to the bone if the insect complement is correct."

"That's fast. But how would you keep away the wildlife?"

"We did it by building a simple wood frame with fine chicken wire over it."

Leigh's head snapped up. "Chicken wire. Like the rolls we found in the coop?"

"Exactly that kind. Make a cage out of wood and chicken wire over the body and seed it with your beetle colony if you have one. No small carnivores, not even mice, could get through the chicken wire. But flies can get through to join in and they'll feast on the corpse and lay their eggs in any open cavities. Those larvae will hatch and will do a huge amount of damage, destroying any flesh they contact. Adult beetles will come in when the soft flesh is gone and they'll scour away whatever is left. Now, it might have been a bit cool at that time of year, so maybe it didn't take two weeks, but three or four."

"What if someone stumbled over the body during that time? You'd think they'd notice a dead body in a cage in the forest."

"He would have kept it here on his own land where he wouldn't expect trespassers and he's a good distance away from any neighbors. For extra camouflage, just cover the chicken wire cage with some of last fall's old leaves and it's out of sight. But the bugs will still get through."

"What about the smell? It's hard to hide the smell of a decomposing corpse."

"You're in the great outdoors, so the smell will dissipate. Once the bugs really get going, it won't be a problem after about a week. Come back in a few weeks and you have a pristine skeleton. Deconstruct the cage into its base parts and it looks like the supplies any farmer would have on hand for his stock."

"Ingenious."

"Effective. If this is what happened, it allowed him to not only hide a body in plain sight, but make money from the end result."

"Until Kiko's sharp eyes caught him at it." Leigh stood and moved to stand with him at the window. Snow covered forestland ran as far as the eye could see, angling steeply up Mount Norwottuck. "If you're right, that closes the case of Brent Pratt. But now we're back at square one again." She met his eyes. "Who killed Del Gerrit and why?"

CHAPTER SIXTEEN:
EFFECTS-BASED OPERATIONS

Effects-Based Operations (EBO): a military concept emphasizing precision weapons, stealth, intelligence, and speed to destroy single targets and disrupt networks. An example of EBO is destruction of power generation facilities and power distribution lines.

Friday, December 20, 5:12 p.m.
Essex Detective Unit
Salem, Massachusetts

"Let me check the knife into evidence, then I'll call Crime Scene Services to take pictures and to do whatever swabbing they need." Leigh led the way through the hallway of the detective unit, Matt following behind her. "Once they're done, it's yours to take into BU to do whatever testing you—"

"*Abbott.*"

Leigh stopped abruptly, holding out a hand to telegraph the move to Matt before he crashed into her. Head tilted, she listened. Had someone whispered her name?

"*Psst. Abbott.*"

The sound came from the open office door they'd just passed. They were walking through the computer forensics unit and that particular door led to Tucker's tiny office. She crooked a finger at Matt—*follow me*—and backtracked down the hallway. She leaned into the doorway to find Tucker sitting at his desk, his gaze locked unblinkingly on the doorway. As soon as he saw her, he rapidly waved her in.

She tugged on Matt's sleeve and jerked her head toward the inner sanctum of Tucker's office. Once they were both inside, she shut the door behind them.

Tucker's office always baffled her. Why on earth did someone need so many monitors when one was enough for normal people? A bank of four screens spread in a gentle arc along an L-shaped desk pressed into a corner. One was a wall of email; the other three were streams of unrecognizable code. Well, unrecognizable to her. She was sure that whatever alien languages they were in, Tucker was fluent in all of them.

The surface of Tucker's desk was surprisingly clean for someone who always dressed carelessly and whose hair was usually standing on end. From his appearance, you'd expect his office to look like it belonged to *The Odd Couple's* Oscar Madison, but instead, the space was nearly sterile. Contributing to this was the well-known fact that Tucker hated paper. If someone brought him a document on actual pulp, the first thing he did was to scan it and give it back so it didn't remain in his office for more than five minutes. He liked everything filed digitally and just a few mouse clicks away; he didn't want to have to actually page through physical documents or risk a paper cut. But what he lacked in paper, he made up with in technology and odds and ends lying on the desk: noise canceling headphones, a teleconference unit that looked like it was sent by the code aliens, plastic models of Captain Kirk and someone else she didn't recognize in a long brown coat, suspenders and a burgundy shirt, his charging cell phone, a bottle of Mountain Dew, and a small bag of what she feared was chocolate covered espresso beans—*no wonder he's always so twitchy.*

She looked up to find Tucker watching her analyze his space with a cocked eyebrow. She cleared her throat, feeling her cheeks flush at being caught. *Time to get back on track.* "What's with the cloak and dagger act?"

Tucker tossed a stress ball in the shape of Pac Man from hand to hand. "I was just about to send you an email asking you to stop in, but you walked by first. I wanted to update you on some new stuff. Pull up a chair."

Leigh and Matt both looked around. There were several

latched, hard plastic crates crammed into the corner, but nothing resembling office furniture beside the chair Tucker occupied. "Tucker, you don't have chairs," Leigh reminded him. "Remember how you don't like people invading your space?"

"Yeah. Right." Spinning around in his own chair, Tucker scanned the room as if really seeing it for the first time. "Pull up a crate?"

Leigh rolled her eyes, but Matt was already lifting down a crate for her to sit on before he dragged one over for himself. He gallantly held out a hand. "Ladies first."

"Don't think I don't know what you're doing. You just want to make sure it'll hold my weight before you try it." She sat down, carefully at first, making sure the crate would support her, but relaxing once it was clear it was sturdy enough. Matt settled himself, but the crate held for him as well. "Okay, now you have us, what's up?" she asked Tucker.

"Hold on." Tucker pushed the teleconferencing unit to the edge of the desk closest to them and then stabbed out an extension.

It rang several times, then "Kepler."

"Sir, it's Tucker. I have Abbott and Lowell in my office. I wanted to update you all, but without calling an obvious meeting. Do you have a few minutes?"

"I do. Hold on." There was a quiet *clunk* as the handset was set down, the sound of footsteps and then the unmistakable sound of his office door closing. He returned in seconds. "Just making sure we weren't overheard. It's good you called because I wanted to talk to you. I've been doing some digging."

"You're working on this on the side?" Leigh couldn't keep the surprise from her voice.

There was a moment of silence that stretched on for a few beats too long. Finally Kepler said, "You didn't think I forgot about it, did you?"

"No, sir." Leigh threw Matt a quick grimace. He waved his hand to her in a circular *keep going* motion. "That wouldn't be like you at all. But I would have understood if it wasn't your top priority."

"It's high enough. We need to decide what to do about this and we need to decide when to bring Harper into it." Leigh started to speak but he cut her off. "That's non-negotiable, Abbott. His people are involved. He needs to know, especially with what I suspect."

Leigh closed her eyes, struggling for calm and trying to stave off the dread that inexorably built every time she thought about bringing Harper into it. *What if he didn't believe her? What if he drummed her out of the force for trying to handle it on her own? What if—*

"Abbott." Kepler's voice broke into her thoughts, surprisingly gentle for such a big brute of a man. "It's going to be okay."

For all his toughness, this was another sign of how well Kepler knew his people. "I'm not sure about that, sir. I may be about to open a can of worms Harper won't want to deal with. And if there are charges to come from it, Saxon won't want to, either. This could get sticky. What if it's a dirty cop?"

"At this point, considering what we've discussed, and what I've recently learned, that's the direction I'm leaning. And if it is, both those men will move heaven and earth to put him away. This is what they've committed their lives to. It's not always comfortable and sometimes it's downright painful. But they're good men who will do the right thing. Have faith."

"Thank you, sir." Leigh pulled in a deep breath, trying to calm her jittery nerves before whatever Kepler had to say would make them worse. "Could you explain what you meant by leaning in that direction because of what you've recently learned?"

"I made a point of dropping by O'Leary's today over lunch," Kepler said. "I thought it might be a good way to finesse some contacts."

Matt moved close to Leigh's ear and murmured, "What's O'Leary's?"

Clearly, he hadn't been as quiet as he'd intended since it was Tucker who answered his question. "It's an Irish pub down by Salem PD headquarters. It was started by a son of one of the

Salem boys and it's a favorite hangout of every cop in town."

"It's a good place to meet a cop if you want to make it look casual," Leigh finished. "Like you were popping in and just happened to bump into someone."

"That was my intent," Kepler said. "There are a couple of cops in the Criminal Investigation Division I've known for years I was hoping to find. I got lucky. They were just waiting for their takeout, so they had a couple of minutes to kill before their orders came up. I asked how things were going in the department. Mostly it's good, no big complaints. But they did pass on an interesting piece of information." He let a couple of beats of silence pass before continuing, "Detective Oakes is up for the Lieutenant position in the CID."

Leigh met Tucker's gaze across his desk. His eyebrows were just about at his hairline. "Is he now? How long has that been in the wind?"

"Officially, only since last week. But they implied there'd been murmurs about it for a few months. When was your first delivery?"

"October."

"Wait," Matt said. "I'm behind a step. Why would that matter?"

"It wouldn't except he was involved in the case and now suddenly he's jockeying for a promotion," Leigh said. "The Lieutenant position runs the whole CID. It's a position of power; he'd answer only to the Chief. Do you know how often a position like that comes up? Once every ten or fifteen years. And then every man in the unit is scrambling to get it. That's if the department doesn't fill the role from another unit, or decides fresh blood would be better and hires an external candidate. Competition is *fierce*." She turned back toward the phone. "Sir, what's their opinion of Oakes?"

"By and large, he's always had the reputation of a solid cop. But they implied he's the golden boy of the department."

"That's not necessarily a good thing. Sometimes that's a designation earned by ass kissing, not because it's truly deserved."

"They never came out and said it, but that's the general vibe I got. He had all the good contacts. He got all the best busts. He's intent on climbing the ladder at top speed. They think he's got his eye on the Chief's job."

"Lofty goal," Matt commented.

"No doubt about it. He's only in his mid-to-late-thirties. Most officers don't get to this level for another decade. All the cards have fallen into place for Oakes."

"Sometimes it goes that way," Leigh said.

"And sometimes other cards get pushed out of the way to make room," Kepler said. "Tucker."

Tucker sat up straighter as if Kepler could see him. "Yes, sir."

"I want you to run Oakes."

"Skim the surface or dive under to get the real story?"

"Dive, Tucker. Dive deep."

"Yes, sir." He rubbed his hands together in anticipation and winked at Leigh. "I love a good dunking."

"Just don't drown while you're down there," Kepler said. "And Tucker?"

"Yes, sir?"

"You get on anyone's radar, there'll be hell to pay."

Tucker's brows snapped together and his lip curled in a near snarl. It impressed the hell out of Leigh when the tone of voice that answered his superior officer was level and reasonable. "Sir, you know better than that."

"Just consider yourself forewarned. To continue on with the analogy, we're in deep waters here."

"Check." Tucker swiveled to face Leigh. "That's one thing I wanted to go over with you. You asked me to review your dad's last case. I did, just after the Ward case, but I wanted to go back to your dad's drive to see if there was anything else."

Leigh looked quickly around the office. "The drive is here?"

"Hell, no. I've got it at home. I have a gun safe. I keep all of my important tech in it."

"No doubt about it, Tucker. You are the king of geeks."

"You say that like it's a bad thing. You just wait, the geeks will rule one day and you'll bow to us."

"Tucker . . ." Kepler's growl came through the phone.

Tucker sent her a look that clearly said *See what you did? Now Dad's mad.* "Anyway, the case is exactly what it looks like. Four years ago, there was a rash of killings in the north end. The reason why there wasn't public panic is because it was drug dealers being knocked off and everyone, especially the media, chalked it up to a turf war. As such, it was barely worth mentioning since the killings were neat and tidy, and no civilians were ever involved. The deaths were considered a small print footnote."

"Are you implying it wasn't a turf war?" Matt asked.

"According to the records, that's exactly what it was. One of the area's major drug kingpins had previously gone down in a hail of bullets and a power struggle followed to determine who could come out on top."

"Power struggle meaning whoever was at the top of each ring was a target," Matt said.

Tucker mimed taking a shot a Matt with his index finger and thumb. *Got it.* "The Salem boys do vice and know those players. But as soon as the deaths started, that's when it became our jurisdiction. Because of the number of deaths and how fast the dealers were falling, Nate became more involved as overall support for his men who were spread over the different killings because there were too many for one person to handle."

"As a good leader should," Kepler said. "Especially with his men going out into that dangerous area."

"Were you on those cases, sir?" Leigh asked.

"No. Now I wish I was so I had more insight, but I was never the officer on call when the murders happened and had a full case load anyway, so nothing got passed to me. What I do remember is Oakes was lead detective from Salem PD. He had a touch with the drug community. Had the best contacts and CIs. Roger Tyson was one of them."

"And that's exactly what Oakes was trying to do the night Nate was killed," Tucker interjected. "He was trying to connect Nate to Tyson, who supposedly had some inside information he was willing to swap, likely for some kind of 'get out of jail free' card. These CIs are great contacts because they're right in the middle of everything. So the meet was arranged. But then Tyson didn't show like he was supposed to and Oakes and Nate split up to look around. Only a few minutes later, Oakes heard the shots." Some of the tension in Tucker's shoulders dropped at the sight of Leigh's composed face. "We've got Oakes's full report. Everything there seems like it should."

"Hold on. The angle I'm hearing here is that we should be looking at Oakes." Leigh turned back toward the phone. "Sir, wasn't there an investigation into Dad's death? Not just yours, but by the force?"

"By both forces," Kepler confirmed. "It was a joint operation, so it was a joint investigation. Both groups would have investigated anyway since it was an officer-involved shooting, even if that officer didn't survive. Oakes was completely open and made himself available to anyone who needed to talk to him. I know he certainly talked to me for my investigation. His story was he wasn't on site when the shooting occurred. There was never anything to disprove that and he was cleared of any suspicion of involvement. You know the final conclusion was that Nate and Tyson took each other out."

"What's the catch?"

"I don't like Oakes." Kepler's words were short and sharp.

Several moments of silence passed as the three in Tucker's office exchanged curious glances.

Finally, it was Leigh who spoke. "Would you mind expanding on that, sir?"

"The best I can tell you is my gut doesn't like him. He seems like an upright guy. You certainly can't fault his conviction rate; it's one of the best in Salem's house. But there's something..." His voice trailed off as if struggling to put his thoughts into words. "He tries too hard. Below the surface, I get the feeling there's nothing... genuine there. That he's always looking for an angle.

That he's calculating. It's subtle, very, *very* subtle. I thought it then and still think it now. But there wasn't a damned thing I could point to."

"Do other people feel this way about him?" Matt asked.

"I'm not sure. Certainly, we're not going to get officers from his house to rat on him out in the open. But I definitely got an edge of resentment from the two guys I talked to today."

"Sometimes character traits are so well camouflaged, it's just years of experience and a very sensitive intuition that picks up on something being off," Leigh said. "Maybe you were sensing something others missed."

"Ah, but that's where you're wrong." Tucker tipped his chair back and wrapped his fingers over the arms. "He's not the only one. Your dad knew something was wrong. It took me a while because I had to go through files on his computer and then some of it was locked down."

Leigh pinned him with an incredulous look. "Something my father locked down gave *you* trouble?"

He glared from under ginger eyebrows. "Of course, it didn't. It was more a matter of sorting through everything on the drive. And then going through each of his deleted files. I wanted all the information. But, as I said, there were files that were password protected." He arrowed an index finger at Leigh. "Do you remember how long it took me to get through Hershey's computer after Bradford killed him?"

In her mind, Leigh could see the stopwatch on the screen frozen on 'oh 0m 37s'. "Thirty-seven seconds."

"Yeah. Maybe half that. And without the password cracker. But it's what's inside that counts. Nate had notes on some cases in there. And he had some suspicions about Oakes."

"Really?" Kepler's voice seemed louder, as if he hunched over the phone in anticipation.

"I've copied the file, sir, and I'll get it to both you and Abbott. But things seemed a little too . . . convenient for Nate. That Oakes always knew where and when to make the bust for maximum effect and to take out as many bad guys as possible. He certainly was making more arrests than anyone else in the unit. Sometimes being a hot shot is hard work, intuition and incredible smarts. But sometimes, it's being on the inside. That's what Nate was leaning toward. But all he had were suspicions at the time."

"Shit." Kepler's expletive burst through the speaker. "Tucker, did Nate ever give any hint Oakes knew of these suspicions?"

"No, sir."

"Why was the file password protected?" Leigh asked. "It was on his personal computer at home. The only person who might have gotten close to it was me."

"But you knew he was working on stuff at home." Matt gave her an apologetic half smile. "You told us yourself he used to work on cases at home. That means you not only found him working on his computer, but you'd seen some of what he was working on. Hypothesize with me for a minute. What if he was right? What if Oakes found out and retaliated? You could have been a target. Leigh, maybe he was doing it to protect you. Maybe he wanted you in the dark."

"And then we circle around to the fact that she'd have stayed in the dark if these packages hadn't showed up," Kepler said. "Why go to the trouble of sending them and risking being exposed?"

"In my opinion, if it was Oakes and he was doing it to keep something buried, then he was handing it off to Abbott to actually do the dirty work so he was completely hands off, with no connection to any of it. But he didn't count on a few things." Tucker counted off points on his fingers. "One—he expected her to bury this to cover for her father at best, or pin it on you, sir, at worst; and that's only if she dug deep enough. My gut says he expected her to bury it so no one could find any trace of any of it. Two—he expected her to be struggling with this on her own, but Lowell's been at her side from the first delivery. That support kept her from drowning in the pain of having to face this again. Three—he didn't know she'd have a wizard at her beck and call." He waggled ten fingers at her and then bowed his head in an at-your-service nod. "And four—he wouldn't have expected her to have you on board. When we identify Oakes, or whoever is responsible for this, it's going to be because we did it as a team."

"Identify him?" Rage snarled in Kepler's voice. "We're going to fucking *bury* him. No one messes with Essex officers like this or taints the name of a fallen hero. *No one.*"

"I couldn't have put it better myself, sir," Tucker said in his mildest tone. "Just give me a day or two. This will be my top priority. Now, let me fill you in on what I've found out because I have a task for you, Lowell. First of all, I went back down to that store across from Bruno's Tavern." He paused, as if surprised by the silence. "No one has anything to say to that?"

"You already know our opinion on it," Kepler said. "No need to keep trying to bash it into your thick skull since the message isn't making it through. What were you going after this time?"

"Our mystery man from the recovered picture. I thought if it's a regular spot for meets, then maybe the guy would show up in some of the other footage."

Matt braced a hand on the crate behind him and propped one ankle over the opposite knee. "You're hoping to identify him from his chin?"

"I was hoping to identify the parka as a first step. Then I was going to let you identify the chin because you're the bone structure expert."

"What if he loaned the parka to someone else?" Leigh asked. "Then you'd be looking at the wrong guy. Or what if he showed up without the parka?"

"That was my biggest concern, but I thought it was worth making the attempt. That's why I knew I'd need Lowell to confirm we're looking at the same man."

"It's a terrible photo, but I can probably do it if you can give me some possibilities." Matt stared at him expectantly. "Can you?"

"I can." Tucker spun around on his chair. After a flurry of keystrokes and clicks he brought up a photo. It was the same black and white security footage they'd seen in the photo sent to Leigh two months ago, but this time it was a warmer time of the year as the man pictured wasn't wearing a parka. "There were a lot of tapes to go through, so it took some time. I concentrated on tapes taken around the same time, as I don't know how long he'd been a regular at that location, if he really was. I totally struck out on the parka though. Bummer."

"It was worth a shot," Matt said.

"I thought so." Tucker spoke for Kepler's benefit. "Sir, you can't see this, so what I'm showing Lowell is a man of approximately the same height as the man in Abbott's corrected photo. Therefore, he's a possibility. But the problem is, so are the other fourteen guys I found." He clicked through a range of photos, each one showing a different man. "Some I could eliminate right off the bat because the height or face shape was obviously wrong. But all of these could be potentials. Then there's the beard shots. There's another five of those." More photos flew by before he swung around to Matt. "I'm not sure where you're going to go with those."

"Shoot them to my email and then give me time to look at them. At the very least, I'll be able to exclude some and narrow the list. From there, what's the plan? Do the same facial profiling you did initially comparing against mug shots to see if any of them are in the system?"

"That's the plan. We don't even know if he's really and truly related to the case. So many of them are just dead ends. This could be, too, but we have to try."

"Yes, we do. I'll get started on it tonight."

"Great. Sir, I think that's it for now. We'll let you know as we get more."

"Same here. Thanks for the update." There was a click as Kepler hung up.

Tucker seemed to deflate, slumping as he ran both hands through his hair, standing the bright red shocks up anew. "He always makes me nervous."

Leigh stared at him, confused. "Why? He's on our side."

"I know. I didn't say it made sense; it just is. What's our next move?"

"I know what my next move is. I want a better feel for what was going down in North Salem four years ago. Tucker, send me everything you have on that case file. I want to read through it tonight. So far, the story we keep hearing about what happened that night is Oakes's. But surely Kepler interviewed others to support it. If we're going to actually investigate Oakes, we need to hear someone else's version of that night."

"Leigh, I don't want to be a naysayer, but don't you think that's going to be tough?" Matt asked. "Remember when we talked to Cabrera during the Ward case and he told us about being taken into custody and having to justify where he was four years before?"

Leigh nodded. She remembered the conversation well because Cabrera had turned it around on her and made it personal.

Where were you four years ago today? Do you remember what you were doing during two hours in an afternoon that long ago?

Four years ago she'd been burying her father, but she had to admit if it came down to a specific day, she wouldn't be able to itemize her actions, either.

"You're going to be looking at essentially the same scenario," Matt continued. "You want to ask people about something specific that long ago?"

"I do, and I get your point." The urge to stop talking and to actually do something became unbearable. She pushed off the crate to pace the confines of Tucker's office. "But I think we have the advantage here. We're not just asking them about any day four years ago. You'd think a cop killing would be memorable."

"You'd think. You're not going down there by yourself though." When Leigh's face darkened and she protested, Matt simply talked over her. "Yes, I know you're a cop. I realize you just want to talk to the residents, so taking the STOP team would be serious overkill, but you're not going alone. I'm coming with you. And I'm bringing the Glock as backup. Don't argue."

Leigh knew that face. When Matt got that expression, nothing shifted him. She paced to a wall, spun, and paced back before she threw a poisonous look at Tucker. "Your office is too small."

Tucker threw up both hands in mock surrender. "Hey, don't get pissy and take out your rage on my poor innocent office." His hands dropped to his lap. "Lowell's right though, Abbott. If you're going to march into that area, off duty, and snoop into the bowels of the underworld there, you're going to need someone at your back. And you'd be insane not to let that someone protect themselves and you, just as you would him. You hope you won't need it, but if you do, you need to be prepared."

Leigh sank down onto her crate. "Yeah, yeah. Message received. Guess it's another fun Friday night working, right?"

Matt gave an easy shrug. "It's what we do. Let's grab your laptop from your place and then drive down to mine so we can both work. We'll pick up takeout on the way."

"Sure." Leigh rose to her feet again. "You'll send me the old case info?" she asked Tucker.

"Right away. You can squeeze this in with your current case?"

"Kind of have to. Hey, here's a question for you. Does it seem right to you that a guy who is a supposed survivalist would have absolutely no technology at his house? No computer, no TV, nothing. I mean, they're prepared for the world to go to hell, but you wouldn't assume they're Luddites."

"They're not Luddites. These are people who understand tech in a completely different way from normal people. They know how it works, and they're often experts in failure analysis. Because if you know what can go wrong, then you know how to protect against it."

"Spoken like someone who knows something about this." Matt stood and pushed his crate back into the corner. "You're not into the survivalist game, are you?"

"Me?" Tucker asked. "Hell, no. Too many crackpots. But I'm buddies with someone who is. And he's not one of the crackpots. Want me to put him in contact with you?"

"That would be great." Leigh hefted her crate into its original position, enjoying being able to expend some of her pent-up energy. "You know, Tucker, you can be a handy guy to have around."

"Damn straight. I'll try to get a hold of him and I'll pass on your cell number. Your evening just got busier, Abbott, but then, that keeps you out of trouble."

Leigh opened the door and tossed her last comment over her shoulder. "You know, people say things like that, and yet, it never seems to happen. Trouble seems to find me."

CHAPTER SEVENTEEN: SHELTER IN PLACE

Shelter in Place: stop moving, take shelter, and stay inside during an emergency.

Friday, December 20, 8:06 p.m.
Lowell Residence
Brookline, Massachusetts

Matt was pouring a second cup of coffee when Teak appeared at his feet, squeezing between his legs and the lower cupboards to sit beside him with a mournful expression. "You can't convince me you're starving to death. I watched you wolf your dinner not even two hours ago." Liquid brown eyes fixed on Matt unblinkingly, and he swore he could see sorrow reflected in their depths. "You don't need a treat," he said flatly.

Teak's head dipped, but his eyes stayed locked on Matt from under the black curve of canine eyebrows as his tail slowly wagged.

Matt lasted about another ten seconds under the weight of that sorrowful gaze. Then he cast a guilty glance toward the empty doorway and reached for the cupboard door. "Okay, just one. And if you give me away you'll never see another treat from me again." He grabbed a sealed container off the shelf, and turned away from the doorway to block it from view. Teak immediately sat straighter, his eyes locked on the cylinder in Matt's hands as the air of sadness disappeared under a quiver of excitement. Matt extracted a cookie and tucked the container onto the shelf just as the soft *shush* of rubber on hardwood signaled his father's approach. He jammed the treat into his jeans pocket and managed to pick up his coffee cup and lean casually against the counter just as his father rolled into the room.

Confined to a wheelchair after a car accident on icy winter

roads that took the life of Matt's mother over a decade before, Mike could have faded into a shadow of his former self. Instead, he had ferociously fought his way back to health. Now, as vibrant and social as ever, he rowed on a regular basis with Matt, delighted in gourmet cooking, and never missed a poker game with his cronies.

"I suspected he came in here." Mike looked down at his dog with a long-suffering expression. "He looks awfully perky. Teak, you mooch. Stop begging for treats." His gaze met his son's. "You didn't give him anything, did you?"

"He's had nothing from me." The near lie rolled off his tongue even as the cookie burned a hole in his pocket. "Maybe he's just happy naturally." *Time to change the subject.* "You want another cup of coffee?"

"No, thanks. I just wanted to make sure you didn't need a hand cleaning up after dinner."

"Already done. Leigh stepped out to take a call, so I finished up."

"Thank her for me for picking up dinner. She's always so kind to include the old man."

"You can thank her yourself, old man." Matt looked over his father's shoulder to where Leigh had appeared in the kitchen doorway.

One hand resting on the doorframe, Leigh glanced from Matt down to his father. "Thank me for what?"

"For including me in your dinner plans. You always go out of your way to make sure I'm not eating alone."

Leigh crossed the room to him, a warm smile curving her lips. "Of course we'd include you. Family doesn't eat alone."

"Spoken by someone who eats too many meals alone," Mike said.

Leigh flushed slightly as the comment struck close to home, and Matt stepped into the conversational breach to give her a graceful exit. "Who were you talking to?"

"That was Tucker's survivalist contact. His name is Max Duffield." She noticed the mug in his hands. "You made coffee."

"I did. I was waiting to pour yours for when you were off the phone." He opened the cupboard again, conscious of Teak's intent gaze following his every move. *Hang on, buddy. You'll get it as soon as we're alone.* He reached down a mug, poured Leigh's coffee, and added cream and sugar. "What did he say?"

"He confirmed what Tucker told us. Basically, survivalists are experts in crucial life systems, and how to manage without them when they fail."

"When?" Mike clarified. "Not if?"

"They always believe it's 'when'. Thanks." She accepted the cup Matt extended, and took a long, slow sip, her eyelids falling to half-mast in enjoyment. "I need to get you to teach the boys at the unit how to make coffee."

"As opposed to the swill you have there currently?" Matt remembered the precinct coffee and shuddered. "I'm not sure I could teach them how to make real coffee when they think they already have it." He picked up his mug. "Why don't we go into the living room where it's more comfortable? Dad lit a fire."

"Sounds divine. It's gotten so cold, so fast, I feel like I can't get warm lately." She waved the notebook Matt hadn't noticed before in her free hand. "I can catch you up."

"Sounds good. And then we have work—I have the pictures to review for Tucker and you have the details of your father's last case to review—but at least we can do it in front of the fire. Dad, don't let us drive you away. You know you're welcome to join us." It was a common understanding after the cases Matt and Leigh had worked together that Matt's father was often included in case discussions. By this time, Leigh knew she had nothing to worry about when it came to Mike's discretion. Discussions never left this house, and often Mike added insights from his years of naval service and his thoughtful worldview.

"Thanks, I will. And maybe I'll have that cup of coffee after all."

"I'll get it for you. You two go on in. I'll be there in a minute."

Leigh and his father disappeared through the doorway and Matt paused to listen to the fading sounds of their voices. A wet nose pushed against his hand and he looked down into the upturned face. "I know, I know. I haven't forgotten you." He slipped the biscuit from his pocket, and held it out to Teak. The dog gently took it, carefully avoiding Matt's fingers. He dropped to the floor, crunching happily. Within ten seconds, not a single crumb was left.

Carrying two mugs of coffee and with Teak gamboling along behind him, Matt entered the living room. His father was in his usual spot near the fire beside the end table. Instead of taking the couch as usual, Leigh had settled in front of the fire on one of the big throw pillows, her legs comfortably curled under her. "You're okay down there?" he asked her, taking his usual armchair on the other side of the table from his father. Teak wandered over and collapsed with a sigh in front of the fire, rolling so his back pressed against Leigh's leg.

"Better than okay. It's heaven." She held out both hands to the flickering flames, wiggling her fingers in the waves of heat. "Well, let me qualify that. It's heaven with case notes." She picked up her notepad and flipped it open. "For starters, Tucker's friend Max considers himself a Prepper, not a Survivalist."

"There's a difference?" Matt asked.

"Apparently. Survivalists tend to be loners and are more the live-off-the-land type. When the world goes to hell, and they're sure it will, they'll survive by hunting and foraging. Preppers, on the other hand, are more organized. They're more likely to live in communities or interact with other Preppers, and make plans with other Preppers ahead of time. It's not that Survivalists don't want to be involved with others, but they tend to have a more 'every man for himself' kind of mentality and will form group connections after the disaster when they need to work together to survive, as opposed to the Preppers who will already have a system in place beforehand."

"So Preppers are the type who would have a vegetable garden and would put up preserves for when they were needed," Mike extrapolated. "The Survivalist would make sure he knew how to hunt and would have the weapons to do so, but would have to actually go out and kill dinner?"

"Close. It sounds like Preppers would also know how to hunt and would have the required equipment, but it wouldn't be their only option. Now, in his opinion, from what I could tell him about Gerrit, is he was more along the Survivalist persona, but Max says we're missing a big piece of the puzzle."

Matt sat forward, his mug locked between suddenly tense hands. "What do you mean we're missing a big piece? We were there. On his property. We looked everywhere."

"We looked everywhere visible. Let me back up. Remember when I asked Tucker about Survivalists as Luddites? Max made it clear that while his crowd knows how to survive without technology—because they're going to need to, potentially someday soon—they're more than happy to use it while they can. Also, they have a deep understanding of how systems can fail and how to compensate. If the sewage system fails, it's not a big deal if you have a working homemade filtration system, right? If you lose power so you can't cold store food, or safely cook it, as long as you have canned goods and dried jerky, you can eat. So no technology of any kind in the house is not indicative of their lifestyle. Yes, he was living off the grid, but he had a generator, so that wouldn't be the reason for not having a TV or a computer."

"Could it have been an issue of poverty?" Mike asked. "He had to sell his electronics to buy food? Matt said he was a seasonal worker. Maybe the seasonal money only held out so long."

"You could be on to something there. But as far as Max was concerned, there's that missing puzzle piece."

"Which is . . . ?" Matt prompted, impatience clawing at him as Leigh took the time to set the stage before hitting the punchline.

"That house wasn't where he was living."

"I know the house didn't feel lived in. We even went through the basement. Minus the cobwebs and the spiders, there wasn't anything there." Matt set his mug down on the end table and braced his elbows on his knees. "But we went through the rest of the property and the best there was out there was a couple of small, empty outbuildings. Is this Max guy implying Gerrit had a second home?"

"Of sorts. Max's point is that when the world ends in whichever way we destroy ourselves, we'll have two choices: running and gunning, or holing up to protect our stuff and our loved ones."

"You don't have to be an ex-soldier to figure that one out," Mike said. "Although those of us who served know firsthand the danger inherent in running and gunning, even your average civilian can figure out it's often safer to hole up with your back to the wall and protect your space and your comrades."

A tiny idea was scratching at the back of Matt's brain, and it was getting louder and louder. "He thinks there's something we haven't found yet. He thinks . . . we missed his hideaway?"

"That's Max's theory. When I explained the whole thing to him, his first question was 'where's his bunker?' I told him we searched the house and found nothing. I told him we went through the basement and the outbuildings on the property. Still nothing. That didn't faze him one bit."

Teak rolled over, rubbing his head against her hand. She took the obvious hint and ran her fingers through his thick fur. The dog released a gusty sigh of pleasure.

"He said they're often on the property. I told him we searched there, too. And he asked if we searched the ground."

"You just told him we already searched—" Matt cut himself off as what Leigh said finally sunk in. "Hold on. Ground, not grounds." He studied her for a minute, her face tipped down to the dog, shaded by the light flickering and shifting behind her. "When he says bunker, he really means it. Like an underground bunker." He flopped back into the armchair cushions. "Hell, I wasn't looking hard enough at the ground to realize the log I was trying to step over was actually a body. There's no way I would have seen the signs of any subterranean dwelling. That's what he means, right?"

"Yes. He said these guys are serious about their bunkers. They can be made out of tractor trailer-sized shipping containers with top entrances buried in pits big enough to completely cover them.

Sometimes they're built into the side of a hill with a side entrance, something we could have in this situation, but it's maybe less likely with a rocky structure like Mount Norwottuck as part of the landscape. Sometimes they're crafted of corrugated metal and shaped like an airplane hangar. The trick apparently is how to take bare metal walls and turn it into a home where you'd be happy to spend the apocalypse. *That's* what we missed."

"It would also totally explain why the house seemed cleaned out. He'd already taken all the good stuff to his bunker. What was left in the house was what wouldn't fit or wasn't truly useful. Except the generator. Why wouldn't he take something useful like that?"

"Part of the point of a good bunker apparently is not only that you can hole up in it, but that you can hide in it. When the apocalypse comes, you don't want your neighbor storming your shelter and trying to take it from you. You heard that generator when it went on. You couldn't hide from a school of deaf kids with that thing. It would be like waving a big red flag and bellowing '*Over here!*' at the top of your lungs."

Matt remembered the roar, and the vibrations rolling under his boots after he started the generator. "Okay, you've got me there. What are the options? You've got to have power somehow if you're underground. Forget about things like lights and heat; if you don't have air, it's game over then and there."

"I think there are more modern, quieter generators now." Mike turned to his son. "You know Jason."

"Poker buddy Jason? The one who won't play without his best friend J.D. at his side?"

Mike chuckled. "That's the one. He and Jack are the best of friends, but only on poker night. He thinks if he drinks it at any other time it will dilute his luck."

"From some of the games I've witnessed, I don't think Jack helps as much as Jason thinks it does."

His father blinked, his head tilted in feigned confusion. "Really? You don't say."

Matt toasted his father with his coffee mug. "Nicely played.

Okay, so what about Jason?"

Mike straightened, the addled expression falling away. "He's a camper. Likes to get out of the city and go out to where he can see the stars at night. But at the same time, he doesn't want to rough it. And since he retired with that big package, he can afford to treat himself to a few extras, so he bought this super quiet generator. He wants to power his electronics while he camps, but he doesn't want to scare away the wildlife and such. Maybe Survivalist guy had one of those and left the loud one by the house for if he ever needed power there or as an emergency backup. But it doesn't sound like it's often since he didn't actually seem to live there."

"That's what Max suggested." Leigh flipped to the next page in her notebook. "A better and specifically quieter generator. And there are other tricks you can do—burying the base of the unit in sand to cushion it, rigging a system of mufflers to deaden the sound, and so on—but the most important thing apparently is to dig a separate hole with a separate door for the generator and then simply run the lines underground. Use a remote starter to control when it runs and you're all set."

"In other words, we're going back," said Matt. "We need another look around."

"We do indeed. Another tip from Max was to make the best of the winter weather if we can. The bunker needs to take in fresh air and exhaust used air."

"Which will be room temperature, or thereabouts, and will melt the snow." Matt finished the thought for her. "That will only help us if Gerrit died after the last snowfall because the generator has to have run out of fuel by now. Any fresh snowfall after that will camouflage it." He stared into the flames, watching them flicker and dance. "You know, as much as I didn't see the body, or just thought I was seeing a log, it made sense in my head because in context it blended in. I think if I'd seen melted snow out there in December in the middle of nowhere in weather cold enough to give me frostbite, it would have stood out."

"How far out did you go?" Mike asked. "You said the property stretched to the mountain itself. Do you know how much of that land belonged to him?"

"We don't," Leigh answered, "and that's an important point now. Before we go back out there, I'll check the title deed and get the plat showing the property lines."

Matt checked his watch. "There's no way the Registry of Deeds would still be open this late on a Friday, and it will be closed all weekend. Can we wait that long?"

"We may not have a choice; we don't want to do this twice. I can ask Tucker to help us with the search, but a lot of smaller towns are still working off paper and haven't digitized. If that's true here, then I'll have to wait for Monday to get the hard copy."

"Is the theory that Gerrit lived in the place full time?" Mike asked. "Are those places built for that?"

"Apparently they are. Some of them are built with just shelving systems for storing the maximum amount of food and water possible but many of them are more like RVs with tables that convert to beds, and storage under the floors. Max said he'd seen ones with separate sleeping and kitchen areas that still had room for a TV, computer, and full radio gear."

"Because you'll need that when the world comes to an end," Matt said. "I bet a lot of these guys are ham operators."

"I guess the only question I have is 'Why was Gerrit in his bunker'?" Mike said.

"What do you mean?" Leigh asked.

"Didn't you say the theory is that you keep your bunker stocked and ready to go for emergencies? Why would he be living there already? Did he think the world was about to end? Did he think *his* world was about to end? Was he scared of something and hiding? Was it because of the man he killed and then sold as a skeleton, or was it something else entirely?"

"All good questions," Leigh said. "He was in crisis mode already. But why?"

"Find that out," Matt said, "and I bet you'll find out why he was murdered."

Leigh's phone rang. She lifted a hip off the pillow and pulled it from her back pocket. "Abbott." She met Matt's eyes and mouthed *Tucker*. "Yes, my place again, ten tomorrow morning. See you then." She ended the call and looked up at Matt, worrying her lower lip.

"What did he want?"

"He says we need to meet and Kepler needs to be there. He's got new information and he's got a plan."

Matt grimaced. "Why does that terrify me instead of filling me with confidence?"

"He also made a reference to Robert Redford and Paul Newman."

"Now that terrifies *me*." Mike had been about take to a sip of coffee, but lowered the mug untasted. "Is he talking about the victorious Redford and Newman in *The Sting* or the Redford and Newman who went over a cliff and then got shot to death by the Bolivians in *Butch Cassidy and the Sundance Kid*?"

Matt wished he could see Leigh's eyes; so often her moods and thoughts were clear to him in her gaze. But she had turned toward the dog at her side and stroked his fur with fresh dedication. Perhaps she didn't want to be that vulnerable now. "Guess we'll find out tomorrow," he said. "This issue is coming to a close. The only question is—what does Tucker have in store for us?"

CHAPTER EIGHTEEN: SHAPING THE BATTLESPACE

Shaping the Battlespace: coordinated military actions taken in advance of a major battle to give an attacking force a decisive advantage. Overnight parachute and glider landings, massive air attacks, and naval bombardment before early morning amphibious landings were an attempt at battlespace shaping by Allied commanders during the invasion of Normandy.

Saturday, December 21, 4:20 p.m.
Harper Residence
Salem, Massachusetts

Leigh shifted from foot to foot on the snow-dusted doorstep, her gaze fixed on the frosted glass panes in the double front doors.

"Abbott, it'll be fine. Simmer down."

She didn't acknowledge Kepler standing at her side, but consciously forced herself to stand still.

Her stomach clenched at the sound of the knob turning, but she kept her chin up and eyes forward. She met Detective Lieutenant Harper's gaze as he opened the door, but he looked past her to Kepler.

"Dan," Harper said.

"Nick," Kepler said. "Thanks for seeing us at home on a Saturday afternoon."

First names. This was already taking a very different turn from what she'd anticipated. It was strange enough to see Harper, with his short cut steel-gray hair a little mussed, in jeans and a long-sleeved T instead of in his usual suit and tie. It was almost as if he had a home life.

Harper held the door open, wordlessly inviting them inside.

Leigh followed Kepler as he entered a comfortable living room to the left of the foyer. A tall, willowy brunette appeared in the entryway to the dining room at the rear of the house. Leigh recognized her from the unit's holiday parties over the years. She gave Leigh a pleasant smile, but brightened when she saw Kepler.

"Dan, it's lovely to see you," Mrs. Harper said.

"Cheryl. How've you been?"

"Good, thank you. Work and the children keep me busy, but it's the best kind of busy."

Kepler sat down on the sofa. Leigh perched on the edge of a cushion at the opposite end, feeling awkward and completely out of her league.

"Mark still showing his team how to really play hockey?" Kepler asked.

"He is." She turned to her husband. "Nick, send him the schedule. Maybe he'd like to come out for a game sometime."

"I'd love that," Kepler agreed.

Leigh was doing her best not to stare at the tall bald man at the end of the sofa. He looked like Kepler, but that was about it. This man was genial and softer spoken and clearly on friendlier terms with the Detective Lieutenant and his wife than anyone in the unit realized.

With a feather-light touch, Cheryl Harper straightened a picture on the wall that already looked level to Leigh. "Is this call business or pleasure?"

"All business today, I'm afraid."

"I'll leave you to it then. Give my best to Kaitlyn." Cheryl Harper disappeared through the dining room into the back of the house.

Kepler's voice and mannerisms instantly morphed into the formality Leigh knew. "I'm sorry to have bothered you at home, sir. But this is a matter of a somewhat sensitive nature."

Back to the normal rank formality. It's time to get down to business.

Harper sat down in a large wingback chair near the cold hearth. "Too sensitive to cover at the unit?"

"I think so, yes. Abbott, why don't you start us off?"

Leigh gave her report like it was one of her official case files— clearly outlining each delivery, when and where it arrived, and what it contained.

Anger snapped almost immediately into Harper's eyes. He only stopped her once, to ask Kepler if he'd seen the evidence. Kepler nodded, saying everything was as Leigh described. With a nod, Harper urged Leigh to continue. His lips tightened at the news of Tucker's involvement, but other than that, he gave no sign, patiently listening till the end of her report, including the details of their meeting that morning and their plans on how to proceed.

Nearly exhausted by the telling, Leigh wound to a close and then sat silently, awaiting her fate.

Harper turned to Kepler. "You're sure about this?"

"One hundred percent. Tucker can be an occasional pain in the ass, but he's sharp and he knows his stuff. Nick, this is Nate we're talking about. No way in hell was he a shady cop."

"Agreed." Harper swung back to Leigh. "I'm sorry about this, Abbott. I can't imagine how terrible it must have been to receive that first photo. And that was right in the middle of the Simpson case?"

"Yes, sir."

"When I was giving you a hard time because of the media circus."

"Which was rightfully deserved, sir."

"At ease, trooper. We're off the official clock here and this goes beyond normal house business. You don't need to defend yourself to us; your record more than speaks for itself."

Leigh blinked in surprised at the compliment, not sure how to respond.

But Harper was already focusing on Kepler. "You want to go after a Salem cop."

"I do."

"You need to be beyond sure of your facts if you're going to do this." Harper stood and walked to the fireplace and, bracing one hand on the mantel, he looked up at the oil painting mounted above the hearth.

To Leigh's shock, she recognized the style and shot to her feet. "Sir!"

Harper turned, his head cocked to one side.

But instead of answering the unspoken question, Leigh moved to stand beside him. She touched the picture frame beneath the signature: Grace Abbott.

"You didn't know Nate gave me this painting when I made sergeant?" Surprise was evidence in his tone.

"No." The word was a near whisper as she stared up at the unmistakable image of the House of Seven Gables, surrounded by a lush summer garden. "I didn't know it existed. It's beautiful."

"Your mother was a talented artist. Stolen long before her time." Harper stood shoulder to shoulder with her as if seeing the painting for the first time again himself. "Nate knew the house and property are special to Cheryl and me. I proposed to her in those gardens. I was honored he would part with such a prize."

"He valued your friendship very much." Even to Leigh's own ears, her words carried a husky edge. "I'm sure it was his honor you'd accept and love this painting as much as he would have. I have one myself that's very like it. It hangs over my fireplace as well."

"A treasured piece of your mother." He turned back to Kepler. "You're sure?" All gentleness left his voice as he got down to business.

The solemn set of Kepler's face and the rigidness of his shoulders telegraphed his answer, but Leigh knew he was not the kind of man to rely on assumptions. "Without a doubt."

"Then I want this son of a bitch taken down. We won't allow anyone, especially another officer, to smear the name of one of our fallen and torment one of our own."

"Sir, what about D.A. Saxon?" Leigh's voice was steady again, having taken the time during their interchange to gather herself. "We need to loop him in on this."

"You leave Aaron to me. Let me assure you, he won't be a

problem. What else do you need from me?"

Kepler rose to his feet. "Just your knowledge of the plan we have so far, your understanding that things are in motion and plans might change at a moment's notice, and your approval to get this done."

"You have it." Harper laid a hand over Leigh's shoulder. "You be careful. If you're right about him, he won't let a little thing like Nate Abbott's daughter stand in his way. Show him he couldn't be more wrong."

"Yes, sir."

"Keep me in the loop as new information arises. These ops can be fluid and you have to think on your feet, but keep me informed as much as humanly possible."

"Yes, sir."

Leigh stood as the conversation ended. There was more to do tonight, a lot more. But if things fell into place, tomorrow would tell the tale. And the stakes couldn't be higher. If this went wrong, she doubted it would only come down to disciplinary action. If it went wrong, she'd be handing in her gun and badge, ending her career in law enforcement.

She couldn't bear to think about that possibility, so she pushed it aside and concentrated on the task ahead.

Tomorrow.

CHAPTER NINETEEN: KILL CHAIN

Kill Chain: a military concept that includes target definition, positioning an attack force, giving the order to attack, and destruction of the target.

Saturday, December 21, 7:34 p.m.
The Point Neighborhood
Salem, Massachusetts

Leigh pulled to the curb on the darkened street and peered through the windshield.

The four-story tenement was built of rough, rust-toned brick. Several front windows were bare and dark; others were covered with ragged curtains or twisted mini-blinds. One was simply blocked with plywood, and Leigh wasn't sure which was the more likely culprit—a brick, a bullet, or a body tossed out the window to the sidewalk below.

It was that kind of neighborhood. Nothing good happened here.

She'd sworn to never come back, yet here she was anyway. She tamped down jangling nerves that suddenly made her palms clammy and set her stomach roiling.

Matt scanned the building through the passenger window. "You take me to the nicest places."

"You wanted to come." Leigh tugged the zipper of her ski jacket higher, unsure if protecting herself from the bitter wind or what was out there. "Ready?"

"As I'll ever be."

"Stick close. I'm not expecting anything, but we're not about to get ambushed. Let's get in, talk to some neighbors, and get out." She pulled a handwritten list from her pocket and scanned the list of names. The flavor of the surnames told the tale of many of the area inhabitants: Menendez, Espinosa, Ramos, Ortega. The Point was overwhelmingly Latino with a high proportion of single parent families, almost always led by mothers, many of whom spoke little English. In a city where tourism was the main commercial venture, the crime, poverty, and violence of The Point made it Salem's dirty little secret and not something the Chamber of Commerce advertised.

Matt looked over her shoulder to read the list by the dim illumination thrown by a streetlight half a block away. "That's the list of current tenants who also lived in the building four years ago?"

"Best the super could remember." She remembered the phone call from late that afternoon. The voice on the other end of the line had been scratchy and carried what sounded like a beer-induced wobble. "It wasn't even one o'clock, but he sounded like he already had a good buzz going, so I'm not sure how accurate it is. But it's a place to start."

"Are you going to tell them you're a cop?"

"Not up front, but I suspect it's going to come out sooner or later."

"Think it'll shut them down?"

"Almost certainly, so I won't be pulling out my badge unless I have to. Let's go."

She reached for the door handle, but froze when Matt's bare hand closed over hers. She turned to find his eyes, dark in the scant light, locked on hers, his expression full of both compassion and concern.

"You're going out of your way not to say anything and you're doing a great job of covering, but I know this is going to hurt like hell. When was the last time you were here? That night?"

Words tangled in her throat, so Leigh simply nodded.

"Once again proving you have more guts than people realize. Most would never come to a place that caused them so much pain." When she angled her face away, Matt brought it back to him with gentle fingers. "I know this is hard for you. Let me help if I can. I'll give you space to handle this your way, but promise me you'll let me know if you need me."

She gripped his fingers, squeezing tight in silent gratitude.

They got out of the car and Leigh circled the hood to stand beside Matt on the sidewalk.

"Lead the way," Matt said, tugging his collar up closer to his ears.

The broken and uneven sidewalk led to a narrow alley that disappeared along one side of the building. Torn, she considered the double front door of the tenement, inset with security windows made of reinforced, wired glass. The urge to storm in and knock on doors was strong, but deep down she knew that wasn't the best approach.

Blowing out a pent-up breath, she screwed up her courage. If she was to have Matt's full backing, he needed to know the whole story. More than that, he deserved the unvarnished truth after all they'd been through together. And how far they still had to go.

"This way." She led the way down the sidewalk and then turned into the alley. Several sets of boot prints marred the snow and indicated their way. "This alley leads to a small park behind the building. It's a known spot for drug dealing, which is a big problem in this area. There's a real split in the neighborhood. A lot of single moms who live here are terrified for their kids, but are trapped because it's one of the cheapest places in town to live. They want the area cleaned up. But the dealers like the rep this area has. I'm sorry to say it's a generally-known fact the cops often turn a blind eye to much of what happens here to save their time and efforts for the big stuff."

"What's small stuff in a place like this?"

"Over-enthusiastic partying, setting off fireworks, small-time dealing, fights, some minor domestic calls, that kind of thing. When you're trying to stop the guy selling ecstasy, crack, and heroin, or the guy who'll take out anyone who tries to take over his territory, teenagers who've had too much beer and are making too much noise don't really register. But it sets the tone for the area. I know the Salem boys; they're doing the best they can with the limited resources all houses have." She stepped from the alley into a parking lot adjacent to a small park. A snow-covered playground was visible in the moonlight near the ghostly, clawing arms of a bare tree.

"This was where they were supposed to meet."

"Your dad, Oakes and Tyson? Here in the park?"

"Yes. It was agreed that if they met out in the open, everyone would feel more secure. But then Tyson didn't show. Oakes says they waited for ten or fifteen minutes and then decided to split up and go looking for him. Tyson lived one block over, so Oakes went that way and Dad apparently headed in the direction of the tenement." She pointed out a slim slip of darkness between two tenements sandwiched next to the cross street. "But something drew him to that alley."

Matt took her hand, his cold fingers winding through hers, but the warmth of his palm bolstered her.

"Show me," he said quietly.

Together, they walked toward the alley.

"This area of town doesn't have lawns. The buildings are separated by small asphalt paths or driveways." Leigh realized she was talking just to hear her own voice and focus her mind on the minutiae instead of the bigger picture of what she was about to confront.

Matt's steps slowed and the backward tug of his hand in hers told her he recognized the site from the photos included in the crime scene file they'd combed over not long ago. She stopped and forced herself to look at it for the first time in four years.

The years fell away, and it felt like she'd stood here only yesterday.

The red and white flash of emergency lights splashed in bursts over brick walls and blindingly into Leigh's eyes as she sprinted over the snow-covered expanse of the park. She darted between police cars pulled in close to the playground and civilian gawkers standing by to revel in the excitement.

"Pig cop is down."

She vaguely registered the callous words of one man as she pushed past him, but they weren't enough to stop her mad need to get there. To save him.

But as she hurtled toward the alley, unmindful of the crime scene tape, a shout had gone up—Stop her!—and hands had reached out with unintentional cruelty to hold her back. She fought like a banshee, struggling and cursing, but they were relentless.

Her father's colleagues. The good, honest men of the thin blue line, many hurting nearly as much as she, but men who would do their job to ensure justice was served. They held that line and kept her behind it while, thirty feet away, Kepler stared at her with dead eyes as he stood over her father's body.

The portable crime scene lamps poured blinding light over the entire scene, making the snow sparkle brilliantly with false cheerfulness. Nate's body sprawled ten feet inside the alley, face down, legs twisted as if he'd spun while he fell, his arms thrown over his head. His service revolver was a foot away, half covered in snow. But there was no mistaking the halo of blood seeping from his head.

Another man lay only ten feet away from the line of crime scene tape. Face up, shadowed eyes staring at the darkened sky, the front of his winter coat was soaked in blood. Boot prints flanked his body and a furrow in the snow led to the gun someone had kicked out of the man's reach.

At that moment, the burly man bent over her father stood and turned toward her. The moment she met the devastated gaze of Dr. Edward Rowe, she knew.

Her father was dead.

"Kepler had an impossible job that day." Leigh could hear the flatness of her own voice, the stark lack of emotion. "I remember looking at him and hating him for being so dead inside. He looked so cold, so remote. I understand now, like I didn't then, that he was shutting everything out simply so he could do the job."

Matt gripped her hand tighter. "To get whatever justice he could for your father, he had to step back from his own feelings."

"Tyson was here." Leigh led Matt to a spot about ten feet from the mouth of the alley. "You've seen the pictures, so you know the set up."

"Yes. Face up, gun kicked that way." He pointed at the wall. "Clean shot through the heart, died almost instantly."

Leigh let go of Matt's hand and pulled her fingers free. She felt his resistance for just a moment, his apparent need to hold on and maintain contact with her, but then he released her.

Alone, Leigh walked toward the alley, her steps slowing as she approached. Gritting her teeth, she forced herself forward, forced herself to confront the memory of her biggest nightmare.

She stepped into the alley, feeling the walls closing in around her as she moved between them. She kept her gaze fixed almost unseeingly on the streetlight shining at the far end of the alley and the flash of the occasional car streaking by. She stopped several feet in and gave herself a moment. Closing her eyes, she took a deep breath. *You're not alone. Matt's here with you. You can do this.* She opened her eyes and looked down, taking in the squalid space where her father had lost his life. Under the snow, refuse lined walls splattered with careless graffiti in a muted bloom of colors. In the distance, the scurry of a small rodent marked its exit at the other end of the alley.

The crunch of snow signaled Matt moving to stand behind her. He didn't touch her, but she felt his presence and drew comfort from it.

"They didn't let me get this close." Her voice was thick and scratchy, drenched with the tears she wouldn't allow to surface, and she furiously cleared her throat to push past the lump. "But the crime scene photos showed everything I couldn't see from behind the tape."

She could see the picture so clearly in her mind's eye—the sprawled body, the gun flung away as he spun, the blood, the gaping head wound, and blood and brain tissue spattered against the brick wall.

"Leigh—"

"Rowe was here." Leigh talked over him. She couldn't take his sympathy; not now, not here where her vital, loving father had become an empty, spiritless shell at the hands of another.

Matt seemed to understand and let her take the lead. "Considering what I now know of Rowe, that doesn't surprise me. Not only a cop going down, but a friend and colleague. He wouldn't entrust the case to anyone else."

"No one had to tell me Dad was gone. I could see it in Rowe's eyes. He wasn't nearly as good as Kepler at hiding his emotions. It flattened him and he didn't care if the world saw it."

"I think in that situation, anyone would understand."

"You'd think so, wouldn't you?" But Morrison had seen her in that moment of unspeakable grief and weakness, and it had set the tone of their interactions from that day forward. She pushed her antagonism toward Morrison aside. "It was clear from standing here that Oakes's story held." She turned around, facing the bitter wind whipping down the alley; it sliced in tiny knives over her exposed face and ruffled her loose hair. "The implication was that Tyson had pulled his gun and Dad shot in self-defense just as Tyson was taking a shot at him." She mimed taking a shot from where she stood to where Tyson's body was found. "They both went down. Oakes says he came running when he heard gunfire, but it took him a minute or two to find them. At first, he only saw Tyson and thought he was just unconscious, so he cautiously approached and kicked the gun away and felt for a pulse, but there wasn't one. It was then that he went looking for Dad and found him here in the dark alley. It was clear from the start Dad was gone, so he didn't get within ten feet, wanting to preserve the crime scene."

"Here's a question. How exactly did Tyson manage a head shot like that"—Leigh winced, but Matt barreled on, as if needing to move past the brutality of this part of his question—"in the dark? Your dad would have been in shadow. Was he just lucky?"

"It was undoubtedly lucky. We assume he was actually aiming for mid-body but was fortunate to hit anything. Another inch or two off and Dad wouldn't have been hit."

"Or might have been seriously but not fatally wounded. But how did Tyson manage to take the shot?"

"I think I know. Walk back to where Tyson's body was found."

Matt trudged through the snow to the spot, then spun to face her. Understanding dawned on his face. "You're backlit by the streetlight at the end of the alley."

"That's what I think. Tyson was aiming at the dark mass in the alley. Where the shot struck was pure chance." She glanced down at the snowy ground at her feet and then walked away, leaving behind the pain it triggered. She stepped from the alley and over to Matt, the rush of wind suddenly diminishing as if she stepped into warmth. "I think we've seen everything we need to see here."

"Agreed. You okay?"

Leigh took a moment to examine how she was feeling. Surprisingly, she felt more balanced than she expected. "Perfectly okay? Not really. But ready to do this? Yes."

"That's my girl." Matt took her hand, kissed the back of it and then continued to hold it as they left the scene of death and tragedy, looking forward toward justice and retribution.

Saturday, December 21, 8:51 p.m.
The Point Neighborhood
Salem, Massachusetts

Leigh knocked on the door, the eighth and second last on her list. Discouragement was running high at this point. Out of seven attempts, two were no shows. In one case, someone had been home and come to the door as the light behind the peephole changed, but refused to answer. The other four times, conversations had been short, with one leading to a door slammed in her face.

"I don't have to announce I'm a cop," Leigh muttered to Matt. "They can smell the badge from behind closed doors."

"I never would have guessed it, but you're surprisingly correct." Matt eyed the battered door in front of them, its once-white paint marred with scuffs and dirty smudges. "It's like some kind of evolutionary coping mechanism. Survival of the fittest and all that. He who avoids law enforcement, survives."

The door was abruptly pulled open by Kalela Jackson, an older African-American woman. Her gaze skimmed over Matt, apparently finding nothing threatening, and settled on Leigh, instantly filling with suspicion. "We ain't done nothing wrong." Her voice was deep and gravelly, as if she'd just come off a fourteen-hour shift as the auctioneer in a smoky hall.

"No, ma'am, you haven't. I was just wondering if I could ask you a few questions." Leigh continued without a pause, not allowing the woman to say 'no'. "I understand you were living in this apartment four years ago."

"Yes."

"You may remember there was a shooting here at that time."

"Lots of shootings around here. This ain't Beacon Hill."

"No, ma'am. Let me be more specific. A police officer was shot and killed behind this building. So was another local man, Roger Tyson. Do you remember that incident?"

Recognition lit the older woman's eyes. "Yeah, I remember."

Leigh pasted on a pleasant smile. "I'm glad to hear it. We're looking for any additional information about that incident or about Mr. Tyson you could provide. We have a logged police report of the incident from Detective Oakes from Salem PD, but we're looking for some eyewitness accounts of that day. I realize it was years ago, but do you remember anything from that time?"

"I know I was at work and I came home to police cars and ambulances. I can't add nothing to the story." She darted backward with surprising speed and slammed the door shut before Leigh could say another word.

Leigh bit back her frustration at another failure, pulled out her list, made a quick note, and started down the hallway.

Minutes later, they were pushing through the main entry doors after the last apartment on their list remained closed. Leigh's temper escalated with each step down the concrete stairs, but she kept it tightly reined until the heavy doors of the tenement slammed shut behind them, blowing snow off the front steps in an explosion of flakes around their feet. Then she whirled on Matt. "Goddammit! Did you see that any time we mentioned Oakes's name, people clammed up and it was like talking to a brick wall? What hold does he have on people here?"

"These are people who are down on their luck," Matt said calmly. "The last thing they'd want is to go up against what looks to them like a popular and powerful cop. He has the power to ruin the rest of their lives. It's easier and safer for them to just shut up and keep their heads down."

Leigh growled with frustration as she stomped down the steps and then crossed the small courtyard in ground-eating strides. When a small, broken piece of concrete appeared in her path, she had the satisfaction of giving it a sharp kick and watching it skitter across the small space to smash into the brick wall.

"Feel better?"

Leigh stopped and let out a deep breath, forcing out some of her frustration and anger. "Not really. Just a bit stupid for being so juvenile."

"Welcome to the human race. Some days, you just need to kick something." He gave her a sly sideways look. "I'm just glad I wasn't the convenient target. Those boots look rather unforgiving."

His attempt to raise her spirits hit the spot and a small chuckle escaped helplessly. "Sorry. Most of the time, I think I've got this. But now, just as things seem almost in reach—" She stretched out her hands, fingers spread and grasping. "—I can't quite make contact. It's frustrating."

"But I know you and—"

"Wait!" said an unfamiliar voice.

They both whirled around at the single word. A gangly teenager was running down the stairs, hurriedly pulling on a battered old jacket over his slender frame.

"You were just talking to my mom." His words came out on puffing breaths.

They'd only talked to one African American woman that evening; he had to be Mrs. Jackson's son.

"We were," Leigh confirmed.

"Can I talk to you about that night?" His looked past them, first one way, then the other. "But not here, not out in the open."

Excitement shot through Leigh for the first time this night. It tasted like hope. "Let's go for a drive."

They jogged to the car. A minute later, they were speeding from The Point toward the downtown core up Congress Street. In another few minutes, Leigh pulled into a nearly deserted parking lot across from the Salem Witch Trials Memorial.

The young man in the back seat blinked out the window. "The Memorial?"

Leigh exchanged glances with Matt. "It's a favorite spot for us. And a world away from The Point and its influences. Now, how about we start with proper introductions." Leigh reached a hand between the front seats. "Leigh Abbott. And this is Matt Lowell."

"Dylan Jackson. Which one of you is the cop?"

"You can't tell?" Matt asked. "From the way we were treated inside, we thought everyone had some kind of radar."

Dylan considered Matt and then Leigh. "It's you," he said to Leigh.

"Trooper First Class with the Massachusetts State Police. What gave me away?"

"I don't know. It's just something about how you walk and talk." He studied Matt. "You're weird. Official, but not cop-like."

"He's a scientist. 'Weird' pretty much sums it up some days." Leigh smiled when Matt threw her a dirty look. She turned back to Dylan Jackson. He sat, hunched, either from the cold or from nerves. The cold she could at least deal with, so she turned up the heat in the car. "What can you tell us about that night?"

"I'll tell you, but you've got to keep this off the record. I'm nearly done high school, then I'm out of here. Got my eye on a scholarship at UMass Dartmouth. This can't get in the way of me going to college."

"Admirable," Matt said. "What's your field of interest?"

"Law school."

"Very admirable," Leigh agreed. "And hard work."

"I'm okay with hard work. If it gets me out of that place"—his tone went scathing—"then I don't object to working my ass off. But I have to be alive to do it, so you have to help me."

"Done." Leigh was willing to spare no expense to get him the help he needed. "Whatever you need, I promise you'll have it."

Dylan's eyes narrowed on her. "How do I know you'll keep your word? Cops in The Point don't have a good rep."

"The cop who died that night? That was my father."

Dylan's jaw sagged as he stared at her, wide-eyed.

"As you might imagine, I'm more than a little over-invested in his death. I'll do whatever you need if what you tell us blows this thing wide open."

"And if it doesn't?" A thread of his mother's suspicion wound through his words.

"I'll do it anyway if what you tell me puts you in jeopardy in any way."

"And I'll do what I can to help you academically," Matt interjected. Dylan looked at him in confusion, so Matt tried to clarify. "I'm a professor at Boston University. I have colleagues I can talk to, or reference letters I can write. Not to mention we have our own School of Law, you know."

"I know." The young man looked embarrassed. "I take back what I said about you being weird."

Matt chuckled. "All makes sense now, doesn't it? Now you know I'm a prof and a lab rat."

Dylan grinned, his body finally relaxing against the seat. "Sure does."

"Okay, then." Leigh was trying to keep her impatience at bay, but was slowly losing the battle. "What can you tell us?"

"I . . ." Dylan took a deep breath. "I saw the murders that night." His words came out in a rush.

The car went deadly quiet as both Matt and Leigh stared at him in shock; only the sound of the heater pumping out warm air filled the silence that followed Leigh's quick gasp. But she recovered quickly. "You were an eyewitness?"

"Yes. The story reported in the news . . . that's not what happened."

Under the cover of the front console, Leigh reached out blindly, but Matt anticipated her and met her hand half way with his. She held on tight, her nails digging deep into the soft flesh of his fingers, but he didn't make a sound, simply gripped back. *This is it.*

"What did happen?" Her voice was surprisingly calm.

"The cop . . ." Dylan stumbled and stopped. "Sorry, your father, he shot Tyson. That part was right. I don't know if Tyson was high as a kite or just panicking because your father wasn't a neighborhood regular, but he was acting totally crazy. Waving a gun around. I was surprised your father didn't shoot him then and there. I wouldn't have waited."

"Dad would never willingly kill someone," Leigh said quietly.

"Tyson was out of control. He didn't have a choice."

"Hold on." Matt's voice seemed sharp in the quiet. "He shot Tyson. Tyson didn't shoot back?"

"No. He was hit and went down."

"Stop. Back up." As much as Leigh needed to know the details, she needed context. Until she had the full story, the cop in her couldn't be sure. "How did you see this? It was during the winter, at night, and it was dark."

"I was out that night. You met my mom. She's a single mom, raising two kids, me and my older brother. She has to work two jobs to make ends meet. So she was at her night job waitressing at the diner. I was fourteen and already running with a crowd that was getting into trouble."

"Bad trouble?" Leigh asked.

Dylan's looked down at this lap. "Mostly stupid stuff. Smoking, a little vandalism, sometimes a fight that got out of hand. That night, a bunch of us met up to hang out. Mom's shift ended at nine o'clock. We don't own a car, so she walked home and would be back about nine-thirty. I wasn't supposed to be out, so I always made sure I was home by a quarter or twenty after nine so I didn't get caught."

"Where was your brother?" Matt asked.

"He would have been out boozing or getting high." Disgust

was heavy in Dylan's tone. "That was his specialty."

"Where were you when the shooting happened?" Leigh asked.

"In the park." Dylan shifted uncomfortably on the seat and then stilled, as if finally committing to the telling of his tale. "I was coming back to the apartment, and I cut through the park. But when I saw what was going on, I ducked behind the big elm tree in the corner. When you see a gun in The Point, you take cover because bullets will fly and you don't want to get killed by a stray shot. But I was young and stupid—" He stopped and shrugged. "Younger and stupider. I watched the fireworks from behind the tree. Tyson went down. And that's when the other cop appeared."

Leigh's lungs froze as if ice was slowly crawling into each tiny air sac. Try as she might, she couldn't pull air into them. "What cop?" she managed.

"Goddamn Oakes."

Oakes. Tucker had been right all along that Oakes was behind it. And now they had their proof. Emotion swept through Leigh, relief and fury trampling over each other in their rush to reach the surface. Matt gave up the attempt to be professional and pulled her hand over the console where he could hold it in both of his to help strengthen her for what they both knew had to be coming.

When the silence continued and Leigh seemed beyond words, Matt spoke for her. "What happened next? Tell us everything you saw."

"Yes, sir." Dylan turned to Leigh. "Oakes held up a hand and told your father to stay there and cover him while he checked on Tyson. Made sure he was out of the picture. He went to Tyson and checked for a pulse, but I guess there wasn't one. He told your father Tyson was dead, at which point your father let his guard down and dropped his gun hand." Dylan's gaze flicked to Matt and then to Leigh nervously. "And then Oakes picked up Tyson's gun from beside his body and shot your father. He didn't even flinch when he did it."

Leigh's whole body jerked as if physically struck by a blow and a high-pitched whine built in her ears. She could see her hand clasped between both of Matt's but couldn't feel the stroke of his fingers.

"Oakes put the gun back down from where he found it and kicked it away from Tyson's body," Dylan continued. "Then he took off his gloves and put them on Tyson."

"Son of a bitch!" Matt's face lit with incredulity and his exultant laugh rolled through the car. "Leigh, do you see what he did?" He shook her hand a little roughly, trying to bring her back. "He just buried himself forensically."

"What? *What?*" Leigh shook her head, trying to clear the fog and the ringing. "How?"

"Remember the gloves in the evidence box we went through a few months ago? One pair for your dad, one pair for Tyson. They both tested positive for gunshot residue. If the gloves seemed to fit Tyson, no one would have thought to hold up the case for possibly a year or more to test for DNA to make sure they were really his. But now we will because Oakes's epithelials will be inside those gloves. We'll run DNA and nail his ass to the wall. He's done." He turned back to Dylan. "Finish your story. What happened next?"

"Oakes walked part-way toward her father, but must have been able to tell he was gone. He pulled out his phone and called it in. I could hear him talking. He said that Tyson must have killed your dad and he'd only found him after. I didn't stick around after that. I waited until his back was turned and I split down one of the other side alleys and circled the building to the front. I just got inside when the cop cars and ambulances started pulling in. Other people ran out to find out what was going on. I didn't leave my room for the rest of the night. Told my mom I had homework to finish so she left me alone. She's too sharp. If she'd taken a good look at me, she'd have known something was up."

"Why didn't you say anything?" The ripping agony of years not knowing the truth and seeing Oakes portrayed as a hero and a valuable asset to the department tore through Leigh. "You could have sent him to jail." She whirled on Matt. "There were two separated shots, but Oakes reported two nearly simultaneous shots and no one contradicted him. *Why didn't anyone tell the truth?"*

Dylan drew back sharply at both her words and her tone.

"Leigh, wait a minute," Matt said. "I know you've been blindsided, but try to think this through. He was a fourteen-year old kid, already getting into trouble, who just saw a cop get murdered. That's bad enough, but it was done by another cop. Who'd believe him?"

Dylan stared wide-eyed at Matt for several heartbeats and Leigh had to wonder how many times an adult had ever defended him.

"There's something else." Dylan's words were hushed. "I heard you talking when you left the building that every time you mentioned Oakes's name, people shut up. People know he can ruin them, whether they done something or not. You don't cross Oakes, not unless you want an accident or a charge for something you didn't do. That's why nobody said anything. Sure, others heard two separate shots. But no one would have dared tell the truth."

Leigh went deadly still, and the confusion and turmoil spinning through her settled enough that she could think again. "Dylan, are you saying he runs this neighborhood?" Her voice was quiet and focused now, and out of the corner of her eye, she saw Matt's small smile as she regained control. "Can you be more specific?"

"Only from what I've heard others say."

"I'll take that as a start. What do they say?"

"That Oakes has had a hand in the drug business here for a long time through a dealer everyone calls Black Mamba. That in return for his protection, Black Mamba has never been caught and his competition has slowly died off or got arrested. That he has at least one of the gangs in his pocket and they do his dirty work for him. He orders a hit, a gang member does the killing, and no one connects it to Oakes."

"If everyone is so scared of Oakes, why are you helping us?" Leigh asked.

"A couple of reasons. One, I don't plan on being here long. I plan on escaping this hell hole and getting away from Oakes. But more importantly, my brother died in one of his gang hits. Yes, he was a screw up, but he was my brother and I loved him." Dylan face transformed with an animalistic snarl. "*I want Oakes to pay for what he's done.*"

"You've come to the right place. Matt, we need to find out who this Black Mamba is. And I call bullshit on the fact Oakes would be offering him protection out of the goodness of his heart."

"Hell, no. He'd be taking a good-sized cut of the drug profits in exchange for his information stream and misdirection of the authorities. This must be the real reason he's been sending you those packages. He's in line for a promotion and needs to be so sparkling clean that he damn well shines. He's trying to offload any suspicion of his dirty dealings now, in hopes that you'll be led astray and then will bury the whole thing so well that no one will connect it to him. This way, he keeps his hands clean and has someone else doing his dirty work for him again."

"It's the first explanation that's made any sense." She squeezed his hand and then pulled free, hoping he could read the message she silently tried to convey with her eyes. *Thank you. I couldn't have survived this without you. I'm back now. Let's get to work.*

He smiled at her, and she knew he understood.

She pulled her notebook and pen from her pocket. "Okay, Dylan, let's run it from the top again. I want everything you know about that night and about Oakes in as much detail as you can manage." She pulled out her cell phone. "I want to record this conversation. Would that be all right?"

"Does our deal stand?"

"Yes." Matt and Leigh spoke the word together.

Dylan sat back and crossed his arms over his chest. "Then we're on."

Leigh gripped Matt's forearm. "You know what this means?"

"You bet I do. This means Tucker's insane plan is a go. God help us all."

CHAPTER TWENTY: ISOLATED RETREAT

Isolated Retreat: a private homestead or shelter that is mostly self-sufficient.

Saturday, December 21, 11:34 p.m.
Abbott Residence
Salem, Massachusetts

They blew through Leigh's front door on a swirling gust of winter wind. Leigh shut the door behind them, and then leaned back against the wood. A long exhale escaped as her eyes fluttered shut. Above her coat collar, her face was pale and there were smudges under her eyes.

"Hey, you okay?" Matt tipped her chin up. The soft glow from the overhead hall light cast even darker shadows over her skin.

Her eyelids rose slowly, revealing clouded green eyes. She shrugged.

"It's been a hell of a night," he said. "You know the truth for the first time, but you have to be exhausted, physically and mentally. Time to shut things down for now."

"You're driving back to Boston tonight?"

"Not a chance. I texted Dad an hour ago to tell him what happened and that I was staying with you." He cut her off when she shook her head. "It's not a night to be alone."

"What if that's what I want?"

Surprise jolted through Matt at the sharp edge behind Leigh's question. "Then I'll sleep on the couch. But someone will be in the house with you tonight," he said, taking care to keep his voice even in response

Leigh dropped her face into her hands and rubbed her fingertips over her forehead, hard enough to furrow the skin. She blew out a long breath, her shoulders sagging. "I'm sorry. You're being kind and I'm being bitchy."

He pulled her hands from her face and held them in both of his. "You're exhausted and overwhelmed. And you spent most of the night trying to hide every ounce of emotion you were feeling while you went through hell."

"I didn't do a good job of it," she muttered.

"Give yourself a break. You relived every aspect of your father's murder. If it didn't touch you, I would have wondered what you're made of. Maybe you stumbled once or twice, but you made it through, and you got the job done on top of it."

"Because of you. You stepped up when I was in trouble. I'm not sure I could have done it without you."

"You always do what needs doing. I just helped steer the boat a bit while you were getting your sea legs. We're a team, Leigh. We work together. Tonight was just another example of that."

"It certainly gave us everything we need to finish off Oakes. Dylan's story is pure gold and will open a whole new angle on the investigation. Which is great news, considering that the faces Tucker gave you to review from the security footage look like another dead end."

"There just isn't enough to make any conclusive matches. Lack of data on top of bad lighting in the original picture, and a hodgepodge of angles and lighting in the comparison shots." Matt freed her hands and yanked down the zipper of his ski jacket. "But Tucker was certainly over the moon about Dylan's story. I thought he'd leap out of his chair and run around his apartment when we filled him in, especially when you started naming names." He shrugged out of the jacket and hung it in the front hall closet.

"I think it will give him the push he needs because I don't think he's going to step away from the computer tonight until he has every detail ironed out."

Matt held out a hand for Leigh's jacket. She obliged him with a weak smile.

"He'll have to make sure he's accounted for every detail. It's not him going into the line of fire." Hanging up her jacket, he purposely kept his back to her. "I don't mind telling you I'm not happy with his set up."

"You mean me meeting with Oakes?"

A small smile tugged at the corners of his lips in response to the thread of outrage in her words. *That's the spirit.* But when he turned around, his expression was serious. "Tucker's not the one sitting across the table from him. He's not even going to be in the room. You're going to have Oakes's back up against a wall and he's a wild card. What if he tries to take you out?"

"There's a risk, but if it had been your father, you'd stop at nothing to get justice."

"You know it. And I know you have to do the same. But I appreciate that you don't object to me being on scene. I'm not going to rest easy until this is over."

"I hope you being there is overkill, but you're a face he won't recognize, so you'll be less conspicuous backup than Riley. You're also a handy guy to have around in sticky situations."

"Speaking of Riley, it was nice of him to step in like that to watch Dylan's place tonight."

"Riley's a good man. He asked what was going on, but when I told him I couldn't fill him in yet, he didn't fuss. I needed him, so he was there."

"You don't actually think Oakes will go after Dylan?"

"No. He doesn't know about him—yet. But I'm not taking any chances. Dylan is putting his neck way out for us; I want him safe." Leigh rubbed her hands up and down her upper arms. "This is stupid. I can't get warm and it's not even cold in here."

Matt had seen similar shock-like reactions before from comrades after battles and losses. He held out a hand to her. "Come on, I know just what you need."

She put her hand into his as if acting on pure autopilot. "You do?"

He tugged her toward the stairs. "It's late, you're tired, and shell shocked on top of it. You need a fire, a cup of tea, some TLC, and then some solid sleep." He pressed the back of her hand to his lips. "Let me take care of you."

Her weak smile in response only highlighted her exhaustion.

Wrapping his arm around her waist, he led her up into the darkness and away from the stress of the world, even if only for a few hours.

CHAPTER TWENTY-ONE:
SURGICAL STRIKE

Surgical Strike: a precise attack on a specific target, intended to cause minimal collateral damage.

Sunday, December 22, 7:14 p.m.
O'Leary's Pub
Salem, Massachusetts

Leigh sat near the rear of the pub, tucked into one of the booths, unblinkingly watching the front door. She hoped Tucker, who was plugged into an obscene amount of electronics in the van down the street, couldn't hear her pounding heartbeat through the microphone taped between her breasts. Tucker would never give her away to the guys in the unit, but she always felt she was fighting to be considered worthy in their eyes; an attack of nerves now would never do.

For the umpteenth time, Leigh forced her attention away from the entrance, turning to casually people watch inside the pub. She lifted the lowball glass to her mouth, took a sip of her nearly finished soda, and scanned her surroundings. The place was full of plain-clothes and uniformed cops, off duty and in civvies. The pub was done in typical English—or, in this case, Irish—decor with dark wood walls, high-backed booths with thickly padded leather bench seats, high tables surrounded by barstools, wide plank flooring, and a roaring fire in the fieldstone fireplace along one wall. A shiny oak bar ran nearly the length of one side of the pub, backed by a long stretch of mirror reflecting bottles of every size and description, filled with every color of liquor imaginable. Heavy frosted glass lanterns threw a warm glow over the room.

There was a crackle of static in her earpiece. "Leigh," Tucker said. "I've got a visual on Oakes. He just parked his car. He's on his way in."

"Roger that."

She looked across the bar to find warm hazel eyes fixed on her. Matt sat alone, nursing an almost untouched beer. He was also mic'd and wore an earpiece to hear Tucker's instructions.

A roar of raucous laughter drew her attention. At a table near the door, four cops were flirting with the waitress who was giving as good as she got. She flashed them a wide smile and a toss of her blond hair, then strutted away with an exaggerated sway of her hips.

Leigh followed her path across the pub to the bar, but her attention was drawn back by the door opening.

7:15. Right on time.

A towering man stepped through the door. Despite the cold and the snow, he wore only a black leather jacket. His hands and head were bare. Dark eyes scanned the bar and then stopped on her. She met his eyes, taking in the short-cropped sandy hair, heavily lined forehead, his narrow face, and thin lips.

This was the man who had taken her father from her. The sudden urge to pull out her service revolver and put a bullet between his eyes was overwhelming, the ferocity of it startling.

Her earpiece crackled to life again. "Abbott, play it cool. Lowell says you look like you're going to bolt."

She raised the glass to her lips to cover their movement. "That's not even close to what I'm thinking," she murmured. "Now shut up, Tucker, and let me work."

Upon spotting her, Oakes broke into a magnanimous smile and strode across the floor as if he owned the place. Leigh noticed the shifting gazes from other officers behind his back after he passed. She also caught the daggers Matt sent his way. *Down boy. And to think you're worried about me losing it.*

"Trooper Abbott." He held out his hand and then pumped hers.

It took every effort to not flinch and give away how her stomach rolled at his touch.

"Even if I hadn't seen your face splashed all over the papers in the last few months," Oakes said. "I'd still know you anywhere. You look very much like your father."

"Thank you, Detective." Leigh motioned to the bench across from her. "Please, join me. Sorry for the table in the back but"— Leigh glanced at the empty tables around them—"I wanted a private conversation."

The blond waitress came to their booth at the sight of the new arrival. "What can I get you?" She took Oakes's order for a draft beer before asking the question Leigh had primed her for. "Another rye and Diet Coke?"

"Yes, please." She handed the waitress her empty glass. Better for Oakes to think she was leaning on alcohol to bolster her courage.

As the waitress hurried away, Leigh looked back across the table. "Thank you so much for meeting me, Detective. I appreciate you giving up your Sunday night."

"It's quite all right. And, please, call me Ian. May I call you 'Leigh'?"

"Of course." She looked down at her hands and realized she'd unconsciously been twisting her cocktail napkin. She ran her fingers over it to flatten out the worst of the creases. "I feel a little silly asking you here."

"Nonsense." He laid one hand over hers to stop the nervous motion. "What can I do for you?"

It took every effort to not yank her hand away, make a fist, and break his nose; the crunching sound of breaking bone and cartilage already echoed in her head as if she'd actually done the deed. Instead, she pasted on a nervous smile. "You're too kind. You don't know me."

"You're Nate Abbott's daughter. He was a good man and great cop, so no kindness is required. What can I do for you?"

"I'm wondering if you could help me with something." She purposely looked down and fiddled with her napkin again, prolonging the moment and hopefully making her seem both distraught and somewhat unstable. "Someone is sending me threatening packages."

Concern filled Oakes's eyes and he leaned in over the table, his hands braced against the edge. "Really? Do you know who's responsible? Or why they're doing it?"

Oh, he's good. This is how he pulls it off, by seeming completely genuine. If we didn't already know, I'd almost believe him. Leigh gazed up at him, blinking a few times as if battling back tears. "I don't know. Whoever it is, they haven't made their identity known."

"Why have you brought this to me?"

This was where she would make or break her case. Either she'd sell it to him and the plan would move forward, or she'd tip her hand and it would all go south.

The waitress arrived with their drinks before Leigh could answer, and she took the time to take a large swallow. Oakes studied her over top of his pilsner.

Leigh set down her tumbler. "I'd like to show you something. This came in the first delivery. Because of your experience and your contacts, I think you can shed some light on what I'm looking at here. This isn't my department and I'm feeling a little out of my league." She reached into the messenger bag on the bench beside her, pulled out the first photo she'd received—her father's death scene—and slid it across the table.

He carefully examined the photo, a mixture of surprise and fury splashing over his face. "Jesus Fucking Christ." He met her eyes. "*This* is what they sent you?"

"This was the first delivery. Turn it over." She waited while he flipped the photo over and read the words on the back. "Someone is trying to smear my father's name."

"Nate Abbott was a solid cop. He wasn't dirty. What do they think he was involved in?"

"The local drug trade, from what I can tell. But there's a problem."

Oakes set the photo face down on the table between them. "Which is?"

"You're right—Dad wasn't dirty. Someone is just trying to make it look like he was."

Oakes fixed his narrowed gaze on her while he took a long slug of his beer. "Any idea who?"

"I think so." Leigh took the time to play with the swizzle stick in her drink, stirring the ice around in concentric circles. *Let him sweat for a minute.* "Whoever sent me the packages didn't know I had an extra piece of information he or she didn't have access to."

"Really?" Oakes folded his hands together, looking as if he didn't have a care in the world. "What's that?"

Careful, Oakes. You're trying too hard. "Dad's old computer. I still had it and could access everything on it. See, the person responsible for this found a way to hack into the state police computer system or hired someone to hack in for him. And he changed small details in some of the files. Little things like names of investigating officers, but nothing to do with actual case details. He also got into the Salem files so that any joint cases matched."

"These weren't any of my cases, were they? Is that what this is about?"

"No, no." Hoping she wasn't laying it on too thick, Leigh reached across the table to lay a hand on his arm. Over Oakes's shoulder, she caught a glimpse of Matt's eyes narrowed in fury. "Nothing like that. I'm actually hoping I can draw from your experience to get to the bottom of this. Let me finish laying it out for you first."

"Sure."

Leigh pulled back and ignored the urge to wipe her hand off on her pants. "He knew it wasn't kosher, but Dad used to bring work home some nights. You know how it is, when a case gets its claws into you and you can't just shut it down when you clock out."

"Oh, yeah."

"He had files on his computer. Original versions that I could compare to what's on our server now, and I found those alterations. Based on that, I think I know who's responsible."

Oakes held utterly still except for the intrigued upward curve of his eyebrows. He remained silent, clearly waiting for Leigh to continue. But a small vein throbbed in his temple.

"My sergeant, Daniel Kepler." She kept her voice flat, unemotional.

It was small, and she would have missed if it she hadn't been watching specifically for a tell, but Oakes's frame relaxed and his whole manner became more open and sympathetic. "Kepler? But I know him. That doesn't seem like the kind of thing he'd do."

"I didn't think so, either. Until names started to surface and I began to dig deeper. The deeper I dug, the more I realized there was a cover-up. But it wasn't until last week that I understood I needed to move on this, and move on it fast."

"What happened last week?"

"Kepler sent me into a firefight where we lost one of our guys."

"The shooting in Haverhill? You were there?"

"Yes. I had nothing to do with the case until that day when Kepler decided we needed to send additional men, and he chose me."

"From what I heard, you were lucky to get out of there alive."

"I was. But Tapley didn't." Leigh let bitterness and a touch of real grief creep into her tone. "I was there with him. I did everything I could to save him, but he bled out under my hands."

"I'm sorry. I didn't know him personally, but it's always hard when we lose one of our own."

"Yeah." Leigh took another gulp of her drink to soothe her suddenly dry mouth. "But it made me realize that until I close this, Kepler has the authority to put me into situations where I can be taken out and it will just look like the job. But it's how he'll silence me."

"Can I help you? To wrap it up faster?"

"I think so. Right from the start, this whole thing hasn't made sense. Why would someone take something long forgotten, bring it out into the light, and point the finger at a dead hero? And then we found the answer."

Oakes immediately latched on the term Leigh was banking on. "We?"

"I asked one of the computer forensics guys to look into this. He's a whiz."

Through her earpiece came Tucker's muttered *Yeah, baby!*

Leigh didn't smile, but she wanted to. "He's the one who traced the case to WITSEC."

"Witness protection? How did he get there?"

"He's good, that's all there is to it. So good, he's already tracking the guy who hacked our system and says he'll have him nailed within the next few days. He's doing it on the down low, of course, because we don't want Kepler to know. Once we find the hacker, we'll get him to roll on Kepler, strengthening our case. But back to WITSEC. Apparently, the Feds have someone in custody who's willing to trade information in exchange for safety inside the witness protection program. Tucker's still running the details, but it's a federal drug trafficking case and it leads to Salem and a dirty cop inside the drug circles here."

"Kepler's the dirty cop?"

"His name is what you find if you dig down deep enough in Dad's original files. And it makes sense. Kepler's aggressive and arrogant and has had his eye on Harper's chair for a long time. Harper will likely retire in five or six years and Kepler wants his job."

"But he won't get it if his record is tarnished."

"Exactly."

Oakes braced his arms on the tabletop. "So he's pinning the whole thing on your father." His tone was conspiratorial.

"My guess is Kepler went clean four years ago when he made sergeant. Probably had to. But he's dirty from long before that, and when that gets out, it's going to end his career. And if it's four years since he went clean, then who better to pin it on than the man who died and can't defend himself, allowing Kepler to step into his shoes?"

Oakes sat back and crossed his arms over his chest, looking thoughtful. Leigh had to once again tamp down on the fury simmering just under the surface. He was actually enjoying himself, enjoying the fact Leigh had figured out what he was doing but somehow managed to pin it on the wrong man. If that story became the truth, she was essentially setting him free.

Too bad for Oakes it wasn't actually the truth.

"So Nate's tragic death at the hands of Tyson was just a convenient detail for Kepler?"

Leigh's vision lost focus. *You son of a bitch. You just want to make sure we still think that's how he died. You're actually pumping me for information.* Leigh covered the spike of rage with another swallow as she forced herself to calm down.

She pushed aside the curtain of red clouding her vision and focused on Oakes. "That's what it looks like." She let enough of last night's sorrow surface in her eyes to be convincing. It wasn't hard to let it show; the rage might be simmering close to the surface, but the grief was still there and just as raw as it had been the night before. "You were there. You know what happened." *You know what* really *happened.*

Oakes's mouth flattened into a thin line. "I do. And I live every day wondering how things might have gone differently if we'd stuck together or if I'd stayed to search the park and Nate went to Tyson's apartment. Tyson would sometimes go into these paranoid rages. If I'd been there, maybe I could have calmed Tyson down. Maybe it would have ended differently. But that's behind us. How can I help you bring this back to Kepler?"

"There's one name that popped up again and again in Dad's notes. But it's a street name and we don't know who it really refers to. You've been in the CID for a long time and no one in the department has local contacts like you do. Does the street name 'Black Mamba' mean anything to you?"

Oakes nodded solemnly. "Everyone in CID knows Black Mamba. He runs one of the biggest drug rings in town. He's known for being brutal to his competitors. Well . . . was known."

The bottom fell out of Leigh's stomach. "He's dead?" *This can't have all been for nothing.*

"Missing. He's been MIA for a while now. That's kind of his style, he moves around, never in one place long enough to get caught, but he stays in touch with his contacts so business continues. But he's been out of sight for a while now. And we're beginning to wonder if someone finally knocked him off. There were rumors of a gang war a few weeks ago and Mamba taking a hit."

"We really need to track this guy down. It sounds like he's the linchpin able to blow Kepler's dirty past wide open."

"I don't know where he is now, but let me talk to some of my contacts. They may be able to shed some light on his location. Or his status." He stood and held out his hand.

Leigh slid out from the bench to shake hands. "Thank you, Detective. It's hard for me to put into words how much this means to me. Not only to put away a dirty cop, but to clear the name of a good man who deserves better than this."

"I couldn't agree more."

Oakes pulled out his wallet. When Leigh protested, he simply held up a hand. "Let me. It's the least I can do." He tossed a twenty on the table, more than enough to cover the entire bill. "I'll let you know in a day or two what I've been able to find out."

Leigh watched him leave, then she sank down onto the bench. The wheels were now in motion; it would either work or fizzle into nothing. No matter what, they had Oakes cold on first degree murder. But to also have proof of his extortion and dirty dealings through the years would be the icing on the cake.

There was a crackle of static, and then Tucker's near shout filled her earpiece. "Abbott, he's on the move. We're tracking using the GPS in his vehicle but you have to move now. He just peeled out of here and he's not headed to Salem HQ. He's headed to The Point."

"Doesn't know where Black Mamba is, my ass." Leigh jumped to her feet and sprinted for the exit knowing Matt would be right behind her.

The chase was on.

Sunday, December 22, 8:03 p.m.
The Point Neighborhood
Salem, Massachusetts

Leigh inched along the dingy hallway, gun extended, and one shoulder brushing the wall. The air was rancid with the odors of marijuana and cigarettes, spoiled milk and dirty diapers. Somewhere down the hall, a baby wailed. The atmosphere was hazy with smoke—she didn't want to think about what kind—and faintly gritty between her teeth. She stepped carefully, watching her boots on the threadbare and torn carpet. One slip of the foot, one small sound, and Oakes might be onto them and into the wind.

Riley, identically outfitted in a bulletproof vest and flak helmet, crept silently behind her, while Morrison brought up the rear, watching their six. It flashed through Leigh's mind that the last time she and Riley had done this, just over a week ago, they'd both nearly been shot and a fellow officer had died. It made her grateful Matt was in the van with Tucker where he could listen to the op, but not be involved.

"You know you can't come with me." Leigh donned the helmet, tugging it over her low ponytail, and secured the chinstrap.

"I know." Matt frowned at the ubiquitous white van at the curb. *"Police action and all that."*

"This has to be letter perfect. If this flies right, we'll not only be bringing down a dirty cop, but also ripping open the biggest local drug ring in the area. There can't be any reason for a judge to toss this case out."

"*And there won't be. Just promise me you'll be careful.*"

"*I will.*" His hand shot out to grasp her arm as she tightened the straps of her bulletproof vest, making her head jerk up in surprise. "*Really, Matt, I'll be careful.*"

"*It's just . . .*" He stepped closer. "*He's going to have his back against a wall in there. And he'll do anything to get out, including shooting anyone in his way. Remember what he did to your father. He won't hesitate to do the same to you.*"

"*Trust me, I'm aware of that. He has almost no connection to me, while he knew Dad for years and still had no trouble pulling the trigger. He'll stop at nothing to get what he wants. And when he realizes what's happening, it will become very dangerous.*" She looked over his shoulder to the men in body armor twenty feet down the sidewalk. "*That's why Riley and Morrison are with me. They won't let it get out of hand.*"

"*I don't like that Morrison's a part of this.*"

"*Didn't think you would. But as much as you don't like him, and as much as he doesn't like me, he's a good cop. I saw his face when Kepler briefed us. He was* pissed *someone would go after an Essex cop like that, especially my father. He'll do what needs doing, even if that means having my back.*" She checked her sidearm. All set. "*I have to go. You'll be in the van?*"

"*Listening to every word. Be safe.*"

"*I just hope this new Sting Ray tech Tucker is using to track Oakes's exact location is as good as he says it is, or we're going to blow this thing by busting into the wrong apartment.*" She squeezed his hand and went to meet with her team.

The door coming up on their left displayed the number '24' in crooked gold metal numerals. Leigh scanned to the end of the hallway—still empty, thank God. The last thing they needed now was a civilian getting into the mix. She paused, met Riley's eyes, and pointed to the door just in front of her. *That one.* She slipped past it silently, and then hugged the frame, pressing against the door, closing her eyes to concentrate on any sounds inside. God bless the cheap, hollow doors and paper-thin walls in shabby, low-rent buildings.

"You can't stay here. You need to get out of town now." Oakes's voice. "Abbott has your name and she knows you're involved with a cop. Once she tracks you down, it won't take her long to connect the arms of the operation. And that leads directly to me. If she can't find you, she can't find me. Disappear for a while until things blow over. Then we can pick up where we left off."

"Why don't you just take care of her? That'd solve your problem."

"Because she's not alone. She's got at least one other guy working with her. If something happens to her now, it's only going to crank up the heat. But you need to be gone either way."

"Where do you expect me to go?" The voice was deep, gravelly, and laced with strain. "I can't travel like this."

"You're going to have to. That's non-negotiable."

"You can't tell me what to do."

Oakes's voice had dropped and Leigh had to lean in and press her ear against the wood.

"Let me make this clear. I'm the reason you're still out on the streets doing business. I'm the reason your competitors were always raided, but never you. I made sure drugs and guns from those cases got channeled into your hands and not into the evidence room. I made you. You owe me *everything*."

"Fuck you. I made myself and you got a healthy cut of every transaction, so I owe you nothing. Now get out of here. I can take care of myself."

"You're not going to leave?"

"No, I—WAIT!"

Leigh didn't need any other incentive. It was clear what was about to happen on the other side of the door. She motioned to Morrison who quickly holstered his gun, pulled the small ram from where he wore it slung across his back, and forcibly smashed it against the lock. The lock gave way and the door exploded inward with a resounding crash. Leigh and Riley went through the door shoulder-to-shoulder, leading with their firearms.

"Police! Freeze!"

They burst into a short hallway. Across the living room, a Latino man with a shaved head lay sprawled on a couch in faded sweats. A dark red-brown stain marked one side of his sweatshirt. Oakes was down on one knee in front of him, the mouth of a gun pressed under the Latino man's chin.

His intention was clear—one shot, precisely placed to look like a suicide. He would have been long gone before anyone called it in and the cops showed up, and the only prints on the gun would be Black Mamba's. A quick glance showed Oakes's service revolver was still on his hip. The weapon he held to the other man's head was probably a stolen gun, likely confiscated during another bust, with no way to trace it back to Oakes.

"Oakes, stop." Leigh's voice was firm but calm. One finger twitch and the Mamba's head would be blown to bits.

"Abbott, thank God you got here. This is the guy you were looking for. I just got his gun away from him when he tried to kill me."

"Fuck you, I—"

"Oakes, put the gun down. We have you covered. He isn't going to hurt you."

But Oakes didn't move, possibly sensing this was his only leverage. Leigh, Riley and Morrison crept closer.

Leigh didn't dare take her eyes off Oakes. "Morrison, have you got Mamba?"

"Check."

In her peripheral vision, she could see Riley's gun fixed on Oakes as well. "Stand down, Oakes."

Oakes's gaze shot sideways toward them and Leigh could read the calculation there. He was estimating his chances of shooting Mamba and then successfully rushing the door. There was no way to do it without someone dying in the attempt to escape or to stop him.

Leigh figuratively slammed that door on this charade once and for all. She raised her gun and aimed it straight at Oakes's head, knowing Riley still had the more practical body shot, but the idea of a head shot carried more weight. "You know how easy it would be to take this shot," she said with deadly calm. "It's the same shot you used to kill my father."

Oakes's eyes widened, but he didn't move otherwise.

"It's a harder kill shot to make, but it's a statement and there's no way I'll miss at this range. You'll be gone just as quick as he was. *Now drop the gun, Oakes.*"

There was no mistaking the lethal warning in her tone, and Oakes inched the gun to the floor.

"Push it into the corner."

For a few seconds, she thought he wasn't going to comply, could see the struggle waging within him. One last chance to escape. But then he looked down the barrel of her gun, and gave up the struggle, sending the firearm sliding into the corner. He raised his hands into the air.

"Riley, got him?" Leigh asked.

"You bet."

Leigh holstered her weapon before she pulled Oakes's service revolver from his holster. She handed it to Riley, putting it into the free hand he held out, while in his other he kept his gun trained on Oakes. With great pleasure, she yanked Oakes's arms behind his back and slapped her cuffs around his wrists. She then handed him over to Riley, who now had both hands free. "Hold him for a minute." She turned to Morrison. "What have you got?"

Morrison was bent over Mamba, his sweatshirt pulled up. Underneath, a dirty, blood- and pus-soaked bandage encircled his middle. "This isn't fresh, and it's not good. From the smell, it's going gangrenous."

Leigh met Mamba's angry dark eyes. "How old is that?"

"I'm not telling you anything, bitch."

He let out a howl of agony as Morrison applied pressure to the wound. "Try again," Morrison growled. "This time with a little more respect."

"About ten days." The words that came out were choked with rage and pain.

"Never treated?" Leigh asked.

"No."

"Guess not. You probably needed surgery and would have been under arrest by the time you came out from the anesthetic. Now if you don't have it, you'll probably die." She pulled out her phone. "This is Abbott. I have a GSW and need an ambulance now." She rattled off the address, ended the call, and slipped her phone into her pocket. She looked around the room. "Looks like we're done here." She met Oakes's furious glare. "Looks like you're done for good."

Sunday, December 22, 8:31 p.m.
The Point Neighborhood
Salem, Massachusetts

Leigh slammed the doors of the ambulance and then stepped onto the curb to watch it drive away carrying Black Mamba and two Salem CID officers. Glancing across the street, Leigh spotted troopers putting Oakes into the back of a state cruiser. Salem PD could have their drug lord; Kepler had made it clear he was still the investigating officer in the case of Nate Abbott's death and he would be closing the case. Oakes was theirs.

She turned away from Oakes and from the remains of the hell he'd put her through for the past three months. It was time to close that door for good. He'd stand trial and would go down for first-degree murder in her father's death. There would be other charges, perhaps even more murder charges levied against him, but her father's death was the only charge that personally mattered to her. She was confident a judge would hand out a harsh sentence for killing a fellow officer. Oakes would never see freedom again.

She headed for the electronics van. When they followed the paramedics out with Black Mamba, Leigh was shocked to find not only Detective Lieutenant Harper in the van with Kepler and Tucker, but also Salem PD Chief Robert Mosley. Mosley, known in the area as a well-respected and fair leader, immediately approached and extended his hand to thank her for her work and apologize for his officer's conduct and any involvement his department had in her father's death. Then he had turned his back coldly on his own man, an officer he was considering for promotion up until just a scant few hours ago, and walked away.

Harper and Kepler both had warm words for her, but then moved on—Kepler to his prisoner, and to officially reopen the investigation into Nate Abbott's death, and Harper to meet with his press officer to deal with the media storm that was about to break.

Leigh found Matt waiting for her on the sidewalk with Tucker. Their matching wide grins made her burst out laughing, feeling for the first time the relief of finally getting to the bottom of months of anguish. She took off her helmet, pulled out her hair band and shook out her hair, finally feeling like the op was truly over.

"Abbott, I have to say, that was damned impressive," Tucker said. "You got both of them without a single shot fired or any civilian involvement."

"That last was pure luck." She glanced at the rundown apartment building. "But in a place like this, most people keep to themselves. Safer that way." She turned back to Tucker. "Thank you for everything. You've stuck by me for months, trying to figure this out. And then spent all last night finally getting to the bottom of it. Without the WITSEC info, we never would have had him on the drug charges. We never would have figured out why he was doing any of it."

"You know what works best—put enough of the truth into the lie that it seems real. And you carried it off beautifully. You told him the exact story, except you had him convinced you had the wrong guy. And since he had no idea what was on your father's hard drive and couldn't take the time to steal it and find out, he had to believe you were telling the truth."

"He likely didn't want to believe anything else," Matt said. "It was his ticket out of the whole mess, so he latched onto it. All he had to do was get Black Mamba out of the picture and he would be in the clear with someone else going down for his crimes. He would have happily let Kepler burn."

"He had no problem killing my father, so sending an innocent man to jail wouldn't register for him," Leigh said. "Where he made his mistake today was with Black Mamba. It would have been smarter if he'd just killed him. But he got greedy and didn't want to kill the golden goose he'd cultivated for so long. He tried to get him out of the picture temporarily in hopes he'd re-establish himself when things cooled down. But in the end, that greed got him caught."

Tucker slapped her on the back, nearly knocking her off balance with his enthusiasm. "A job well done. Now, I have to get this van back to the Unit before they notice it's gone."

Leigh gaped at him. "You didn't requisition it?"

Tucker flushed a dull red up to his bright orange hair. "Uh . . . no. Didn't have time for the paperwork."

"Or didn't want to risk being turned down?"

Tucker winced. "Yeah. That, too. Considering we had Kepler and Harper with us on the op, I can't see there being trouble. Still . . ."

"Go. Get it back where it belongs. And if you run into trouble, let me know and I'll straighten it out."

"Thanks." Tucker started to step away but Leigh caught his arm. "What?"

She threw her arms around him for a quick hug, holding his stiff body tight. "Thank you," she whispered.

When she stepped away, Tucker was more flushed than before. With a muttered *you're welcome* he scurried off toward the cab of the van.

"I've never seen Tucker that particular shade before," Matt commented casually. "I didn't think it was even possible to turn that color."

"Leave it to Tucker. If anyone could, it would be him. I really embarrassed him." She laid her hand on Matt's arm. "I owe you an even bigger thanks." Reaching up, she pressed her lips gently to his. "That doesn't even remotely cover it."

"You know I don't need thanks."

"Maybe not, but I need to say it anyway." Her smile dissolved and she looked down at her boots. "I had him, Matt. I had my gun pointed at his head."

"I know," he said gently. "I heard the whole thing."

"I could have done it. I could have ended it all right there."

He grasped her securely by both shoulders until she looked up to meet his eyes. "You're human and it had to be a temptation. But that's not you. You'd never have taken the shot unless you had to. You'll let the courts decide his fate and let him pay for his crimes. Because it's the right thing to do."

"Part of me wanted to." Her whisper carried an edge of shame.

"Remember who you're talking to. I went to war in Afghanistan after 9/11. I know the pull of retribution. You didn't take the shot because you're a good person and because your father wouldn't want you to avenge his death. Feeling the temptation and acting on it are two different things."

Leigh stared up at him. "How do you always know the right thing to say?"

"My father must be rubbing off on me."

Over Matt's shoulder, Leigh saw Morrison exit the building and start down the sidewalk to where their cars were parked around the corner.

"Hold on." Leigh stepped around Matt. "Len."

Morrison stopped and looked back at her suspiciously. She moved closer, holding out her hand. "Thank you."

His gaze flicked down to her hand. "For what?"

"For helping bag a dirty cop. For helping to clear my father's name. I know you don't like me, but I know you thought the world of Dad. I appreciate it, and I know he would have as well. So . . . thank you." She extended her hand further and stared Morrison down. *Come on. Meet me halfway.*

The conflict and hesitation was clear in his face, but finally he stepped forward, slapped his hand into hers, pumped twice, and let go. Then he strode away from her.

Baby steps.

When Leigh turned around, Riley had joined Matt and they were headed toward her.

"I'm going to mark this day down on my calendar," Riley said, grinning.

"Really? Why's that?" Leigh fell into step with them.

"As the day Len Morrison finally acknowledged your presence in a positive way. Nowhere to go but up, right?"

Leigh grinned. "You got it."

As they passed the front entrance, she looked one last time at the apartment building where they had finally shut Oakes down. He was in custody. There would be no more packages in the mail, no more suspicion, no more anguish.

It was over.

CHAPTER TWENTY-TWO: PREPPER

Prepper: a person who actively prepares for catastrophic events, disasters and SHTF situations by stockpiling food, water, weapons, and emergency supplies.

Monday, December 23, 2:11 p.m.
Gerrit Residence
Amherst, Massachusetts

Matt pulled his SUV up in front of Gerrit's rundown house and cut the engine. "Here we are. Talk about no rest for the wicked."

"You got that right. It was a hell of a weekend and we're back at it again. Too bad I had paperwork to finish this morning. I'd have liked an earlier start."

Matt stared into the sky. Ominous clouds rolled in, and bare tree branches danced in the gusting breeze. The sprinkling of snowflakes that started shortly after they'd left Boston was now coming down harder and at a steep diagonal angle, driven by the wind. "We're going to have to move fast. If forecasters are correct, there's a hell of a storm coming in."

"Thanks for driving. I'm not sure what our ride home is going to be like."

"My SUV will manage better than your Crown Vic. If it gets bad, we'll find a hotel and stop for the night. I told Dad I'd let him know and we'd just play it by ear. But if we don't search the grounds today, we'll have to deal with up to two feet of snow by tomorrow and it'll really be like finding a needle in a haystack. Right now, it's just an inch or two, so we should still be able to locate the bunker."

"If it exists. It's also possible it's not here."

"True. But according to Tucker's buddy Max, it's probably nearby; we just didn't find it on our first sweep. But now we know what we're looking for."

"These will certainly help." Leigh pulled several folded papers from her jacket pocket and flattened them against her knee. "This is the plat that goes along with the property deed for the land. Gerrit would have built the bunker on his own land, or he'd have run the risk of losing it if a neighbor found it on their property."

"I get the impression the neighbors are few and far between here."

"But I think he'd still be careful. So this"—she tapped the plat—"is what we have to cover." She circled the northernmost end of the property with an index finger. "Here's the driveway and the house. And this . . ." She indicated the elongated, nearly rectangular extension of land with a smaller outcropping on the west side. "This is all Gerrit's land." She pulled a second sheet from behind the first. "This is the topo map of the area. Considering the terrain, I thought it would be useful to put Gerrit's land in perspective. I've sketched his property onto it."

Matt considered the contour lines that crossed the land. At first, they were spread out, but were drawn closer together toward the southern boundary. "From the contour lines on the map, you can see where the land rises to become part of Mount Norwottuck. Really, that cuts down on our search grid considerably because there's no way he'd successfully excavate an underground bunker in basalt without attracting attention by blasting. Not when coming one hundred feet closer to the house would ensure you're digging mostly in dirt."

"Makes sense to me. Let's search closer to the house. Ready?"

"Just about. Just so you know, I packed the Glock." Reaching across, he tugged open the glove compartment. Inside, nested into its holster, was his C23.

"Why do you think you'll need that?"

"I don't. But think about that last day on the Ward case. We thought we were going out to do a suspect interview and ended up on the top of a tower struggling for our lives. Someone killed Gerrit, someone we haven't identified yet. I'm not taking any chances today.

"I honestly don't think we'll see a living soul. You carrying is overkill, but I'm okay with it." She pinned him with a mock severe look. "Just remember the rules."

He was instantly taken back to their first case together—the two of them huddled behind a fallen log after Matt had tackled her, driving her off her feet while bullets flew overhead. Back when Leigh hadn't known his history in the Marines. Before they'd become a team. *You go left, I'll go right. Keep your eyes open. Do* not *shoot me. Preferably, don't shoot period.* "Oh yeah, I remember. Try not to shoot you."

"That would be nice." A particularly strong gust of wind rocked the SUV and Leigh reached into the back seat to retrieve her gloves and hat. "Suit up. We don't know how long we'll be out there so dress like it might be a few hours."

"Between losing the light and the storm moving in, we don't have a few hours to look."

A few minutes later, they were trudging through the rapidly darkening afternoon. Matt pulled the hood of his ski jacket further up around his knit watch cap and bent his head into the wind. The snow mixed with ice pellets and the flakes were like tiny daggers drilling into his skin.

"This is brutal." Beside him, Leigh's voice came muffled through the scarf she'd wound around her neck. "And the temp is dropping fast."

"They're calling for a low of minus five tonight. Feels like we're getting close to that now with the wind."

"Another reason to do this as quickly as possible. Let's find this place, find out whether we can get into it, secure it, and leave."

They circled the house and stood by the shed, scanning the terrain around them. A forest of bare trunks stretched out as far as they could see. Directly south, the slopes of Mount Norwottuck rose high overhead.

"Look for anything man-made, any ventilation ducts, any signs of a generator," Leigh said, her teeth chattering. "From what Max said, they need a fair amount of space to bury a bunker, so look for a clearing large enough to hold a shipping container. Let's split up and cover the ground."

"Got it. Stay in sight, though." Squinting into the thickening snow, Matt frowned. "I don't want us getting separated. In your navy state police jacket, you'll blend in as we lose the light."

"Good thing you're wearing bright yellow. I'll keep an eye on you."

"That works. Call me the moment you lose sight."

"I won't lose sight. Let's go."

They separated to roughly ten yards apart and slowly covered the ground in careful parallel steps, looking for anything out of the ordinary in a winter forest.

Matt scanned the area around him, shaking his head. This just wasn't right—the trees were thick with only sparse gaps, and it was just too close to the house and the road. It had to be further out. But he kept walking and searching. Ten minutes later, when he and Leigh met on the slope of Mount Norwottuck, she was of the same opinion.

"This isn't working." She had to raise her voice to a near shout to be heard over the wind which had risen to a howl. "This land isn't right for the kind of structure we're looking for."

"You brought the map?" When she nodded, he said, "Can I see it?"

Her gloved fingers were clumsy, but she fought with both pocket and page to extract the map. She clutched it tight in both hands as the wind ripped at it, flipping the edges wildly.

Matt helped her steady it. "What about this area here?" He circled a small offshoot from the property on the west side. Holding one hand out to block the snow swirling into his eyes, he scanned the distance, through the trees. "It's that way. I think we need to get out of the trees."

Leigh awkwardly folded the paper and jammed it back in her pocket. "Agreed."

They cut due west, winding around trees and clumps of low brush. The wind was biting, the kind that snuck into the lungs to steal a person's breath. Matt turned his back against the wind for a couple of steps, taking several sheltered deep breaths before he turned into it again.

They broke from the trees into a slightly more open section of land. No longer in the dubious shelter of the denuded forest, the wind picked up.

Matt surveyed the area. "This is exactly what we're looking for." Approximately fifty feet wide and a hundred feet long, a line of mid-sized pine trees and brush backed by barbed wire fence bordered the land on one side. "Keeping his neighbors out. Clearly delineating what's his."

"Also sheltering it from prying eyes. Notice the evergreens." Leigh looked back the way they'd come. "Pretty much every other tree on this property has lost its leaves."

"Until you get a lot higher up, deciduous trees are the majority of the forest. Mount Norwottuck looks high enough that there's probably a point where it's mostly fir trees from that point on."

"You don't have to tell me that. Remember, when the weather is good, I like my rock climbing to be outside the gym. Let's check this area out. I'll take the far side."

They started at one end of the open area and slowly covered its length.

Partway along, Leigh stopped and called out, "Look at this." She stepped sideways to reveal a stake protruding a foot above the snow. "It's a garden stake. Part of this area was used for growing vegetables."

"Fits in with the lifestyle. And makes me more sure the bunker is here. He'd want his food source nearby."

Ten feet further along the ground went hard beneath his boot. Certain, he'd found the first clue, he hunkered down and wiped away the mounting snow to reveal the edge of a square metal hatch. "Son of a . . ." He drew in a breath to call for Leigh when a faint sound from below reached his ears. His head snapped up and he shot to his feet. Leigh noticed the motion, but he silenced her with a gloved finger to his lips. He waved her closer. As she approached, he knelt, tossed back his hood and lowered an ear to the ground. It was there, not easily heard over the scream of the wind, but a low hum was audible. He pulled off his glove and laid his bare hand on the frigid metal. He winced at the contact but forced himself to hold it there to the count of five as he measured the vibrations. He pulled his hand away, thankful it hadn't frozen to the metal and hurriedly pulled the glove on, almost sighing in relief as warmth returned.

Leigh moved in close. "What do you hear?"

"A generator. There's no way it's still running from when Gerrit was killed. And there'd be no reason to refuel and have a generator running unless someone was currently living in the bunker and actively keeping it warm. The bunker and buried generator are kept separate, but if this is the generator, then that means the bunker is literally only feet away because he wouldn't want to run the electrical lines between them too far." He grabbed Leigh's arm and moved toward the tree line.

"But it was Gerrit's bunker. He lived there alone, as far as I know." Leigh's eyes narrowed on the shallow hatch inset into the ground as Matt pulled her into the trees. "What if the bunker is the key?"

"The key to Gerrit's murder?"

"According to Max, a bunker is the most important thing in a Survivalist's life. It makes the difference between life and death in a crisis. What if the murders have all been related to this lifestyle? Pratt sells Gerrit down the river to get himself out of a jam and Gerrit's assets are seized. Gerrit's only a seasonal worker, so he doesn't have a lot and the little he has is now gone, making him even less prepared in case of disaster. Gerrit kills Pratt in retribution and then uses his body to earn back some of what he's lost."

"Talk about paying for your crimes. If that's true, Pratt paid twice. Once with his life and once with his bones."

"But now we have someone using Gerrit's bunker, a bunker we didn't know about and isn't officially registered anywhere. Maybe it was known inside the Survivalist community."

"And you think maybe someone coveted it enough to kill Gerrit for it? That's not over the top?"

Leigh turned her back to the wind and tugged her hood closer around her cheeks, hunching her shoulders against the cold. "Not from how Max described it. A solid and defensible bunker is what will save your life and is worth more than gold to some of these people. He also said there are Survivalist communities online and in person. Perhaps Gerrit shared details of his bunker in one of those places. Maybe he was already feeling threatened in some way because of it and that's why he'd abandoned the house to live in the bunker full time."

"You should get Tucker to work some of his magic and see if he can track down any online clues. Or, once we get down into the bunker, if there's a computer, he can just do his analysis from there. But I think you're on to something. If Gerrit was showing off and bragging about his great place, maybe someone took an interest in it."

"But to what end? Gerrit owns the property. We didn't even know he was dead until last week."

"And maybe that's the key. Right from the start, I've wondered why anyone would leave the body out in the open like that. Maybe the answer is because the killer wanted it found. Once it's found, then the owner of the property is known to be dead and the property can change hands."

"If there's a will, then it will be left to someone," Leigh protested. "So unless it's left to the person who killed him . . ."

"Ah, but you're forgetting something. This is someone who doesn't trust The Establishment and who stays off the grid. Is he going to have a will in a safety deposit box in a bank? Filed with his lawyer?"

Leigh's eyes went shrewd. "He'll have it in his bunker. Where it's safe. Where no one will find it."

"Except the guy who's taken over his bunker. Who's likely destroyed it by now. There's no will and an obviously dead property owner. We showed up early, otherwise, Gerrit might not have been found until spring or later. In the meantime, Bunker Boy is comfy and warm in his new, ultra-safe home no one knows about. And what if Gerrit doesn't have any relatives?"

"I haven't been able to find any so far," Leigh interjected.

"Then the property will revert back to the state. The state can then sell it for the income it will produce."

"And without anyone knowing about the bunker, it will basically come along free for the price of a broken-down house on a remote piece of land that can't be worth much."

"It could be a steal of a deal. Bunker Boy just needs to make sure he's the one to buy and his home away from home is now officially his. Pretty damned ingenious when you think about it."

"Except we caught him."

"And now he's holed up in one of the safest places ever. If he finds out we're out here, he'll stay holed up. If we try to storm the bunker, he's got the advantage and may very well kill at least a few officers before someone picks him off or he runs out of ammo. Remember what Max told you about the gunrooms a lot of these places have. He could just sit tight and pick off anyone who climbs down his ladder. We'd have to tear gas him out and he'd still likely come out shooting."

A movement caught Matt's eye, drawing his gaze toward the line of pine trees. A man stepped through the trees and out into the open space leading toward the bunker. He wore a dark coat and work boots, carried a compound bow, and had two dead rabbits slung over his shoulder. His eyes went wide at seeing them and the rabbits fell from his hand. He swung the bow up and targeted them.

"*LOOK OUT!*" Matt grabbed Leigh and, spinning, jammed her against a tree, pressing his body against hers as the *thunk* of something heavy hit the tree trunk, sending reverberations vibrating through the frozen wood.

Leigh squirmed beneath him and pulled her weapon from its holster. Matt yanked the Glock from his waistband at his back under his jacket.

Explanations weren't needed. They'd caught the killer outside the bunker and had to apprehend him before he locked himself inside. He was armed and ready to fight. They had to go on the offensive before he could put them on the defensive.

She indicated with a pointed finger that he should go south while she would go north. She met Matt's eyes, nodded, and then they simultaneously burst from behind the tree.

CHAPTER TWENTY-THREE: INCH

INCH: a Prepper acronym for "I'm Never Coming Home." In an INCH situation, the survivalist will leave home and flee, becoming a refugee willing to "burn his bridges."

Monday, December 23, 2:49 p.m.
Gerrit Residence
Amherst, Massachusetts

As Leigh shot from behind the tree, she instantly caught sight of a dark blur disappearing into the evergreens across the clearing. She was certain it was no misunderstanding—he'd fired a crossbow bolt at them after all—but she gave him a chance with the obligatory call out: "Stop! Police!" The only response was the cracking of fallen tree branches under fast-moving feet.

Clearly, not stopping.

Leigh sprinted head-down between the pine boughs after him. Staying with him was crucial. He knew this land and they didn't; if they lost sight of him, they might never find him again.

Just beyond the pine trees, the compound bow lay discarded on the ground. *Thrown away to allow for a faster escape, no doubt. Could this mean he was now unarmed?*

The snow was falling harder now, several inches already on the ground, making for precarious footing as the wind whipped flakes into tiny vortices swirling along the ground. But in front of her, boot prints sketched a path leading directly to her prey.

Their suspect couldn't know for sure they'd found the bunker, but by his trajectory, he was leading them away from it anyway. Perhaps, he hoped to circle back once he lost them, and then disappearing by literally going to ground. But right now, the boot prints were leading in just one direction—straight toward Mount Norwottuck.

Matt's footfalls were a rhythmic thump behind her, and his breath a grating rasp. Her lungs were burning with the effort required to run in the treacherously slippery snow. The need to suck frigid air into lungs starving for oxygen was a constant shock to the system, with each lungful a stinging cluster of tiny needles. Leigh tugged her scarf away from her mouth, praying it would make breathing easier. Instead, damp skin instantly frosted with exposure to the icy air.

She wove through the trees, following the prints in the snow. The terrain under her boots angled upward and chunks of lichen covered rock, iced with snow, jutted into her path. Ahead, a fallen tree blocked the route. As she leaped over it, a shot rang out. *Not so unarmed, after all. Must have been why he abandoned the crossbow.*

Scrambling, frantically trying to find her footing in the snow, Leigh darted behind the closest tree, desperately searching for Matt. She finally found him, pressed against a trunk, on the other side of the path about ten feet behind her. She held up a palm, indicating he should stay there.

Leigh needed to report in, so she took the time to dial 911 on her cell, and reported her rank, position, situation, and requested local Hampshire County State Police backup. They were heading up Mount Norwottuck and would be going silent, but would confirm a new position when possible. She hung up and jammed the phone back into her pocket with clumsy fingers. Cold seeped into her bones and shivers shook her frame, whether from the frigid temperature or adrenaline, or both, she wasn't sure. Either way, it would play hell on her accuracy with her gun. Hopefully, it would affect his aim as well.

She peeked around the tree trunk, trying to catch a view of the path beyond. A bullet drilled into the trunk beside her head and bits of bark exploded at her face, scraping her cheeks. She pulled back, breathing hard. *Too close.* But now she knew his approximate location.

She angled around the other side of the tree, and got off two quick shots in succession. She darted back to safety as another shot rang out, this time going wide. But it came from a different direction. She found Matt leaning out slightly from his hiding spot, staring intently into the trees.

"He's on the move," he hissed.

"Stay with me. Keep as low as you can." She had to pause to drag air into her lungs, this time nearly reveling in the pain of the Arctic blast. Pain meant she was alive. "He's trying to lose us because he knows he's leaving a trail a mile wide."

"Sounds like a handgun, but we don't know what else he might be carrying. Whatever he has, he's still going to have limited ammo."

"Us, too. I have a spare clip, but that's it."

She realized Matt was looking at something only a few feet from her and followed his gaze. A circle of vicious metal teeth pierced the snow, a small raised platform in their center. "Is that a trap?"

"Leg trap. Possibly for wolf or coyote. If he's got the property booby-trapped, we'll need to be extra careful or we're out of the race then and there."

Ignoring the hazard of the trap, Leigh closed her eyes, listening for any sound through the scream of the wind. The faintest noise of a branch breaking reached her ears and she was off, Matt hot on her heels. She cut through the underbrush, ignoring the boot prints in the snow. If he was zig-zagging, the fastest way to catch him was a straight line, so she followed her ears instead of her eyes. She crouched low, balancing the need for speed with the need for silence and watched for half-hidden threats.

She was rewarded moments later with a glimpse of a dark jacket slipping between trees on a path that abruptly slanted upward even more. She glanced back at Matt. His gaze was fixed over her shoulder before he dropped it to meet hers with a nod of approval.

They'd gained some time.

Clambering over icy rocks, Leigh pursued as quickly as she could, but the dark shadow moving up the hill had already disappeared beyond a small ridge. Caution was called for now because he could be just out of sight, waiting to pick them off. She scanned the terrain rising ahead and cut right instead of left.

There was barely a path to follow. Anyone familiar with the terrain would pick both the easiest route and the best defense, leaving them to improvise. Heading directly uphill was a death sentence. She had to find options until they were left with no other choice.

But this was not an easy route. The track forced them away from any well-worn path, and instead up and over fallen branches and rocky outcrops. When her boot caught under an arching root, hidden beneath a drape of snow, Leigh tripped and went down hard. She barely managed to hold onto her gun, catching her weight with her left hand on a rocky surface, pain lancing up her arm. With a muttered curse, she climbed to her feet. She caught Matt's look of concern, but waved it away.

Moving forward, she ducked under a massive fallen tree, snapped off eight feet above ground level and lodged in the 'V' of a neighboring tree. As she straightened, she chose her path, twenty feet upward, nearly in a straight line, to where the hill leveled out. She quickly took in the route ahead—rocky, uneven, possibly worse than anticipated because of obstacles hidden by the snow. It was dotted with scrubby brush and that meant handholds. But it also meant she had to holster her gun; she would climb better with both hands free.

So be it.

She jammed her gun into her holster and started uphill, using the stubborn stems as leverage to pull herself up. Ten feet. Fifteen. A quick glance showed Matt was close behind. When she was five feet from where the land rounded the crest of the hill, she pulled her gun out again and went the rest of the way one-handed. She poked her head carefully over the top—*clear*—and scrambled up.

"Where is he?" Matt climbed to his feet beside her.

"Not here, damn it. We lost valuable time going around."

"And if he was sitting at the top and we marched right up,

we'd both be dead. It was worth it." Matt scanned the area. "Look, there." He pointed to a very faint line of track going due south. "He's used the time to get as much distance on us as he could."

"Let's go, then."

They set off at a jog, using the boot prints as an indication of how far behind they were since snow was rapidly blanketing the tracks. He had a good lead on them now, so they could chance staying hard on the trail.

For the next twenty minutes, they didn't speak, simply maintained the chase, knowing that any slowdown increased the risk of losing their suspect. But exhaustion was closing in and Leigh found herself increasingly short of breath. Finally, she put up her hand, signaling a stop and pulled back behind a wide trunk for cover. Matt drew closer and bent over, bracing his hands on his knees and puffing hard.

"I don't . . ." She had to stop for several gasping breaths. "See him. He's . . . up ahead . . . still."

"We have to keep going." Matt's last two words were strangled and he straightened again, sucking air in hard. "He's still in front of us. Still climbing."

"He's following an established path." Leigh tipped her head back against the trunk and closed her eyes, her breath blowing hard, her heart banging against her ribs.

"How can you tell?"

"We passed a marker on a tree about fifteen minutes ago. Number 203. That was when the trail went straight uphill."

"What do you think his plan is?"

"Not sure." Her breath was coming easier now and the rush of blood in her ears was diminishing. "He's familiar with this land. He may use this mountain for regular exercise for just something like this. He's likely hoping to lose us because we can't keep up with him."

"Unluckily for him, he's being followed by a trained rower and a climber. Still, it's a hell of a workout."

"He's good, but he can't be so good he's not stopping to rest occasionally like this, too. But he's probably banking on staying ahead of us—if he can do that, even leaving boot tracks, all he has to do is get down to a road that's cleared and we'll lose him for good. I think his goal is to pick us off somewhere near the peak. After that, it's all downhill and we'd have a better line of sight on him than the other way around, and the defensive advantage will be with us. It's what I'd do if our positions were reversed. Find the highest location and defend it. Assuming whoever is following can make it all the way up there." Leigh looked out through a break in the trees. Far below, the undulating hills of the surrounding mountain range were visible through a screen of blowing snow. "And we will. We have to be at least a thousand feet up. The peak can't be much higher."

"You should call in our position. Who knows where help is, but they won't find us on this mountain without some specifics."

"Good idea." Leigh quickly called in her updated position as best she could and was told cars had been dispatched. But the worsening weather was making it difficult for officers to get to their location. Leigh ended the call and looked at Matt. "The weather is a problem. We have to assume it's just us."

"We've done it before. We can do it again. There's two of us and one of him."

Leigh cupped her hands over her mouth and blew hard. She couldn't feel the heat of her breath through the gloves and frostbite might be a real possibility. She wiggled her toes inside her boots; feeling was sluggish there as well. They might be keeping up the kind of pace that would keep their torsos warm, but their extremities were in real jeopardy.

Time to get moving.

She ran her tongue over lips chapped from the cruel whip of the wind. "Ready?"

"As ready as I'll ever be. I think we're nearing the end if your theory about the peak is correct. If so, be careful, and be ready."

"You, too."

The last part of the trail to the top was treacherous. The climb went nearly vertical, narrow bits of pathway that wove between what looked like a seasonal creek lined with jagged rocks flowing downhill. It took extreme care to pick their way through the rocks, making sure not to slip or turn an ankle. The last thing they needed in a blizzard and more than a thousand feet up a mountain was a broken ankle. Someone could die from hypothermia before help arrived.

But they hit a wall when the boot prints disappeared at the bottom of a sheer rock face.

"How the hell are we supposed to get up that?" Matt paced at the bottom of the nearly vertical wall. "How did he?"

The snow was now falling so thick and fast, Leigh couldn't see clearly to the top of the rock face. She yanked off her glove, running her mostly numb fingertips over the wall, feeling with her experienced climbers touch for the perfect handhold. And then she felt it, a divot and scrape in the rock. Her heart sank. "He's got crampons."

"You mean those spikes you strap onto your boots for walking on ice?"

"Or climbing, depending on the design. His boot prints haven't indicated it before now, so he must have been carrying a pair of cleats in his pocket in case he needed a little extra traction while hunting. Gives him a hell of an advantage." She considered the wall and the terrain around it. "Okay, no help for it. It's throw up our hands and surrender, waste a huge amount of time trying to find another way up, or just get the job done. I'm going up." She holstered her weapon, pulled off her other glove, and stuffed them in her pockets. "You'll need bare hands for this. God, I wish I had chalk. This is going to be brutal between the icy holds and the temperature of the rock. Remember everything I taught you at the rock wall. How to find holds. How to set your feet. Keep your center of gravity close to the wall. We're not wearing proper climbing shoes, so we're at a huge disadvantage." She looked up at the wall, dread filling her with a chill that went even deeper than the temperature. All her experience climbing and she wasn't sure she could do it, not with the gear at hand. And if she couldn't manage it, Matt was dead in the water.

No choice.

"Watch everything I do. If I backtrack, only go with what works. If this was inside, I could have it cold in about two minutes flat. This is going to take longer. And there are no mats. I need you to spot me until I can find the safest way."

"And if you fall?"

"Do your best to protect my head. And yours. We're in a really bad place to require medical attention." She rubbed her hands together, blew on them for a last bit of warmth, and then wiped off any dampness on her jeans. The roughness of the denim was only dimly registered by her fingertips. She tried to tamp down on her rising anxiety, but the question pushed at her. If she couldn't feel her jeans, how was she going to hold onto frozen rock?

Reaching up on her tip toes, she brushed snow off a tiny outcropping and gripped the rock. Finding a toehold for her bulky hiking boot, she boosted herself up, already scanning for the next hold. It was all about finding the right path, the right combination of hand and foot holds to get up the wall. She'd done it a thousand times at the gym, but there the path was marked out by little colored flags. Here she was on her own.

Hand hold. Foot. Next hold. No, that wouldn't work. Backtrack.

It was an immensely frustrating process when she wanted to fly up the cliff and find the man responsible for ending another man's life. But unless she wanted to fall onto the rocks below, or, worse, watch helplessly as Matt did, she'd have to find the safest route. Matt showed promise and had the strength needed in a good climber, but he lacked experience.

Leigh was getting close to the top when she slipped, her right hand losing its precarious hold just while she was transferring weight between feet. Her body slid down the rock face until she dangled with only her left hand bearing her weight. A cry burst from her lips as pain wrenched through her left shoulder, but she held on. Rough, icy rock ground against her left cheek, scraping skin. She vaguely registered Matt's shout as he shuffled his position under her, trying to find the best way to break her fall.

No way in hell was she going down.

With a grunt, she swung her right arm up, catching a hold farther out. Once both handholds were cemented, she got a toehold in place. Then she took ten seconds, her face pressed against her sleeve, just to breathe. When she took her cheek away, the wetness of blood stained the dark Gore-Tex of her jacket.

Another four combination holds and she was poking her head cautiously over the top, finding it clear and scrambling over. Clumsily, she fumbled her gloves back on before looking at Matt, who stood at the bottom, looking up at her.

"You okay?" His gaze narrowed on her cheek. "You're bleeding."

"I've had worse. You followed the route?"

"Yes."

"Then come up. Carefully. It's a hard climb. I'll coach you as best I can from here."

Matt's journey up the rock face was slower, but more of a straight line than hers since his route was established. At the end, she held out her hand and hauled him up the final few feet before they both stood.

Matt ran a finger over her left cheek. "That has to hurt like hell."

"I can't feel it as much as I should, which isn't a good thing." She flexed her cheek—the skin felt tight but there wasn't much pain from the deadened nerves. "Might be a mixed blessing right now." She unholstered her gun, clutching it with mostly-numb fingers. "Let's go bag this guy if he's still anywhere on this damn hill."

Matt squinted up the path. The wind screamed like a banshee and snow drove nearly sideways. "I'm think we're nearly at the top. Look. Nothing but pine trees and open sky. No dirt underfoot, just rock. What do you want to do?"

"He'll assume we're going to continue to follow the path. So we can't." Holding her hand over her eyes to do her best to shield them from the snow, she scanned the surrounding area. "Let's go that way." She indicated for them to circle the peak from their current level. "Quietly. And maybe we can sneak up on him from behind or from the side."

His cap was pulled low over his eyes, but concern furrowed Matt's face as he stared down at her. "You're banged up and really pale. Want me to lead the way for a while?"

She shook her head. "If anyone has to take him out, it needs to be me unless there's no other choice. I'll lead." But even as they cut further south, rounding the top of the peak, her steps flagged and she stumbled. *Pull it together, Leigh.*

They crept between trees and around rocks, slowly circling the summit. The cold was definitely dulling her senses, and Leigh had to focus too much on putting one foot in front of the other. She almost wished they would suddenly confront him, just to get a jolt of adrenaline to clear her head and finish the job.

As if the universe heard her, she thought she heard over the wind the sound of a falling rock ahead. She held up a hand, and, behind her, Matt stopped instantly. She turned around, a finger over her lips and then waved her fingers in a 'follow me' motion. *Forward. Quietly.*

They crept soundlessly around boulders and between the few scraggly pines that dared to grow in such harsh terrain. But Leigh was grateful for their presence, affording them a small amount of cover. Granted, the blizzard was doing a good job of that on its own, and visibility was down to less than ten feet.

A large rocky outcropping, shrouded in snow, blocked their path. There was no way over it; their choices were to skirt around it at this level or to try to climb down to a lower level and then up again on the other side. Not sure how they'd get back up again, Leigh slid around it, leading with her gun hand, inching slowly and carefully. She exchanged glances with Matt, who gave her a nod that he was with her, and turned back, extending her right foot to ease forward.

The large crevice in the rock was filled in with snow, so Leigh didn't know she was stepping into thin air until she was already falling. She threw her weight forward, turning her body into the fall, trying to work with her own inertia instead of against it, scrambling for any hand or foothold she could manage. She burst out from behind cover and only had a brief view of a dark shape silhouetted against the white snowscape.

The man shot to his feet from where he perched on a narrow, icy ledge behind a large rock formation. Leigh quickly registered they'd been right; his position was not only sheltered, but also directly opposite the path they would have followed up the peak had they not detoured. But now they were in the direct line of fire.

Still off balance, Leigh tried to get her gun hand up, but the crack of gunfire split the air, even as she crashed onto the rocks.

A cry burst from her lips as agony ripped through her body, first icy cold and then flaming hot. Memory flashed through her— a vortex of pain and sinking blackness. She'd been here before.

"Leigh!"

She threw up a hand, holding Matt in place as she appraised her surroundings. Down where she was, she was out of sight of their suspect, who was still exposed.

It was now or never. He'd already be scrambling for cover. And she was afraid she wasn't going to make it much longer.

She held up a finger to Matt. *One . . . two . . . three!*

She pushed to her feet, clearing the rocky cover and catching sight of the man just as he was scaling the ledge, attempting to get out of sight.

Her gun wavered as she locked her knees, desperately trying to steady herself, and took the shot.

Matt's shot sounded nearly simultaneously. The man's hands flew up, the gun spinning out of his grip and into the air to sail over the edge. His body jerked, driven several feet off the ledge. For a moment, Leigh thought he'd catch himself as he landed. But he slipped off the icy surface, crashed down onto the ledge, and fell away into the pine trees below.

Gone.

Shaking, Leigh lowered her gun, but then it slipped out of nerveless fingers to fall to the rocks at her feet. Even as Matt rushed toward her, she ripped off her right glove, and pressed her hand to her side. When she pulled it away, blood stained the pale skin of her ice-cold fingers. She looked up, meeting his terrified eyes, her vision narrowing as the black closed in.

She crumpled as her legs gave way.

CHAPTER TWENTY-FOUR: SHANK'S MARE

Shank's Mare: an eighteenth century Scottish colloquialism combining the verb "shank"—meaning to go on foot—and *naig* (a horse). This later evolved into the Appalachian saying "I haven't got a horse of my own for the journey, so I'll use Shank's mare to get there."

Monday, December 23, 4:04 p.m.
Mount Norwottuck
Amherst, Massachusetts

"Leigh!" Matt leaped toward her and caught her as she fell. She was alarmingly limp in his arms, her face pale and slack, snowflakes already gathering on the dark sweep of her lashes. A dark smear stained the palm of her right hand. He lowered her to the ground and knelt down to cushion her body against his thighs. He thrust his Glock into its holster and yanked off his gloves.

He hated to do it, but he didn't dare move her until he knew what was going on. The zipper of her coat was caked with snow, but he pulled it down and pushed the right side of her coat away. The sky blue thermal shirt she wore underneath was soaked with blood and a ragged hole about four inches above her waistband near her hip marked the entry wound.

Raw terror clawed at him at the confirmation Leigh had been shot, but it quickly dulled as a familiar calm settled over him. This was known territory—during his years as a field medic with the Marines, his Fleet Marine Force training, and then in Afghanistan with the Fifteenth Marine Expeditionary Unit after 9/11, he'd seen more than his fair share of gunshot wounds and knew this kind of triage like the back of his hand. Of course, in the sands of Afghanistan, hypothermia and frostbite weren't a concern, and he'd always had a fully stocked medical kit with him. Now he was on his own, more than a thousand feet up a mountain, in a blizzard, and without even a first aid kit.

This wasn't good.

Don't think about that. Get her stabilized and then decide what to do.

He fell into the old routine with surprising ease. He assessed her breathing and checked her pulse, which was thready but regular. Then he had no choice but to lay her down on the rocks to do a full assessment, cushioning her head as best he could with her hood while he checked for other injuries. He was near certain there were no other wounds, but he couldn't risk missing anything. Indeed, the gunshot wound was the only injury. Small blessings there—it was a through-and-through. At least now, he didn't need to worry about the bullet shifting while he carried her down the mountain. But the exit wound was a nasty, ragged hole of torn skin, shredded muscle, and drenching blood, the wound tract running on a diagonal toward her flank. From the entrance wound, he estimated the bullet had been in the .40 caliber range, corroborated by the size of the exit wound.

Two things to worry about now—blood loss and exposure. Moving her was going to be hell, so he hoped she'd stay unconscious, but Matt didn't see a choice even if she were awake. If it had been the middle of summer, he'd have called for a rescue chopper with a basket to pick them up there at the summit. He looked into the roaring blizzard, the snow whipped into a wild frenzy by the winds. They'd never send a chopper up in this weather. He was going to have to get her down the mountain and out by ambulance—and that would cost precious time. Time Leigh might not have.

He had to minimize the blood loss while he moved her. She was bleeding constantly, but not, he thought, consistent with a major vessel being hit. But from the wound location around the seventh and eighth ribs, her right kidney had likely been hit and possibly the large intestine. But if the liver had even been nicked . . . He forced himself not to consider that option, because that was a death sentence he'd be helpless to stay. As it was, if a renal vessel was nicked, the moment he moved her, she risked bleeding out. But if they stayed put, they'd freeze to death.

No choice. She might die if you make the attempt and certainly will if you don't.

What he wanted was sterile bandages and fluids. What he had was the scarf she wore around her neck. Made of thickly woven wool, it was long, winding twice around her neck and then tucked inside her coat. He could use it to make a tamponade. He quickly weighed the issue of hypothermia, which was a mixed blessing. While her dropping body temperature would slow both her heart and the bleeding, it would also cause the blood to be shunted to her torso, which would inversely increase the bleeding. If he packed the wound with snow, the blood vessels would constrict, but it would bring on hypothermia even faster. Damned, no matter what he did.

He carefully lifted her head, slipped the scarf free, and then wrapped it twice around her torso as a makeshift compression bandage. He twisted the ends in a half knot and then looked down into her slack face. "This is going to hurt like hell. I'm sorry." He pulled brutally tight and she came to with a ragged gasp, her eyes blinking, and her mouth working soundlessly. Trying to turn a blind eye to her struggles, Matt tied off the scarf as snugly as he could. Reaching under his coat, he yanked open his belt and pulled it off with clumsy fingers. He wrapped the belt over the scarf, pulling it tight and increasing the compression. He then zipped her coat, and slid her glove on her lax fingers, desperately trying to keep her as warm as possible.

Don't let her see how worried you are. You need to keep her calm and her heart rate down.

He took a deep breath and buried his fear beneath the armor of the medic. He'd worn it often and it slipped back into place as if it had been mere weeks rather than a decade since that was his role.

Only then did he let himself meet her eyes.

———————

Monday, December 23, 4:19 p.m.
Mount Norwottuck
Amherst, Massachusetts

The world was a red haze of agony, touched at the edges with ice.

"Leigh? You with me?" Matt's voice, imploring.

She needed to follow that voice. There was safety there.

She squinted, trying to focus on the face above her. The red haze cleared, leaving her in a world of white, but she still couldn't quite focus.

"There you are. That's my girl." Matt kissed her forehead, but she couldn't feel the touch of his lips. She blinked a few times, but the white fog remained. Reality slammed into place on a wave of pain as it all came rushing back.

Snowstorm.

Mount Norwottuck.

Gerrit's killer.

Shot at the peak.

"Where is he?" Her words were raspy and laced with pain.

"He went off the cliff. One or both of us hit him."

"We need to make sure he's dead."

Leigh could see the battle in his eyes, but Matt gave her a sharp nod and rose to his feet, striding into the curtain of snow so she could only barely see his outline. He returned and knelt down at her side. "It's hard to see, but that area is a little sheltered from the wind. I couldn't spot his body, but I think he went a long way down. If the shot didn't kill him, the fall probably did. It's nothing but rocks down there."

Leigh tried to push herself into a sitting position, a groan of agony ripping from her at the movement. She got as far as propping herself up on one elbow and screwed her eyes shut, fighting dizziness brought on by waves of pain. "Where's my gun?"

"You dropped it when you fell." He retrieved it and slipped it safely into her holster. "We have to get off this mountain. You've been shot and need the kind of medical attention I can't give you.

There's no way they can get a chopper up here in this storm, so we have to get down to the road."

"I can make it."

"Yes, you can. But you're going to need a lot of help."

He wouldn't meet her eyes. Add that to his suggestion she needed airlifting out and the situation had to be dire. Knowing Matt, he was trying to shield her from the reality of her status for as long as possible.

"How bad is it?" She pressed when he hesitated. "The truth, Matt."

Now, he met her gaze and held it. "It's not good. It's a single shot through-and-through. I think it may have hit your kidney."

"Am I going to bleed out?"

The gleam in his eyes was nearly feral. "Not if I can help it." The light dimmed a bit, but the intensity was still there. "But we have to move. Now."

"Call 911. Tell them what's going on. They need to—" Pain arced through her and she hissed in a breath. "Send . . . help. Use the . . . GPS . . . to track our location."

"I will." He gently laid her down. "Stay still and save your strength. You're going to need it."

She closed her eyes, gritting her teeth against the pain that radiated in waves through her. *It's going to be a nightmare getting off this rock.*

She only hoped she made it. If she died on Matt's watch and in his care, she was terrified about what it would do to him.

———

Monday, December 23, 4:32 p.m.
Mount Norwottuck
Amherst, Massachusetts

"Stay here for a minute." Matt pushed to his feet, and picked his way over the rocks to the far side of the peak. The sheer rock face they'd scaled awaited them if they tried to go back the way they come. Standing at the top of the peak, buffeted by wind and battered by blasts of snow, Matt stared at the only other way down—a path that wove steeply down the other face of the mountain.

To go back the way they'd come would mean somehow lowering Leigh down that rock wall without dropping her or jarring her wound. But it also meant the final destination of Gerrit's house and his waiting SUV. *If you can find your way there.* The other way was a path uncharted, but possibly smoother and easier to manage.

As much as she said she'd help, he knew he couldn't allow her to try. He needed to manage the way down bearing her full weight; anything else would take too long.

He made a snap decision. He'd take his chances on the new path and not waste time trying to find his way back to Gerrit's property, which would be lost by now anyway in a world of white. He'd get her down and then get help to come to them.

He climbed over to her. She lay where he'd left her, her face turned away from the worst of the driving snow, but her skin was already touched with white in a way that spoke of frostbite. *No more time to lose.*

"Leigh, I need to get you up now. Leigh!"

Her eyes opened blearily, dulled with pain, but she nodded.

He slipped one of her arms around his neck and bent low. "I'm going to lift you on the count of three. It's going to hurt like hell, but I have you no matter what. Okay, here we go. One . . . two . . . *three!*" He lifted her straight up, hardening himself against her cry of pain to set her on her feet. He gave her a moment to steady herself, feeling the stiffness in her body as she fought the pain. Unfortunately, it was about to get worse. If she was lucky, the pain would be bad enough she'd pass out.

Grasping her hips, he bent and put his shoulder against her right hip and lifted her into a fireman's carry, draped over his shoulders. She gave a ragged gasp and her body went limp, her arms hanging loose to his waist. *Thank God.* Slipping his right arm between her legs, he wrapped it around her thigh before grasping her wrist and holding it across his chest. He carefully picked his way across the rocks and down the path that hopefully led to safety.

For the first twenty minutes, the descent was slow but steady. The path was often steep, but Matt figured out the best way to balance their combined weight and never trusted any surface to be anything but icy. Part way down, he found a sturdy branch he co-opted as a walking stick for his free hand which he used for balance and to help support their combined weight.

His breath came in harsh pants; carrying her down the mountain proved to be nearly as strenuous as climbing up on his own. His upper body shook from the effort, but he ignored it, calling on his years at the oars to steady them both.

Part way down, he gave himself two minutes to lean against a tree while he called in his updated position. Relief flowed through him when he learned an ambulance had been dispatched and State Police had sent in officers in proper search and rescue gear to find them. Help was coming. He just had to keep moving forward to meet it because either with assistance or without it, he had to get Leigh down to the bottom of the mountain. He pushed away exhaustion and kept moving.

A few minutes later, she shifted slightly and he cursed under his breath. He was hoping she'd stay unconscious the entire time. He wanted to stop, to check her wound and test for hypothermia, but knew that would only waste time when he couldn't do anything to fix either problem. So he kept going.

He estimated he was nearly half way down when he hit a rock formation that stopped him in his tracks. Two giant boulders with only a narrow pass between marked the edge of a fifteen-foot drop down to the rocky path below.

There was no way around it. A sheer rock wall shot skyward to his left. To his right, a massive overhang extended out over the forest floor below before it fell away at a sharp angle. Down in the forest, there were trees and brush, and a long stretch of open pathway that wound through and down until it disappeared in the blinding snow—likely the established hiking path. Having seen several markers, Matt knew he was following it. And he'd stayed with it, knowing it would be the best-defined path off the mountain. He'd been able to call in his position not only by GPS but also by path markers. Help was still a long way off, but he wanted to make sure they knew where he was in case he got lost.

He looked back the way he'd come. He couldn't afford the time to backtrack up to the top. But the way down . . . In summer, this was likely a steep, tricky, but manageable climb. Now, during winter, with the rocks coated with ice and sleet, there was no way he could carry Leigh down without risking both their lives. And no way could Leigh manage it by herself.

There was no choice but to drop her over the edge.

Monday, December 23, 5:03 p.m.
Mount Norwottuck
Amherst, Massachusetts

Leigh moved in and out of consciousness, the waves of pain alternately tugging her to wakefulness and pulling her under into blackness. One moment she seemed numb, but was aware of the lurch of Matt's body moving under hers as they left the mountain peak, his careful steps carrying her to safety; the next, agony was tearing through her, ripping her apart.

She thought they'd only been climbing down from the peak for mere minutes, but she had long since ceased to feel her extremities. In moments of lucidity, she knew her body was shutting down, from cold, blood loss, or both. At first, the fear was overwhelming—she had so much left to do both for herself and with Matt—but now there was a dull buzzing in her ears and she was tired. Exhausted. If he'd only put her down, she'd close her eyes and let darkness take her. There was peace in the darkness, and no more pain.

She heard Matt's voice, but couldn't focus on the words. Then her body was tilting and she was on her feet. Dizziness struck as the blood pooling in her head suddenly flowed south. Her knees buckled, but she didn't fall. Instead, her body was slowly lowered to the frigid ground. Her head fell back dazedly against hard rock.

Hands tugged at her clothing and then cold air wafted over her torso. Matt's low curse told her everything she needed to know about her wound.

She was dying. To an honorable man like Matt, a man who would give everything to save her, this failure would destroy him.

Because, despite his best efforts, he was failing.

She reached out to stroke his cheek with her gloved fingers, but focused on his eyes. She needed to grant him her forgiveness now, so he'd give it to himself later. "I'm sorry."

He was struggling to hide it, but the fear banked in his eyes shone back at her. "You have nothing to apologize for. Just hang on. I'm getting you out of here." When she blinked at him dully, he gave her a little shake. "Stay with me." Pain exploded again, clearing the fog in her brain, giving her a moment of clarity.

Matt moved away, and squeezed through a gap in the rocks and to study what lay below. From the stiffness in his shoulders and the tight set of his mouth, he wasn't happy about what was coming next.

Returning, he hauled her to her feet, not giving her time to get her balance. "We have to get down to the next level and there's no way down but between those rocks and then down the hill. You won't be able to climb down, but I'll lower you as far as I can, and then I need you to land as well as possible. I'll make this as easy as I can, but it's going to be rough and it's going to hurt. Can you do it?"

She clearly heard in his terse words what he didn't say—that the fall could kill her. She could tear open her wound, or crack her head open on the rocks below.

Maybe it was a blessing. She'd go faster this way than if she slowly faded. Then Matt could worry about saving himself, instead of dying out here with her. Because right now that was a real possibility, and she didn't want him to die. She wanted him to live. And to remember her and what they had. She blinked back tears. So many hopes and dreams, stillborn.

She nodded.

"After that, I think we're through the worst. It looks like we're down to straight forest after that." He half carried her to the edge when her sluggish body couldn't help him. Looking down through the sheets of sleet, she could see the ground below. The cushion of snow looked deceptively soft, but she knew jagged rocks underneath could tear tender flesh and break fragile bones.

"Matt?" Her voice sounded weak to her own ears.

"I'm here."

She turned to face him, to meet his eyes as she told him one last time. "Thank you for trying; I know you've done your best." Her mouth was suddenly dry and she had to stop to try to wet it. "I love you."

Fury whipped across his face, but it was fear that flooded his words. "Don't you dare tell me that now. We're not done, do you hear me?" His voice cracked. "Don't you give up on us."

She didn't say the word, but let the tiny smile that curved her lips say it for her. *Goodbye.* Then she turned to face the open air beyond.

He lifted her to sit on the edge of the drop. He grasped both her hands in his and lowered her out into thin air. She nearly blacked out from the agonizing pain stabbing through her as the weight of her own body ripped at her wound. She hung momentarily, buffeted by the wind, before he released her right hand to drop her a few more inches toward the rocks below. Already strained and exhausted, his arms shook even more, but he held on to lean outward, lowering her down as far as possible, until she still dangled feet above the rocks and where a bad landing was inevitable.

"Please . . ." Matt's voice. A prayer.

Then she was flying.

Leigh . . .

Was that her father calling?

Then there was nothing.

CHAPTER TWENTY-FIVE: SERE

SERE: a U.S. military program emphasizing survival, evasion, resistance, and escape using caution and basic survival skills.

Tuesday, December 24, 4:27 p.m.
Baystate Medical Center
Springfield, Massachusetts

Leigh swam through layers of fog, the mist slowly clearing as she drew closer to the surface. Her eyelids felt weighted with lead, opening only a slit before closing again. But something prodded at her. She needed to wake up. There was something she needed to do, someone she needed to see.

With effort, she opened her eyes again, squinting against the bright glare of overhead fluorescent lights.

"Leigh."

Her head was unsteady on the pillow as she turned toward the gentle sound of a man's voice. Even so slight a movement had her head swimming and she clenched her eyes shut, willing the room to stop spinning. She opened her eyes again at the warm touch of a hand wrapping around hers. A man was beside her; he didn't stand over her, but instead sat nearby. He seemed vaguely familiar, but she couldn't place him.

The mist was warm and dark as it lapped at the edges of her consciousness, threatening to pull her under. She fought against it. *Not yet.* She focused on kind green eyes, recognizing both concern and relief there.

"You have no idea what a relief it is to see you awake," he said.

Just gathering herself to speak took tremendous effort, but she concentrated hard, forcing her lips to form the words. *Where am I?*

What came out of her mouth was only a low unintelligible

rasp.

The man released her hand. "Let me get you some water." He moved away from the bed and she stared after him, her brain sluggishly making connections as he rolled away in a wheelchair. The final connection was made just as he spoke from across the room. "I sent Matt back to the hotel a few hours ago. He was determined to stay until you woke up, but he was dead on his feet. I told him I'd stay so he could go grab a hot shower and some shut-eye and I'd let him know as soon as you were awake." Mike returned to the bed with a small covered cup with a straw. Coming in close to the bed, he offered the bent straw, slipping it gently between her parched lips. "Small sips. Don't overdo it."

A tiny pull and cool water blessedly flowed down her parched throat. After a few sips, she angled her face slightly away and Mike removed the cup. She tried to curve her lips around the questions she so badly wanted to ask, but Mike, ever intuitive, patted her hand gently.

"You probably want to know what's going on. Do you remember anything?"

It was all a jumble of images and feelings. Of snow and bone chilling cold. Of blood and agony and Matt's panicked eyes. Of the certainty she would die.

Mike seemed to understand her silence. "You and Matt went out to Del Gerrit's house to search for a survivalist bunker on his property. From what Matt said, you inadvertently found the guy who murdered Gerrit, chased him up a mountain, and then there was a firefight at the top. One or both of you shot the suspect and he went off a cliff, but you were also shot. Matt somehow managed to get you down the mountain where he was met by officers and an ambulance. Springfield has the nearest level one trauma center so they brought you here. You needed surgery to repair the damage from the bullet, but you're going to be just fine."

Leigh's head was spinning and the grey haze was closing in on her again. She understood Mike's words on one level, but their meaning still seemed to elude her. She pushed against the haze, trying to stay awake, trying to understand.

Mike's comforting voice flowed over her, saying, "It's okay, don't fight it. There's lots of time to make sense of it later. For now, just sleep."

The weight of her eyelids overcame her and she dropped into darkness once more.

Wednesday, December 25, 2:53 a.m.
Baystate Medical Center
Springfield, Massachusetts

A soft beep roused Leigh from sleep. This time, when she opened her eyes, the suffocating fog stayed at bay. The room was dimly lit, and only the rectangle of light falling through the partially open doorway shed a faint glow in the room.

She closed her eyes again, taking stock, concentrating on every part of her body. The burning in her side was still there, but muffled, the radiating pain mostly quenched. The skin on her cheek was tight and stiff but mostly pain free. Her limbs felt sluggish as exhaustion draped heavily over her, but there was no more confusion and her brain was clear with full memories of what happened at the peak of Mount Norwottuck.

She opened her eyes to lazily scan the room. A jagged green line danced rhythmically across the black screen of the heart monitor beside the bed. A host of numbers running down one side had to be her other vital signs. A tall silver pole held a cluster of IV bags of various sizes, their lines running into the IV pump mounted on the pole below. A long winding tube led from the pump to the needle inserted into the back of her left hand.

A watercolor painting of a pond with water lilies graced the wall beside her bed, and, at the foot of the bed, a table held a small, oddly decorated Christmas tree. Only about a foot high, it was covered with small paper decorations that looked like snowflakes, and yet . . . weren't. Small tubes of colored liquid dangled from the branches and an odd plastic model served as the star at the top of the tree. Several small, cheerfully wrapped gifts were tucked under its tiny branches.

Her gaze dropping lower, she suddenly realized she wasn't alone in the room. A familiar shape hunched at the side of her bed, his dark head resting on crossed arms beside her hip. In the dim light, his face looked pale and lines of strain were etched around his eyes. Sliding one hand along the sheet, she reached out weakly to stroke her fingertips through his tousled hair, to feel him warm under her touch. Alive.

She hadn't meant to rouse him, but Matt was often a light sleeper. He jerked awake at her gentle touch, his head rising several inches off his arms to blink sleepily at her. Seeing her eyes open and fixed on his, he came instantly awake, a relieved grin lighting his face.

"There you are." He rose from the hard plastic chair to settle one hip on the side of the bed where his head had rested. He leaned over her, cupped her unscraped cheek with his palm, and studied her face. He must have been satisfied with what he saw there as he visibly relaxed, his shoulders falling on a sigh. "You scared the hell out of me."

"You got me out." Her ragged croak had him reaching for the water glass beside the bed.

"Just a little at a time. But it will help your throat." He helped her take a few swallows, before he pulled the glass away. "Better?"

"Yes." Her voice was steadier, clearer. "You got me out," she repeated.

"I did."

"I . . . I didn't think I'd make it."

His shaky exhale told her more about the relief he was feeling than words ever could. "You said goodbye to me up there; don't think I didn't know it." He dropped his head down to rest his forehead against hers. "I couldn't live with that."

"The way I was feeling, I didn't think you'd have an option."

"You were going into shock and were suffering early stages of hypothermia. Which in the end actually worked to our advantage because it slowed your heart rate and that reduced the bleeding. Otherwise, you might not have made it."

"What happened after you dropped me off that cliff?"

Matt winced and pulled away. "That wasn't one of my more brilliant moves."

"What choice did you have?"

"None, really. You wouldn't have survived if I had to climb back to the top and gone down the other way. Not to mention, the rock face we climbed on the way up would have posed the same problem. In the end, we went down the easiest way. But you could have cracked your head open or broken something when I dropped you. It's a miracle that nothing like that happened. I think you passed out before you hit; unconscious, you didn't tense up before hitting bottom. That helped. I jumped down behind you, got you over my shoulders again, and was just starting down the last part of the climb when four Hampshire officers met me on the path. I was getting tired at that point, but they took turns carrying you and we moved much faster. Not to mention they knew those trails. They radioed in to make sure the ambulance met up with us. After that, we had you warm and rehydrating within twenty minutes, and in Springfield inside a half hour after that. A surgical team was waiting and they got you on the table immediately. And here we are."

It took some effort, but she reached up to touch his jaw with her free hand. The rasp of his stubble under her fingertips told her how little time he'd taken in his rush to get back to her. "You saved my life."

He caught her hand, brought it to his lips, and then held it against his cheek. "I didn't think I'd manage it," he confessed on a whisper.

"You had me fooled. You were the one who wouldn't give up." She curled her fingers over his, gripped as tightly as she could. "I don't know how to thank you."

"You're here. That's all the thanks I need." He squeezed her fingers. "You should rest. You look exhausted."

"Soon. I need to know the rest of the story first. Did the

Hampshire boys find our suspect's body?" Leigh's stomach dropped when Matt's face clouded. "What?"

"The Hampshire State Police went in as soon as the storm ended yesterday. They combed the place. And Kepler sent Morrison and Riley in to help in your place. Leigh, they didn't find him."

"What do you mean they didn't find him?" She tried to sit up in alarm, but moaned as pain arced through her.

Matt grasped both her shoulders and eased her back against the pillow. "I'm not telling you any of this unless you stay calm. I probably shouldn't be telling you this at all."

"Matt . . ."

"All right, all right. I was able to give them the exact location of where he went over. They found evidence of a body falling through the tree cover, breaking branches, but they didn't find him. They found his semi-automatic lodged in some rocks and traces of blood where he fell when they dug down into the snow, but he was gone." He met her gaze. "We hit him, but we didn't kill him. At least not right away. But we know who he is."

"How?"

"Riley called me late yesterday afternoon for an update on your status and to let us know what he'd learned. They pulled fingerprints off the gun and found a match in the system. His name is Glen Baldwin, and he's apparently a well-known survivalist in the area. No known permanent address. Before he went off grid, he was an EMT with search and rescue training, which goes a long way to explaining Gerrit's fatal wound. Someone with that knowledge would know exactly where to land a knife strike for maximum damage."

"If he's an EMT, he'll be more than capable of taking care of his own wounds if they're non-fatal. And of finding a way to disappear, maybe permanently. Gerrit aside he has a charge of attempted murder of a police officer on his head, so he's in the wind for sure. He won't go back to Gerrit's because he knows we'll be watching. He'll just disappear." She loosed a long sigh, defeat a heavy weight on her chest. "He beat us."

"Yeah, he did."

Leigh looked up in surprise. She expected Matt to placate her, to put a positive spin on it to boost her spirits. Instead, he was being brutally honest.

"He beat us fair and square. He had the skills and smarts to not only almost get away with murder but also to get away with his life. He knows how to live off the land and he's an EMT with search and rescue skills. He knows how he'll be tracked, and he'll do what's needed to stay off the grid, something he's already familiar with."

She closed her eyes, discouragement flooding her. Her eyes flew open again at the gentle stroke of his fingers on her cheek. "But are we done? No. Is the mystery of the case over? Sure. We know who the players are, both victims and killers."

"And where they overlapped."

"Exactly. You got to the bottom of it. Did it have the ending we wanted? Absolutely not. But you know better than I do that not every case is solved the way you want. Welcome to the reality of real-life law enforcement. But there's hope. This isn't a cold case. We know who he is and what he's done. Assuming he's still alive, and we don't actually know that, the hunt is only just beginning for him. He tried to kill you and you survived. You even got some of your own back."

"Or you did. We both fired at the same time."

"Either way, he was definitely hit. We lost this round Leigh, but the war isn't over. And you've survived to make sure of that."

"I guess."

"Also, there's more evidence being collected. Riley and Morrison got into the bunker and it's a gold mine. All of Baldwin's stuff is there, but so are Gerrit's belongings. They've already got a good candidate for the knife used on Pratt. It will go for full testing and I made sure Riley knew about the guy you suggested in Sudbury to look at the blade striations. That will further cement Gerrit's role in Pratt's death. It may also have been the weapon used on Gerrit himself, but you'll need more details from Rowe before that call can be made. If not, they took several other knives into evidence that might be a better fit."

"They did well."

"They did. They're capable investigators, so you can let go of the case for now knowing it's in good hands and they'll keep you in the loop every step of the way. You just need to concentrate on getting strong again."

Exhaustion was closing in and she knew she needed to rest, but her attention was caught by the strange little tree on the small table. "What is that?"

Matt chuckled when he realized what she was looking at. He wheeled the table a little closer. "When Kiko, Paul, and Juka found out what happened, they hit the road and came out as soon as the highways were clear. Kiko didn't want you spending Christmas in the hospital by yourself with no festivities, so she brought you the tree she had on her desk in the lab." He slipped a finger under one of the 'snowflakes'. "Origami viruses and tree balls of centrifuge tubes with different colored pH controls." He tapped a spiky ring at the tree's apex. "Organic model of benzene. It's the ultimate lab geek Christmas tree."

"It's perfect. I love it. Are they still here?"

"No, they stayed for a few hours, but then I sent them home to continue on with their Christmas plans. Paul, by the way, won their bet about the snowfall amount in spades and ribbed them about it the whole time they were here. They're planning to come out tomorrow, and I bet he'll still be at it. But before they left, they made me promise to make sure you knew that these were for you." He tapped one of the gifts under the tree. "One from each of them."

"That's really nice of them."

"You'll have to wait until we get home to get mine. This wasn't exactly how I thought we'd be spending Christmas."

Leigh tried to smile, but it turned into a grimace as the healing scrape on her cheek pulled painfully. "That's an understatement. You'll be waiting for yours, too. It's at home under my tree." Her sigh was full of exhaustion. "I'm sorry I've ruined your Christmas. And your father's. How did he get here anyway?"

"Dad's got a buddy with an off-road four-wheel drive who was thrilled at the challenge of getting him across the state in such terrible weather. They made it safe and sound while everybody else was still hiding at home. And you haven't ruined our Christmas. We always planned on spending it with you. It's just going to be here, instead of in Boston. Where we are doesn't matter." He bent and dropped a kiss onto her dry lips. "I nearly lost you. I'm not worried about where we are as long as you're with me." He pulled back. "Now, you need to rest."

"What about you? You can't sleep here in that chair."

"Watch me. I'm not leaving, so don't even try. Go to sleep. And when you wake up, I'll still be here."

Her brain was fuzzy and sleep was closing in whether she wanted it or not. She relaxed against the pillows as he tucked the blankets in around her and then settled in the chair near the bed. He threaded his fingers through hers and gently stroked the back of her hand with his thumb.

Leigh let her eyes close, the darkness gathering closer.

The last few days had been full of highs and lows. Her father's killer would finally see justice for his crimes, but she'd had to go through her own personal hell to see it finished. And then there were her murder cases, built one on another. Leaving any case unfinished unsettled her, but leaving one so unjustly balanced disturbed her. She'd identified Pratt's killer, but Gerrit had been murdered before Pratt's death had been discovered. And now Gerrit's killer ran free. Someday he'd make a mistake and she'd be there to see his downfall. She looked forward to that day.

Down the hall, she heard the soft strains of a Christmas carol. She felt the strength of Matt's presence and the warmth of his hand in hers. For the first time since her father died, she'd spend Christmas with family, even if it was in a hospital bed. The thought filled her with happiness.

At peace, she drifted off into the silent night.

ABOUT THE AUTHORS

A scientist specializing in infectious diseases, **JEN J. DANNA** works as part of a dynamic research group at a cutting-edge Canadian university. However, her true passion lies in indulging her love of the mysterious through her writing. Together with her partner **ANN VANDERLAAN**, a retired research scientist herself, they craft suspenseful crime fiction with a realistic scientific edge. Their Abbott and Lowell Forensic Mysteries include *DEAD, WITHOUT A STONE TO TELL IT*; *NO ONE SEES ME 'TIL I FALL*; *A FLAME IN THE WIND OF DEATH*; *TWO PARTS BLOODY MURDER;* and *LAMENT THE COMMON BONES*. As Sara Driscoll, they also write the FBI K-9s series, including LONE WOLF, BEFORE IT'S TOO LATE, and STORM RISING. The fourth book in the series, NO MAN'S LAND, will release in December 2019.

Ann lives near Murphy, North Carolina with four rescued pit bulls. Jen lives near Toronto, Ontario, with her husband, two daughters, and three rescued cats. You can reach her at jenjdanna@gmail.com or through her website at http://www.jenjdanna.com.

Made in the USA
Monee, IL
20 January 2020